Also by Jill McGown
in Pan Books

A PERFECT MATCH

Jill McGown

Redemption

PAN BOOKS
in association with
Macmillan London

First published 1988 by Macmillan London Ltd
This edition first published 1991 by Pan Books Ltd,
Cavaye Place, London SW10 9PG
in association with Macmillan London
1 3 5 7 9 8 6 4 2
© Jill McGown 1988
ISBN 0 330 32088 2

Printed in England by
Clays Ltd, St Ives plc

Hail, O ever-blessèd morn!
hail, redemption's happy dawn!
sing through all Jerusalem:
'Christ is born in Bethlehem!'

Chapter One

Lloyd finished the last chapter of his library book, and closed it with relief, wishing that it was in his power to abandon books half-way through. But no matter how obvious the plot, how stilted the dialogue, he was obliged by some natural law to finish them. The worse they were, the more likely he was to devour them, reading into the small hours to get them out of the way. Good books relaxed him, and he would fall asleep with them in his hand, but no such luck with the lousy ones.

He balanced the book on top of the others on his bedside table, and ran his hand over his hair to smooth it down. It was habit – he couldn't get used to his hair being so short now. He had decided that people who were rapidly losing their hair should not draw attention to the fact by keeping the remaining hair long. He still thought it looked odd; Judy said she liked it. He had wondered about growing a moustache, to make up for the shortfall on his head – he craned his neck to see himself in the dressing-table mirror, and pulled a face. His unshaven face held the ghost of what a moustache might look like, and he didn't think it would do. Tall, military types could carry off moustaches, but he had come in at the low end of the regulation height. Too small and dark, he decided. He'd look like a bookie's runner.

He lay back, wide awake, aware that the pile of work

which awaited him was being added to as he lay doing nothing. Added to by pre-Christmas burglars who helped themselves to the presents under someone else's tree – added to by the ones who stole the trees, come to that; the chain-saws got stolen around August, the trees in December. Added to by the drunks, added to by the jolly Christmas spirit that brought out the pickpockets and the handbag snatchers, the credit-card frauds and the conmen in the market square.

One small, striped package and the odd Christmas card were the only hint of Christmas in Acting Chief Inspector Lloyd's flat. Not that he had any objection to glitter and tinsel – in fact, if he were truthful with himself, which he quite often was, he was a bit of a sucker for jingle bells. But there was another natural law which decreed that no man be alone at Christmas, and he would once again be made welcome by Jack Woodford and his nice, comfortable wife in their nice, comfortable house. Lloyd didn't really know if they actively desired his presence at their festivities, but they knew that they had to ask him, and he knew that he had to accept. And he would give their grandchildren presents that their parents would insist were too expensive, as he had done for the past three Christmases, and the collective Woodfords would give him a bottle of malt whisky.

He liked buying presents for the children; his own were grown up now, and just got presents like everyone else's. He had missed his annual excursion into the magic world of children's toys. His Christmas visit to his own offspring consisted of an hour or two on Boxing Day, with Barbara making polite conversation as though they hadn't been married for over eighteen years before it all came to pieces in their hands. So he was glad of the Woodfords' goodwill, and he enjoyed the cheerful, noisy family Christmas. Especially this year, now that his father was beginning to get used to the idea of being a widower, and had decided to go back to Wales to live, which he'd wanted to do ever since he'd left. What with that, and

Judy about to have her in-laws staying with her, Lloyd would have been very much alone.

Judy was the detective sergeant with whom he'd worked, off and on, for seven of the fifteen years since he'd met her. He had been married then, and the twenty-year-old Judy had rejected his advances, her eyes sad. Eventually, she herself had married, and moved away. Because Barbara had wanted it, and because it might have saved his marriage, Lloyd had requested a return to Stansfield, but the divorce had happened anyway. Then, eighteen months ago, Judy had arrived back in his life, a brand new detective sergeant. Since then they had, with a sense of inevitability, become lovers. Occasional lovers, he thought, with an audible sigh. Very occasional.

When Michael was at home, he and Judy weren't lovers. And Michael's promotion had ensured that he was home for considerably longer periods than before. Michael, a computer salesman turned sales director; Michael, to whom Judy professed an unexplained wish to remain married.

The covert nature of their relationship was beginning to irk Lloyd, though Judy seemed happy enough with things as they were. He wished she was with him now, in his three o'clock in the morning wakefulness, though even that pleasure would have been qualified by her ability, figuratively at least, to keep him at arm's length. He looked at the little gift-wrapped parcel on the dressing table. It ought to be tied with ribbon, he decided. And under a tree. He'd get one tomorrow. And some lights. Tomorrow was Christmas Eve; today, he corrected himself. Judy was on leave to play hostess to Michael's parents. He probably wouldn't even see her until after the holiday, but her present would be under a bloody tree if he had to keep it there until March.

He switched off the light, and closed his eyes. He wondered if it was still snowing, as it had been when he'd retired with his dreadful book. A white Christmas – it looked pretty, but the roads hadn't been gritted, and the traffic lads would be busy. His thoughts dwelt on work until at last his mind began to shunt itself into a siding for what was left of the night. Filtered through the fog of sleep, the sighing of the wind reached his ears, and his last conscious thought was for the traffic division, if the snow drifted.

George Wheeler rubbed his eyes as the early morning sun glinted on the snow. Not so early morning, he realised. It was ten o'clock, and he still hadn't written a word.

'I'm sure *you* understand, Vicar, being a Christian.'

Perhaps it was when those words were addressed to him by someone whose motives he had no desire to understand, and with whose values he had no desire to be aligned, that George Wheeler had stopped believing. Not in God, for he knew that he had never honestly believed in God as a being, an entity. As a force for good, perhaps – something inherent in man – but not as some sort of super-caretaker.

Stopped believing in himself? No, that wasn't right either. George believed in himself, for there he was, flesh, blood and bodily functions. And bodily desires – was it perversion to find himself appreciatively eyeing the young mothers at the church play group, or mere perversity? Was it middle-aged conceit that made him imagine that young Mrs Langton was seeing past his clerical collar to the man, or a sign that soon he would be roaming the streets of Soho, a *News of the World* headline *manqué*?

He put down his pen, and sat back in his chair, the better to contemplate the prospect. He had played a bit of soccer in his youth, and he still did some refereeing when he got the time. He'd kept in shape, more or less. Good enough shape for the lovely Mrs Langton to fancy him? He smiled to himself. Chance would be a fine thing. Though he still had all his hair – its sand colour was diluted here and there by silver, but that was distinguished, according to his wife. George believed in himself enough to be vain about his appearance, so that wasn't it.

No, he had stopped believing that he believed. It wasn't

something that it had ever crossed his mind to wonder before. His family went into the Church. His grandfather had made it to Bishop, and there had even been rumours that he was on course to make it all the way to Canterbury, but George rather thought that his grandfather had started those himself. At any rate, he didn't. It was taken for granted – by George as much as anyone else – that he would go into the Church. It was a career decision, if decision it could be called, not a spiritual one. There was the Church, the armed services, the Civil Service. George had chosen the Church.

He addressed himself once more to the pale lines of the A4 pad in front of him, but inspiration, divine or otherwise, eluded him. George had been expected to do well, to rise through the ranks as had his grandfather before him, and as his nephew was doing even now. But George wasn't a company man. He was well enough connected to have secured a living in one of the prettiest villages in England, complete with a vicarage about which anyone might be moved to write poetry. Verdant lawns, bushes, shrubs, climbers; light-filled rooms with elegant lines, and old, good furniture. Wonderful views from its hilltop site, across three counties which today all lay under a shifting blanket of snow. And just twenty-five minutes from Stansfield, with its new-town bustle, its supermarkets and cinema, trains and buses. The best of both worlds, and for twenty-nine years George had clung tenaciously to his well-behaved flock and his uncomplicated life. Lack of ambition, said his superiors. Pure selfishness, George knew now.

It would take rather longer than usual to get into Stansfield today, George thought, glancing out of the window as the wind whipped up the fallen snow. It was drifting badly on the road, and the cars were already having trouble on the hill.

It was no crisis of faith, for there never had been faith, but it was a crisis of the heart, and the words for the midnight service simply wouldn't come. He put down his pen, and stood up, holding out his hands to the one-bar electric fire. Central heating would make the vicarage truly a poem.

11

As it was, there was still a sliver of ice on the inside of the study window. The parish couldn't afford central heating, and neither could he. Until now, he had accepted that as his lot, just as he had accepted everything else.

He had accepted God, to the extent of praying to him in church, and sometimes out of it. Praying for the rescue of people in peril: physical, in intensive care, or spiritual, in the back of a Vauxhall Chevette. Prayer perhaps helped those who prayed, but that was all. And then there was worship. George had never worshipped God. He had taken part in acts of worship – if saying a few words about the sanctity of life and tossing off a couple of hymns to the less than talented Jeremy Bulstrode's organ accompaniment counted as worship. But it didn't. Not in George's book.

Worship was naked, open adulation, to the point of total selflessness. George had never lost his sense of self, not even on a morning like this, when the elements combined to put man firmly in his place. Not even when he had fallen hopelessly in love, at thirteen, with his cousin from Canada, five years his senior and only in the country for a fortnight. Not in the throes of more mature passion, or grief, or anger. And not, certainly not, in the pulpit of St Augustus.

And yet he knew how it felt, this loss of self, this giving over. Once, long ago, he had felt it. He walked to the window, and ran his finger down the sliver of ice, which melted to his touch. It wasn't a woman, he thought, with a smile at himself. A few courteous and cautious walkings-out before Marian, and marriage. A happy, fulfilled marriage, but not worship. Joanna? No, not even her. He loved his daughter with all his heart, but it was still *his* heart. It was long ago, before any of that, before adulthood.

The dog. Of course, of course. His grandfather's dog, whom he had had the privilege to know all his life until the old soldier died, when George was eleven. Perhaps only a child could truly worship, for he would have died instead, if he could have. So, he thought, as the sun shone blindingly

12

on the white carpet below him, he had broken the first commandment.

Come to that, he had spent all summer spraying greenfly in a deliberate act of destruction. Did greenfly count? Birds did.

His father had shot birds; George had joined him once or twice on shoots, but he was a miserably bad shot, and had barely inconvenienced the game.

He had loved his father and mother, but that was no big deal. It wasn't hard to love people who loved you, and it certainly wasn't an honour to be thus loved. If honouring them meant putting flowers on their grave on the infrequent trips to his remaining relatives, then it was Marian who did the honouring. If it meant being straight with them, then he had dishonoured them by joining the Church.

And *by* joining the Church, he broke one commandment regularly, every Sunday. The Bible might not count taking Sunday services as work, but he certainly did. Standing in the pulpit, in the ever-present draught that gave him a stiff neck, seeing the same old faces staring back at him, not expecting anything from him. They were there, like him, from habit and custom; presumably they did find something that they needed in the chill air and the stained-glass light, but he never had. Whatever kind of fulfilment he sought, it was not to be found in St Augustus on a Sunday morning.

Could Mrs Langton provide it, he wondered? VICAR IN PLAY GROUP LOVE TANGLE. Except that she probably hadn't given him the eye; it had probably never occurred to her that his mind ever dwelt on such things. But it had. Not *News of the World* stuff, then. A question on a game show, perhaps.

'*We asked one hundred vicars: Do you ever have sexual fantasies about the mothers in your church play group? How many vicars said yes, they did have sexual fantasies about . . .*'

'I've brought you some coffee. You must be frozen.'

13

He jumped at the sound of Marian's voice, and turned from the window.

'Sorry,' she said. 'Were you working or day-dreaming?'

He smiled. 'Qh, day-dreaming,' he said, walking back to the electric warmth.

'I've got the fire going in Joanna's room,' Marian said, handing him the mug. 'It took about six fire-lighters, but it's caught now. And George,' she said, in her scolding voice, 'must you leave your overalls in a heap on the hall floor?'

'Sorry. I was looking at the car.'

'What's wrong with it?' Marian asked.

'Nothing. I was just—' But she had never understood his love for things mechanical, so he didn't try to explain. He put both hands round the mug of coffee, and stared at the empty pad on the desk.

'Are you having trouble?' she asked.

'You could say that.'

Marian wasn't what he thought of as a vicar's wife. Even he saw the situation comedy notion of Vicar's Wife, when he thought of the actual words. Vicars' wives were either dowdy, shy and full of good works, or blue-rinsed, tweedy and full of good sense. Marian had short, curly, dark blonde hair, and mischievous eyes. Her fiftieth birthday had just passed, and those eyes had tiny wrinkles that he supposed had once not been there, but which were a part of her that he felt he had always known. She had the suggestion of freckles on her nose, and a wide, generous smile. She wasn't tall, and seemed even less so once Joanna had grown up to become three full inches taller than her. He smiled. His adulterous thoughts had made him feel quite frisky, and vicars weren't supposed to feel frisky at ten-thirty on a Wednesday morning, especially not on Christmas Eve.

'Which one?' Marian asked.

'Sorry?'

'Tonight's or this afternoon's?'

He stared blankly at her. 'Sorry?' he said again.

14

'Which sermon are you having trouble with?'

'Oh. Tonight's. This afternoon's for the children really. It's easy to talk to children.'

'Well, I hate to break it to you, but Jeremy Bulstrode's on his way over, in a state about something. He can't play this afternoon.'

'He can't play, period.'

'Something to do with his wife's brother,' she went on. 'He's on his way over for high–level discussions. What will you do?'

'See him,' George said, with a sigh. Ah well, it was highly unlikely that the vicar's wife would want to know at ten-thirty on Christmas Eve morning anyway. And it just wouldn't do for Jeremy Bulstrode to come in and find the vicar and his wife *in flagrante delicto* on the study floor. Would that interest the *News of the World*, he wondered? Or would it have to be the vicar's wife who found him and Jeremy Bulstrode?

'I mean about this afternoon. Shall I fix up the record player?'

'Oh – no, that might not be necessary. Mrs . . .' He hesitated over the surname, not in deliberate deception, but none the less deceptively. 'Mrs Langton plays,' he said. 'I believe.'

'Oh, good,' said Marian.

Mrs Langton was a newcomer to Byford; eight weeks ago she had moved into the cottage at Byford Castle, with her two-year-old daughter.

'I'll pop round and ask her,' George said.

'But Jeremy's coming.'

'After Jeremy,' he said.

'I can go, if you're busy.'

'No,' he said. 'I'll go. It'll be a good excuse to get rid of Jeremy.' He pushed away his pad. 'Maybe visiting someone will give me an idea for this,' he said.

'What about tomorrow? Have you still got to write tomorrow's as well?'

'No. I say the same things every Christmas Day.'

'Do you?' She frowned. 'I hadn't noticed.'

'More or less,' he said. 'It's the midnight service I like to get my teeth into. But the one I'd written won't do.'

'Why not?'

He looked at her. He couldn't tell her she was married to a fraud. He couldn't tell his congregation that they had been listening to a fraud all these years. He didn't know what to say to her, or them. Perhaps seeing Eleanor Langton would help. He found it easy to talk to her, to be himself with her, and not the character actor that he had become, even with Marian.

Eleanor had told him a little of herself – she had been a research assistant, and was now employed by Byford Castle to work during the winter on preparing their archives for publication, and to oversee the guided tours in the summer. She was a widow, and she was lonely. She had told him that because he was a vicar, he assured himself; that's what vicars were for. But he felt as though it was vaguely guilty knowledge, because he *hadn't* imagined her interest in him, and she had seen and recognised his in her. Unspoken, unacknowledged, but it was there, and it had been for weeks.

'George? Are you feeling all right?'

He smiled, almost laughed, at himself. 'Just considering my suitability for getting into the *News of the World*,' he said.

'Do you *want* to get into the *News of the World*?'

'Other vicars do,' he replied.

She smiled. 'You haven't developed a passion for choir boys, have you?'

'Good Lord, no. Nasty little brutes. Can't think what all those unfrocked vicars see in them.' He moved reluctantly from the arc of warmth, back to his desk. 'And that's another commandment gone,' he said, sitting down.

Marian bent down and sniffed. 'You've not been drinking,' she said.

'No. But I took the Lord's name in vain. I do it quite a lot.'

'Yes,' said Marian.

'I suppose,' he mused, 'if I worked my way through all ten commandments – that might qualify me for inclusion.'

'Well,' Marian said, picking up his empty mug. 'I don't care how much you covet it, you're not bringing that ox in here.'

Judy Hill switched on full headlights as the drifting snow swirled round the car, reducing visibility to what seemed like three feet. Mrs Hill senior sat beside her in the car, and Mr Hill sat in the back, tutting at the weather. Judy felt as though she was somehow being blamed.

'Idiot,' she said, as a car swept past her through a gust of snow-filled wind.

'I'm looking forward to seeing the new house,' Mrs Hill volunteered, after a moment.

'We haven't finished decorating yet,' Judy said. 'But it's looking pretty good.'

'Michael says he's thinking about converting the loft,' said Mr Hill from behind her.

Judy slowed down still more as she felt her tyres become unsure of their grip on the deepening snow. 'Yes,' she said absently, peering through the flakes which were falling yet again. The windscreen wipers worked hard, piling snow into the corner of the windscreen, but the weather was beating them. 'I'm not sure why,' she went on. 'There's more than enough room for us as it is.'

'Maybe he's thinking of the future,' Mrs Hill said.

Judy hooted angrily as a car cut in ahead of her. The future? My God, it wasn't a granny flat she had in mind, was it?

'Adds to the value,' came the voice from the rear. 'When you sell.'

Oh yes. Nobody actually bought houses to live in, not in Michael's world. You bought them as a rung on some socio-economic ladder.

'It would make a nice nursery,' said Mrs Hill.

'Not too far now,' Judy said, hearing a note of desperation creeping into her voice already, and they weren't even installed

17

yet. Michael didn't even *want* his parents' company over Christmas; he just wanted to show off his enhanced lifestyle. She signalled left with a mental sigh of relief. Almost there.

The little road was almost clear of snow, and her heart sank as she saw why. The driveway was inches deep, with snow piled up against the garage door. She pulled into the pavement, and stopped the engine.

'Oh dear,' said Mrs Hill. 'Someone will have to get busy with a shovel.'

You? Judy thought sourly. 'Yes,' she said, brightly. 'Let's get you settled in first.'

Mrs Hill got out, and fiddled unsuccessfully with the front seat.

'I'll do it.' Judy tried hard to keep the edge out of her voice as she tipped the seat forward to allow Mr Hill to clamber out.

'There's a present here, ducks,' he said, handing it to her.

Damn, damn, damn. She had meant to go via the police station, and drop it in to Lloyd. The weather had driven all thoughts out of her head, save picking up the Hills and getting them home in one piece. 'Thank you,' she said, putting it in the glove compartment. 'It's for someone at work.'

She led the way up the path, and kicked away the snow from the front door. 'Go on in,' she said, realizing that she had left her car lights on. 'I won't be a moment.'

Back at the car, she switched off the lights and opened the glove compartment, as if staring at his present would somehow magic it to Lloyd. She couldn't just leave the Hills there, even if the thought of just driving away again did have a certain malicious charm. With a sigh, she closed the car up.

'It's a lovely big room,' Mrs Hill was saying, as Judy went in, shaking the snow from her dark hair.

'It's a bit of a change from the last one,' Judy said. 'We swing a cat every now and then to celebrate.'

'Pardon?'

'Nothing,' Judy said, taking out her cigarettes.

18

'Oh, now – I thought you'd given that up,' said Mr Hill. 'You should read what it says on the side of the packet before you light that.'

Judy lit it without improving her mind. 'I only have one very occasionally,' she said truthfully. When she felt she needed one. Like now. 'I expect you'd like a cup of tea. Or something stronger?' she added, hopefully.

'Tea,' Mrs Hill said firmly, as Mr Hill opened his mouth.'Thank you.'

Michael came in while Judy was in the kitchen, and she could hear his mother fussing over him. He wasn't, apparently, wearing warm enough clothes.

'The driveway's blocked,' he said, when he joined her.

'I know. What are you doing home?'

'Office party,' he said. 'It started at about half past eleven.' He leant on the fridge.

Judy pushed him to one side as she got out the milk. 'Aren't you supposed to stay?' she asked. 'To mingle with the common folk?'

'I pleaded bad weather,' Michael said. 'I can think of better things to do than trying to get my hand up some typist's skirt, even if Ronnie can't.'

Judy laughed. 'Ronnie doesn't turn into an office Romeo at Christmas, does he?'

'Does he not.' Michael looked through his double-glazed window at the weather. 'I'd better start digging,' he said. 'I can't leave the car out in that.'

'The car' was his car. His company car.

'You won't be able to get it out again if you put it away,' Judy pointed out.

'What you've just said would have had Ronnie in stitches,' Michael said, with a smile. 'Do you blame me for running away?'

Judy smiled too, shaking her head.

Michael stood, still looking out, momentarily lost in thoughts which Judy knew she didn't share, his thin face slightly pink

19

from the cold air. They were doing well, so far. A good five minutes without a cross word. She set mugs on a tray, and Michael, back in the real world, looked pained.

'What's the matter?' she asked.

'We do have cups and saucers,' he said.

And still, teeth gritted, Judy didn't allow the very cross words she was thinking to pass her lips. They would have shocked Michael even more than the mugs had.

'George – come in.' Eleanor Langton had decided to stop calling him Mr Wheeler the last time they had spoken, but she hadn't had the nerve. She waited apprehensively for his reaction, as though he might tell her off.

'Thank you,' he said, brushing snow from his coat as he came in.

'I'd take my coat off, if I were you,' she said. 'It's a bit warm in here.'

'Thank you,' he said again.

'Is this a social visit?' she asked, as he slipped off his coat. 'You're in civvies.'

He smiled. He really did have a lovely smile, she thought. It made him look about six years old.

'I've come to beg a favour,' he said.

'Anything. I must owe you several favours.'

'What for?' he asked.

Eleanor indicated a chair. 'Listening to my moans,' she said.

'You don't moan. And if you did, it's a vicar's job to listen.'

Eleanor brushed her blonde hair back from her face. 'What favour?' she asked.

'My organist has let me down, or turned up trumps, depending on your ear for music,' he said. 'In any event, he can't play, and I've got a children's carol service this afternoon. Nothing tricky,' he added. 'Just the usual carols to the usual tunes.' He paused. 'Will you play for us?' he asked.

'Oh,' she said. 'I only play an electric organ.'

20

'It is electric,' George said. 'It used to be a harmonium, but I didn't see why the church shouldn't move with the times.' He smiled again. 'No pumps, no bellows,' he said.

'I'd love to,' said Eleanor. 'I was taking Tessa anyway.'

'Wonderful.' He sat back. 'Where is she?'

'At the film-show. Mrs Brewster took her, bless her.'

'Oh, yes. In the church hall. I'd forgotten about that.' He sat forward a little. 'Eleanor,' he began, slightly hesitant. 'You – you're not going to be alone tomorrow, are you?'

'No. Richard's mother's coming – well, she was. If this goes on much longer . . . ' She shrugged, glancing out of the window at the snowflakes dancing through the air.

'Well, the vicarage is at your disposal,' he said. 'Marian always buys an enormous turkey – it lasts until about April.'

Eleanor laughed. 'That's very kind of you,' she said. 'Will you have a Christmas drink with me? It's almost lunch time.'

'I'd love to. I feel as if I'm playing truant,' he said.

'Why?' Eleanor stood up. 'What should you be doing?'

'Writing tonight's sermon.'

'Oh dear. You're cutting it a bit fine. I can only offer you whisky or sherry, I'm afraid.'

'I'd better have sherry,' he said.

'Is the sermon proving difficult?' She handed him his sherry, and sat on the sofa.

'Yes,' he said, getting to his feet. 'Do you mind if I take my jacket off? It's a little—'

'It's very,' Eleanor said. 'The boiler has two modes – off or equatorial.'

He took off his jacket, but he didn't sit down again. He walked over to the sideboard and picked up the photograph of Richard. 'Your husband?' he asked, turning.

Eleanor nodded.

'Is this your first Christmas without him?'

'Not really.' She could talk about it now. There had been a long time when it was impossible, when the tears that were denied her at the time would suddenly surface. But she was

21

over that now. 'Richard was in a coma for a very long time,' she explained.

George carefully replaced the photo. 'I'm sorry,' he said.

'Tessa never knew him, not really. I took her to the hospital when she was born, but—'

George looked horrified. 'Oh, forgive me,' he said. 'I didn't know the circumstances—'

'It's all right,' Eleanor assured him. She took a breath. 'It was a motorbike accident. Head injuries.'

Driving without due care. That was all the driver had been charged with. Her life was shattered because someone drove without due care. It was anger that she felt now, more than grief. More than anything. But that would pass too.

'He only died in October,' she said. 'But – well, this is the third Christmas without him.'

George sat down beside her. 'How dreadful for you,' he said.

'It was,' said Eleanor. 'To start with. They said I should talk to him – you know? At first, you feel self-conscious, but in the end, it became—' She paused. 'A habit, I suppose,' she said, looking away from the hazel eyes that she was saddening. She hadn't meant to talk about Richard. 'After he died,' she heard herself saying, try as she might, 'I kept a diary. Telling it the things I would have told Richard.' She looked up. 'But I haven't had to do that since I started working here.'

George stroked his upper lip for a moment before he spoke. 'Did you have your family to help you?' he asked.

'Richard's mother. I'm not from Stansfield. My brother came down as often as he could—' She broke off. 'I'm sorry,' she said. 'I really didn't mean to bend your ear with all this.'

'I told you,' he said gently. 'That's what vicars are for.'

'I don't think that's why I'm telling you,' she said quietly, and there was a silence.

The man wasn't just married, he was a vicar. A *vicar*. The first man in whom she had had a flicker of interest, and he was a married vicar. 'I'm supposed to be listening to your problems,' she said, her voice sounding false, even to her.

'My problems?' He loosened his tie slightly.

'With your sermon.'

'Oh, that.' He sighed. 'That's easy. I don't think I have the right to preach to people.'

'Then don't,' she said. 'Just tell them what's on your mind.'

He looked at her, into her eyes, and smiled. 'I don't think that would be a very good idea,' he said.

Eleanor closed her eyes for a second; George loosened his tie some more. Another silence. She had to say something, do something. 'I'm sorry it's so hot,' she said.

'Have you had anyone to look at it?' he asked.

'The castle said they'd get someone, but they haven't yet.'

'I could look at it for you.' He smiled. 'I'm quite good at that sort of thing.'

'Would you?'

He put down his drink. 'Lead the way,' he said, getting up.

'Oh – but you're too busy just now.'

'It might just be that the thermostat's set too high,' he said, following her into the little outhouse which had been tacked on to the cottage. The cottage itself had been built on just after the Civil War, to accommodate the family while they repaired the ravages of Roundhead occupation.

George caught his breath as he walked through the wall of heat to which Eleanor had become acclimatised. 'You could grow tropical fruit in here,' he said.

Eleanor watched as he pored over the yellowing manual, and she fetched screwdrivers and pliers when requested, like a nurse assisting a surgeon.

He mopped his own brow, however, and stood up. 'Why they want to put the damn thing in the most inaccessible—' he said, and bent to his task again, his tie trailing in the dust at the back. He stood up again. 'Would you undo my tie?' he asked. 'It's getting in the way, and I can't let this go.'

He kissed her as she undid his tie, as she had known he would. Just a gentle kiss.

She slowly pulled his tie from his collar.

23

'A dog-collar wouldn't have afforded me the opportunity,' he said, with a little laugh. 'Maybe that's why I came in mufti.'

Eleanor didn't speak, because she couldn't.

'Are you angry with me?' he asked, after a moment.

She shook her head. There were so many things she wanted to say. About the months and months of willing someone to live, but waiting for him to die. About the relief when the end finally came, and the resultant guilt at that relief. About being locked into a kind of limbo, neither married nor widowed, with a baby to bring up. A limbo where you shrivel up inside. About how it simply wouldn't do for the person who broke through that terrible barrier to be him, of all the men it might have been. Her tongue couldn't find the words. Any words. But she reached for him, and it found a different kind of eloquence until the doorbell made them spring apart.

'Tessa,' Eleanor said.

He nodded. 'I think I have mended your boiler,' he said. 'It wasn't just a ploy.'

Eleanor stepped back to let him pass. 'We're not going any further with this, are we?' she asked.

George shook his head. 'I don't think we're cut out for it,' he said, as they went along the corridor to the sitting room. He put on his jacket. 'I love my wife,' he said, but it merely undermined the effect of his previous statement.

She handed him his coat.

'But I don't want to pretend that it never happened,' he said quickly. 'I'm not sure what I want.'

'You mean we should keep it in reserve?' Eleanor asked, smiling.

'Perhaps I do.'

Eleanor went to the door. 'What time's the carol service?' she asked, as Mrs Brewster came in with Tessa, who immediately turned shy.

'Here we are,' said Mrs Brewster.

'Three,' George said.

'Did you have a lovely time?' Eleanor asked Tessa. 'Stay and have a cup of tea, won't you, Mrs Brewster?' She turned back to George. 'Three?' she said. 'I'll get there for about half past two, then. All right?'

'Lovely.' He ruffled Tessa's hair, and passed the time of day with Mrs Brewster. 'Thank you again, Mrs Langton,' he said, as he left.

And beyond the door, where the others couldn't see him, he smiled at her again. And *winked*.

Eleanor turned back to Mrs Brewster. 'You couldn't possibly keep your eye on Tessa for another ten minutes, could you?' she asked. 'I have to make a phone-call.'

Marian stared coldly at the young man on her doorstep.

'I just want to talk to her,' he said. 'She is my wife.'

'I'm aware of that.'

'We can't go on like this for ever,' he said.

'She isn't here, Graham. Not at the moment.'

Graham Elstow looked every inch the successful young accountant that he was. He dropped his eyes. 'I've got to see her,' he mumbled.

There were steps up to the vicarage door; Graham had retreated after ringing the bell, and for once Marian had the luxury of looking down at someone. The parting in his well-cut fair hair was neat and straight, like a schoolboy's. Behind him, beyond the porch, the weather grew wilder, and Marian began to be a little worried about Joanna, who had gone into Stansfield to do her Christmas shopping at the last minute, as usual.

'When will she be back?' Graham was asking.

'I've no idea.' Marian scanned the whiteness, hoping that she wouldn't see Joanna's car, hoping that she would. It was a perilous world.

'Can I come in and wait?'

'No, Graham,' she said. 'You can't.'

He looked surprised. He actually looked surprised.

'I've got to talk to her,' he said again.

'Then I suggest you come back when she's here.'

'But—' He turned and waved a helpless hand at the blizzard.

'I can't help that. I don't want you here. I'm sorry.'

He dropped his eyes again. 'I can understand that,' he said.

Then go away, Marian thought. Go away and leave Joanna alone.

'I'll never forgive myself.'

Marian didn't speak. All she could do was pray that Joanna wouldn't forgive him. Not this time. Surely not this time.

'Is it all right if I come back after lunch?' he asked, half turning to go. 'If I get something at the pub, and come back? Will she be back then?'

Marian wouldn't answer, and he walked through the snow back to his car. She watched until it had driven away before she closed the door, her legs weak, her hands shaking. For a moment, she stood with her hand on the door-handle, gathering herself together.

It was about half an hour later that Joanna appeared, pink-cheeked and bright-eyed. 'It took me over an hour just to drive from Stansfield,' she said, depositing bags round the kitchen, where warmth could be ensured in the draughty old house. She unwound her scarf, pulling a face at the wet folds of wool. 'I'd better hang this up,' she said. 'It'll drip everywhere – that was just coming from the *car*.'

'Graham was here,' Marian said baldly. There wasn't any way to dress it up.

Joanna's smile vanished. 'When?'

'A little while ago. He says he's coming back.' She watched as Joanna sat down at the table, her fair hair bedraggled, her hands tight around the scarf. 'He says he wants to talk,' she carried on, sitting beside her. 'You don't have to see him, Jo.'

'I do,' she said.

26

'Not yet. Not today.' Marian took the wet scarf from her, and hung it over a chair. 'You can see him when *you're* ready.' She held Joanna's hand in hers.

'Now's as good a time as any,' Joanna said, as the front door banged. Her grey eyes looked apprehensively into Marian's.

'We're going to get snowed in,' George said, as he came in, rubbing his hands and walking to the fire. He stood with his back to it, and looked at them, frowning slightly. 'What's up?' he said.

Joanna let go of Marian's hand, and left the room.

'What's wrong?' George said again.

Marian told him. He exploded, as she had expected.

'Coming back, is he?' he said, angrily rebuttoning his coat. 'That's what he thinks. The pub, you said?'

'George,' Marian said wearily. 'Joanna wouldn't thank you.'

'I'm not looking for thanks! I won't have that little rat in my house – not today, not ever.'

'He's her husband.'

'Marian – he'll talk her round again. She'll go back with him.'

Marian rubbed her eyes. 'She's got more sense,' she said.

'She didn't have more sense the other times!'

'She hadn't left him.'

'She forgave him, though.'

'But she hadn't left him,' Marian repeated. 'It's been two months. She won't go back to him. She hasn't even said she'll see him.' She stood up. 'Now,' she said briskly. 'Lunch is ready. Give Jo a call.'

George stared at her. 'How can you behave as though it wasn't happening?'

Because it was the only way she could deal with it. George could fly into rages, could go marching off to the pub, and make a scene. But Marian had to think about problems, and work out a strategy for dealing with them.

'You still have to eat,' she said stubbornly. 'He isn't here now, so there's nothing we can do.'

'There's something I can do!'

27

'But you're not going to,' Marian said, deliberately barring his way. 'Take off your coat, and tell Joanna her lunch is ready.' She looked up at him, aware suddenly of their relative strength; aware that the only reason she could actually stop him leaving was because George, like most men, operated a voluntary handicapping system.

He reluctantly unbuttoned his coat again, and threw it over the chair with Joanna's scarf.

They ate lunch in near silence, until George gave up his brief attempt at minding his own business. Minding other people's was his job when all was said and done, Marian supposed.

'Well?' he said belligerently, looking up at Joanna.

'I've got to talk to him,' she answered.

George stabbed a piece of potato. 'I don't want him here,' he said.

Joanna laid down her knife and fork. 'There's nowhere else,' she said, reasonably enough, in Marian's opinion.

'You don't have to see him at all.'

'I do, Daddy! He's right. We have to talk. If it can't be here, then I'll have to go there.'

Marian, her head turning from one to the other, saw the angry colour rise in George's face.

'Well then,' Joanna said, putting away her volley. Advantage.

'If you're seeing him, I'm going to be here.'

'No,' said Joanna. 'Anyway – you've got the carol service.'

'That can be cancelled.'

'No, it can't,' said Joanna. 'And how do you expect me to talk to him with you and Mummy outside the door, listening for—' She broke off. 'Just go to your service. And you go and do your Santa Claus bit,' she said to Marian. 'I'd much rather be alone when he comes back. He finds it difficult here anyway.'

'He finds it—' George began, his face purple.

'It's my problem, Daddy. I'll deal with it.' Game. Joanna pushed her plate away. 'Thank you,' she said, getting up. The

28

handshake at the net. 'I know you want to help. But I'm just going to talk to him, that's all.' And she left.

George looked at Marian. 'Are you still going out?' he asked.

'I have to, George. And I think I should. I don't want her to feel she's got an audience – it would only make it more difficult for her.'

George sighed, and finished his lunch. Marian was sure he had no idea what he was eating. 'I'd better get changed,' he said.

'Where's your tie?' asked Marian, suddenly realising that it was his open-necked casualness that was making George look different.

His hand went to his collar. 'Oh – I took it off,' he said. 'I must have put it down somewhere.' He stood up. 'Maybe I'll have a more Christian attitude to that little toad when I'm dressed for it.'

Marian began to clear away.

'What if she goes back to him?' George asked.

'She won't,' Marian said resolutely, squirting washing-up liquid into the bowl. 'Not this time.'

But she looked anxiously back over her shoulder when she and George left the house, an hour later. Perhaps he won't turn up, she told herself.

And she kept looking at the phone while she was talking to the matron of the children's home, barely following what the woman was saying.

It's none of your business, Marian Wheeler, she told herself severely, as the matron repeated what she had just said, and Marian still wasn't listening. You *can't* phone her. Wait until you get home. She won't go back with him. She *won't*. She's got more sense.

'You're just not listening to me, are you, Graham?'

Graham picked up her father's decanter, and waved it at her.

'No. And I don't think you should have any more,' she said.

'Mustn't drink all Daddy's whisky? I'll replace it.'

29

'You've had enough, Graham. You'd had more than enough when you got here, and that's your third!'

He saluted her with his glass. 'One of the perks of bachelordom,' he said. 'You can get pissed without being nagged.' He dropped his hand, and sat down, his head bowed. 'I'm sorry,' he said. 'I'm sorry. I just wish you'd come home and we could sort it out on our own.' He looked up. 'I can't – I can't get *through* to you here. It's too—' He shrugged. 'Too nice, too Enid Blyton. I'll bet you're back in your old room, as if I'd never happened.'

'Why have you had so much to drink?' she asked. Drinking, despite what he'd just said, was not one of Graham's faults. 'Why?' she asked again.

'No reason,' he muttered.

'Because you were coming here?'

'No!' he shouted. 'Forget it. Look – Jo. Just come back. Don't stay here. Shouldn't your father be telling you that? I mean – isn't he supposed to believe all that about those whom God hath joined together?'

Joanna's eyes widened. 'Graham – you're talking as if I had left you on a whim.'

'I know,' he said, shaking his head. 'I know what I've done. It won't happen again.'

'It will.' She got up and went to the window, watching the snow fall from a darkening sky as the silence enveloped them. It was cold in the sitting room; she had chosen it as the site for negotiations rather than the cosy, homely kitchen, where she might be lulled into a false sense of security.

'Joanna, I swear. I'll never, never do it again.'

His voice was suddenly close to her, and she turned to find him behind her.

'Don't look like that,' he said. 'Please. Please don't be frightened of me.'

'I am frightened of you.' She turned away again.

'But it isn't me,' he said. 'You're not frightened of me.' He put his hand lightly on her shoulder, and she faced him again.

'Something gets into me. Something just snaps.'

'Then you should see someone. Talk to someone.'

'No. I can work it out for myself.'

'Not with me.' She pushed past him, and put as much distance between them as the room would allow.

'It has to be you. You're my wife.'

'And you think that gives you the right?'

'No!' He drained his glass. 'But—' He sighed. 'All right,' he said. 'I will see someone. I promise.' He waited for her response, which was not forthcoming. 'I *promise*!' he shouted.

Promises. As though they had never had this conversation before.

'What do you *want* me to do?' he asked, striding across the room.

Joanna moved away again, as he picked up the decanter.

She closed the curtains on her reflection. 'Why *are* you drinking so much?' she asked again. 'What's wrong?'

'Nothing. No reason.'

'Is it because of me?'

'Nothing to do with you. I met—' He paused. 'I met someone. Nothing – no one. Forget it.'

He wasn't making sense. 'Don't drink any more,' she said.

'Why not? What do you expect? You walk out on me—'

'I didn't exactly *walk* out,' she said sharply.

'Oh God, Jo,' he whispered. 'I'm sorry. I'm so sorry. Tell me what you want me to do, and I'll do it.'

'See someone,' Joanna said. 'Tell them what happens to you.'

He put down the decanter, his face growing a painful red. 'I couldn't,' he said.

'Because you don't want to admit it?' She took a deep breath. 'Well, that's what you're going to have to do,' she said. 'If you do that – if you prove to me that you're trying to get help . . .'

'You'll come back?' he said eagerly.

'You have to do it *first*,' she said.

31

'I will, I will.' He came towards her. 'Don't walk away from me, Jo,' he said. 'Help me. I'm not sure how—' He waved a hand. 'You know. How to go about—'

'I'll do that. I'll find out who you should see. And I'll go with you. To the doctor, or whatever. We'll get advice.'

'Yes. Good.' He put down his empty glass. 'Thank God,' he said.

Joanna looked at him for a long time. 'It's your last chance, Graham,' she said.

'I know. I know.' He took her hands. 'I know,' he said again, kissing them. He smiled, and kissed her on the cheek. 'Let's go,' he said.

'No, Graham. You've got to make the first move.'

'But you said we'd do it together.'

'We will. But you've promised before, Graham. I'm not going back until I know you're doing something about it. I will help you. I will. But I'm living at home until I'm sure.'

The clock whirred quietly, preparing to chime, as Graham dropped her hands. She knew the faintly puzzled look.

'What did you say?' he asked, and she knew the tone of voice.

She knew what came next.

Chapter Two

Eleanor had played at the carol service, catching his eye only to indicate in mime, her back to the congregation, that he had left his tie there.

He had told the children about all the people in the world who didn't have turkey and Christmas pudding, and had smiled gravely at the earnest, concerned faces which had looked back at him. If only that concern could last, he thought, into Cabinet Ministerhood. But it couldn't. By then, delicate international situations would seem much more important than feeding hungry mouths.

He locked away the collection money – he must have convinced some of the adults too, because there was even a fiver in there. He picked up the cash-box, then paused, and opened it again. Another fiver joined the first, and he locked the box again. He'd make sure it went to Save the Children or someone. The church roof could wait. Church roofs didn't cry.

He walked out into the already black night, and looked up at the starless, snow-laden sky. He'd have to get the tie back some time. He wondered about Eleanor's reasons for not bringing it with her. In case someone saw her give it back? Or because she wanted him to have to go back for it? Either way, it was a complication that he could have done without.

He should have worn boots, for the snow was covering his shoes, and he looked round for clear ground, but there was none. Sighing, he turned up his coat collar as a flurry of snow went down the back of his neck. He needn't worry about his sermon for tonight, he thought. He'd be the only one there.

As he rounded the church, the wind hit him. Head bowed, he set off to where the road could still just vaguely be seen, a faint fold in the white blanket. He heard the car as he walked along what he thought was the verge; he moved to the side, but it hooted. He lifted his head to see Marian.

'Lift?' she said, reaching over and opening the passenger door.

George got into the car, and pulled the door shut. 'Oh boy,' he said.

'The Stansfield road's blocked,' said Marian.

'Great.'

Marian drove a little more quickly than he would have done under these circumstances. As the car shimmied round into the vicarage driveway, she slowed down. 'His car's still here,' she said, pulling up outside the house. She looked at him. 'She won't go back to him,' she said. 'She's got more sense.'

'Not where he's concerned.' George got out and ran up the porch steps. As he opened the front door, he heard the bedroom door close upstairs. 'Jo?' he called.

He and Marian exchanged glances.

'They just want some privacy,' Marian said.

'They could be private downstairs,' George said darkly.

Marian stood for a moment, looking anxiously upstairs. Then her eyes went slowly to George's. 'She won't go back to him,' she said defiantly.

George felt that a closing bedroom door was hardly a sign of irretrievable breakdown. But she couldn't, she *mustn't* let herself be persuaded to go back. He felt helpless; all his working life he had helped people in trouble, and all he could do was fight with Joanna, as though it were her fault.

'What can we do?' he asked.

'Not much,' Marian said, with another glance upstairs. 'I think we should carry on as normal.'

'Go out, you mean?' He and Marian always spent a couple of hours in the village pub on Christmas Eve. It had been Marian's idea – she said you were more likely to get people into church if you were manifestly seen to be a person. 'What if he wants to come with us?'

'We'll cross that bridge when we come to it.'

'Will we?' he said dubiously.

'Yes,' she said. 'Let's go and get changed.'

'Upstairs?' The thought embarrassed him. Joanna's bedroom was at the other end of the landing from theirs, but he still felt as if he would be intruding.

'Well, that's where our clothes are,' said Marian. 'George, I am not going to let him spoil things. It's my house, and I'll go wherever I like.'

He changed, keeping his fingers crossed that the tie wouldn't come into the reckoning, and it didn't. She just told him to take what she called his work shirt down with him when he went, because she would be washing.

'On Christmas Eve?' he asked.

'Why not?' she demanded, a little on the defensive.

Marian always found something useful to do when life got complicated. He held up his hands in surrender. 'Just asking,' he said.

'What do you think?' she asked, holding up a dress he hadn't seen before.

'When did you get that?' he asked.

'It's your Christmas present to me.'

'I've got very good taste,' he said. 'It's lovely.'

'Joanna found it. She said you'd approve.'

George sat down to put on his shoes. 'Why should you need my approval?' he asked.

'What?' Marian came over to him. 'You're still in a funny mood, aren't you?' she said, her arm round his shoulders. 'What is it?' she asked, kissing the top of his head. 'Joanna?'

He patted the hand that rested on his shoulder. 'Partly.'

'And partly what else?'

He looked up at her. She believed in him. She believed he was what he said he was. And she didn't think for a moment that he visited Eleanor Langton because she had good legs and long blonde hair.

'Male menopause,' he said, as she sat beside him, her head touching his. He put his arm round her. 'I wanted to make love to you this morning,' he said.

'Why didn't you wake me?'

'You were awake,' he said. 'But I thought it might embarrass Jeremy.'

She laughed.

'Is this place important to you?' he asked.

Marian frowned slightly. 'The house?' she said. 'Or the village?'

'Either. Both.'

'On a scale of one to ten,' she said, 'I'd give it seven, I think.' She looked concerned. 'Are they trying to make you move to Brixton?' she asked.

He laughed. 'No. Nothing like that.'

Living here was important to her, he thought, tying his lace. Which just made things more difficult. Marian, you're married to a fraud, but I'm an honourable fraud, so I have to resign. He picked up his shirt, and they went downstairs.

'Someone's left the light on in the sitting room,' he said.

'I think it was Easter when we used it last,' said Marian. 'Let's hope it hasn't been on ever since.'

George saw Joanna when he opened the door. She looked up, her face streaked with tears, her eyes already bruising, her mouth swollen.

'My God,' he said.

'George?' Marian came in behind him, and ran to Joanna.

George watched, his brain numb. Joanna burst into tears again, and Marian took her into the kitchen, where she bathed the bruises, her face pale and set. Joanna was mumbling something, rendered incoherent by the sobs. And he just watched, feeling a creeping coldness in his limbs. Then he remembered the closing bedroom door.

'He's upstairs,' he said, making for the door.

'No!' Joanna shouted suddenly. 'Leave him, please. Leave him. He's drunk. He'll be sleeping it off—'

George was out of the kitchen before she'd finished the sentence, but Marian was behind him, her hand on his arm, as he reached the bottom of the stairs.

'George, do as she says.'

'I told him what would happen if he laid a finger on her again,' he said, starting up the stairs, but with a strength that he hadn't suspected, Marian hung on to him.

'It wouldn't do any good,' she said.

'It would do *me* some good!'

'It would get you into trouble! You'd upset Joanna – and what for? It wouldn't undo anything, would it?' Her face, still grimly sensible, looked up into his. 'Come back, George,' she said. 'Let him sleep it off.'

'In my house? He's leaving. Now.'

'He can't,' Joanna said, appearing in the hall.

George looked at her, bruised and battered, and felt tears of rage prick his eyes. She'd even got dressed up for him.

'He can't drive anywhere,' Joanna said. 'He took your whisky up with him. He's had far too much to drink.'

'I'll put him in a taxi when I've finished with him,' George roared, but he still couldn't make any progress on the stair, with Marian clinging to his arm.

'The road's blocked,' Marian reminded him. 'He can't get back to Stansfield anyway.'

'I don't care where he goes, as long as he leaves my house!' George shook Marian off at last.

'Please *leave* him!' Joanna cried, and there was real fear in her voice.

He stopped, and turned, but Joanna had gone back into

the kitchen. He sat down heavily on the stairs.

'What's the point in causing more trouble?' Marian asked, joining him. 'If you hit him, that's all you'll be doing.'

'Here,' he said, pushing his laundry into her hands. 'You wear it.'

'George—'

'I mean it. I'm not fit for it. Not if you're meant to turn the other cheek. Not if you're meant to love someone like him.'

'I'm not being particularly Christian,' Marian said. 'Just sensible. Joanna's had enough – she doesn't need you and Graham brawling into the bargain. She needs us to be with her.' She stood up, and held out her hand.

George looked up at her, and took her hand, heaving himself off the step. 'He's loving all this, isn't he?' he said, with a malevolent look at the closed bedroom door.

'Talk to him when you've calmed down and he's sobered up,' Marian said, leading him downstairs. She stopped at the bottom. 'I'd better make up the bed in the back bedroom,' she said. 'For Joanna.'

'Of all the—' George spluttered. 'If anyone had told me that I'd be offering hospitality to—'

'And I think you should take Joanna out,' she said firmly.

'What?'

'If he gets up, I don't want Joanna here. Or you, come to that,' she added.

'She won't come,' he said.

'Yes, she will – you can persuade her. You know you can.' She patted him. 'Go on. Go and talk to her.'

George sighed, and went into the kitchen, where Joanna was sitting by the fire, ineffectually raking the coals.

'Your mother thinks you should come out for a drink with me,' he said.

She shook her head. 'Like this?' she said.

'Well, that's what I thought.' He pulled a chair from the table and sat down beside her. 'But unless you're thinking of keeping yourself prisoner, you'll have to go out sooner or later.'

'Later,' she said.

'And then they'll see you in ones and twos,' he said. 'Why not come out with me and let them all see you at once?'

She smiled, still tearfully.

'I'll go along with whatever you want to tell them,' he said. 'Will you come?'

She didn't reply.

'It'll look worse tomorrow,' he said, in a matter-of-fact way that was entirely manufactured. He wanted to break down and cry. He wanted to go and ram Elstow's own medicine down his throat. He wanted to run naked through the snow and get into the *News of the World*.

'Is this so as you can talk to me?' she asked.

'I rather hoped you might talk to me,' he said. 'But I don't care if you talk or not.'

'Do you really want me to come?'

He nodded.

'All right,' she said. 'I might be telling a lot of lies,' she warned him.

'Fine,' he said. 'I've been telling a lot of lies for years.'

'What do you mean?'

'Oh – I'll tell you some time.' He smiled. 'When you're older.'

Marian watched Joanna's car move off slowly down the driveway. Perhaps spending the evening together would bring them closer; they had grown apart recently.

She glanced at the bedroom door as she got the bedding for Joanna, then walked quickly downstairs to the back bedroom, frowning in concentration. Had they had this chimney swept? They had had discussions about whether or not to include it, since the room wasn't really used now. Yes, she remembered. She had sensibly decided to get it done, just in case.

Just in case they had to accommodate her daughter's vicious husband.

Eighteen months, Marian thought, as she quickly and efficiently spread the sheets on the bed. Married eighteen months, and already an old hand at being knocked about. It wasn't too bad this time, she had said. Not compared to last time. Marian shook her head, and smoothed out the blanket. Perhaps you got grateful when he only blacked your eyes.

She sat on the bed, remembering the first eighteen months of her own marriage. Discovering George, realising that she wasn't obliged to be his right arm, and finding that she wanted to be, anyway. They hadn't had many rows – they'd been lucky. She'd become aware of his temper, of course, but it was usually aroused by something beyond their domestic boundaries.

The first time he'd actually been angry with her was when they'd been married about six months. She remembered the occasion; where they were when the row blew up. They were in the garden shed, of all the unlikely places for her to find herself. It was something to do with the garden – she had interfered with one of his precious plants, or something. He told her she'd killed it. He was furious. She tried to imagine how she would have felt if he'd attacked her physically, but she couldn't. She couldn't begin to imagine being frightened of George.

She finished making the bed, and set about the fire-building process with rather less efficiency. Twenty-six years of coping with the vicarage fires had done nothing to make her any more expert, but she thought that if it was lit now, it would be just right when she got back.

As Marian scrubbed the coal-dust from her hands, she could hear again what Joanna had said while she was bathing her eyes. Quietly; so quietly that George, still shocked, hadn't even heard her.

But Marian had.

Joanna was getting used to the stares; she had told those who'd asked that she had been to the dentist. She had once seen someone come back from the dentist with black eyes. The swollen mouth added to the effect, but even so, there were one or two polite but old-fashioned looks.

They were in a corner, where they could speak without being overheard. She looked at her father, whose face was still dark with brooding anger.

'He needs help,' she said.

He sipped his beer. 'He needs something.'

'He's going to see someone.'

'Not before time.'

'I'm going back with him,' she said carefully. She paused. 'We're going to get help.'

Her father stared at her, slowly putting down his mug. 'You're not serious,' he said.

She knew what she was doing to him, but she had to go through with it. 'It isn't his fault,' she said.

'I don't *care* whose fault it is,' he whispered fiercely. 'I don't care, Joanna. It's you I care about!'

'He doesn't—' She stopped as the barmaid came along, picking up empty glasses.

'You've been in the wars,' said the barmaid cheerfully.

Joanna smiled weakly.

'Dentist, Bill said. Eye-tooth, was it? I know they can do that to you.' She laughed. 'Your husband must be getting some funny looks,' she said, and went off to pass a few cheery words with someone else.

'He doesn't know what he's doing,' Joanna carried on.

'He knows well enough to stop doing it when he hears someone coming,' her father said. He leant closer. 'What would have happened if we hadn't come back, Jo? It would have been like last time, wouldn't it? Maybe even worse.'

Joanna stared into her barely touched cider.

'He's *dangerous*, Jo. You must see that. You can't go back to him! It's—'

'He doesn't understand you,' she said, interrupting him.

41

George drank some beer. 'I should hate to think that he did,' he said coldly.

'He doesn't understand why you're so against us trying to work it out,' she said. She was hurting her father more than she'd ever hurt anyone, and she loved him. 'He thinks you should be stronger on letting no man put asunder,' she said.

'I think he should be stronger on cherishing,' said her father.

'But you're supposed to believe in all that,' she persisted. 'If I was a stranger, you'd be helping me. You'd be helping Graham.'

He looked shocked; she wished she hadn't said it. But it was true.

'Do you love him?' he asked suddenly.

Joanna looked away. 'He isn't like that all the time,' she said.

'Do you love him?' he repeated.

'I did! When I married him.'

'And do you still?'

Joanna looked round the little pub, full of people in various stages of Christmas cheer. 'I don't know,' she said. 'It's hard to separate one thing from the other. It's not his fault. Yes. Yes, I do.'

'But you didn't make any attempt to get in touch with him, did you? Why not?'

Joanna's eyes were throbbing. She sipped her cider.

'Why not, Joanna?' he asked again.

'I was afraid,' she said. 'I shouldn't have left. It's only made things worse.'

'How can you love someone you're afraid of?' he asked.

Joanna looked over her glass. 'You should know,' she said. 'Aren't you supposed to fear God and love him at the same time?'

Her father sat back. 'I can't help you, Jo,' he said. 'I don't know how, because I don't understand. All I can do is tell you how to fight back. Don't drop your guard – learn how to punch. Learn how to put your weight behind a blow, how to duck and weave—'

'Stop it.' She had never heard him so bitter about anything. 'We're just making one another unhappy,' she said. 'This wasn't a good idea.'

'No,' he said. 'Perhaps it wasn't.' He finished his half pint. 'How can you talk about going back to him when he's just done that to you?' he asked.

'I've got reasons,' Joanna said. One reason. One that she wasn't going to share with anyone.

Eleanor was attempting to assemble the first toy. Didn't people used to buy toys already made? She stared at the instructions for the pedal car. What on earth was a . . . ? She screwed her eyes up to read the small, smudged print, but she still didn't know what it was, never mind which one of the parts at her disposal it was likely to be.

She had finally located the thread of a plastic bolt when the doorbell rang, and the nut slipped backwards and off. Eleanor glared at the door. Trust someone to come just when it seemed she had got the hang of something. She flicked the curtain back, and smiled. George's car – he must have come for his tie. He'd know how to get the car together.

What was it he wanted from her, she wondered. Was this the harmless flirtation that one read about in problem pages? She picked up the tie and, on an impulse, draped it round her neck. Maybe she could get her own back.

She opened the door, and froze.

'Good evening,' said Marian Wheeler.

She couldn't take it off; she'd notice. 'Oh, hello,' she replied, certain that her face had betrayed her if the tie hadn't.

'I'm calling to confirm George's invitation,' she said. 'You'd be very welcome.'

'Thank you,' Eleanor said, still transfixed.

'Please don't hesitate to come over,' Marian went on. 'Any time. Don't worry if there's no one in when you get there –

the door won't be locked. Just make yourself at home.'

'Thank you,' Eleanor said again, as her wits slowly returned. Ask her to come in, she told herself. You'll have to – she's just invited you for Christmas. 'Would you like to come in?' she asked, but it really didn't sound convincing.

'No, thank you – I've got some other calls to make.'

'Well – thank you for coming.'

'Not at all. Oh – and if you did want to contact anyone tonight . . . ' She paused, just for an instant. 'Your mother-in-law, is it, that you're expecting? I'll be pleased to pass on a message – I know you can't leave your little girl.'

Had she seen the tie? Was that why she stopped speaking for a moment? Oh, God, had she? 'It's very kind of you,' Eleanor said. 'But I – no. No, thank you.'

'You're welcome. And do bring Tessa over to see us some time over Christmas anyway. It's a long time since there was a little girl at the vicarage.' She turned to go. 'A long time,' she said again.

Lloyd drained his glass and set it down on the bar.

'Another?'

'No, thanks, Jack.' He looked at his watch. 'I think I'll get off now,' he said. 'Get an early night.'

'It's only ten o'clock,' Jack said. 'I thought you never went to bed the same day you got up?'

Lloyd slid off the stool.

'Got a date, have you?' said Jack.

Lloyd looked at him quickly. Jack had his Dutch uncle voice on. 'I just don't want to miss Santa,' he assured him.

'Judy rang in,' Jack went on. 'She said to say she's sorry she missed you, and happy Christmas.'

That was something, Lloyd supposed. 'I hope she's having fun with her in-laws,' he said.

'In-laws are obligatory at Christmas,' Jack said, and finished his pint. 'You're right,' he said. 'Shouldn't stay out too long on Christmas Eve. I'll go home and surprise the wife. Any chance of a lift?'

'Sure.' Lloyd smiled. Jack Woodford was the most complete family man he had ever met, but he liked to give the impression that he wasn't. Lloyd had been a family man too, once. Before the rows, which weren't so bad because you could always kiss and make up. Before the long silences, which were awful, because the air never cleared, and it got hard to breathe. Before the complaints about the hours he worked, and the accusations of neglect. Now, Barbara seemed almost like a stranger. Perhaps she always had been.

'Trouble with this job,' Lloyd said, holding the door open, 'is that you know your colleagues better than your family sometimes.'

'Or they know you better,' Jack said, as they went out into the dark, slushy car park. 'I mean, there's things you can't talk about to your family – not even your wife. Things they wouldn't thank you for talking about.'

'Things they wouldn't understand if you did,' Lloyd said, unlocking the passenger door. Little things. Minor irritations, minor triumphs, shared with people to whom they did not have to be explained.

'Yeah,' said Jack, mind-reading, as he often did. 'Like that bloody book.'

Lloyd laughed. The Super's ideas of efficiency weren't meeting with general approval. The book was instituted so that the desk sergeant could see at a glance . . . Lloyd couldn't quite remember what. 'Like that bloody book,' he agreed.

'Still,' Jack said, arranging his legs more comfortably. 'You've got all that sorted out, haven't you?'

'The book?' asked Lloyd, puzzled.

'The problem.'

Oh. Lloyd didn't answer, as he negotiated the slippery car-park entrance. Snow began to fall again, and he sighed.

'You and Judy Hill,' Jack said, not one to beat about the

45

bush for ever, if the birds didn't rise. Stick the gun in and shoot them there.

'I thought I was overdue for a lecture,' said Lloyd.

'I'm not lecturing you – just pointing out that it's not very clever.'

'Yes, thank you, Sergeant.' He leant slightly on the rank.

'Don't try that with me,' Jack warned. 'There are promotions in the wind – Barton's getting a shake-up in the new year.'

Jack was ten years older than Lloyd, but he behaved as if he were old enough to be his father. It was Jack, a sergeant at twenty-seven, who had interested Lloyd in making the police his career. Jack himself had never tried to get further than sergeant, having found his niche.

Lloyd switched on the windscreen wipers. 'I'm not all that ambitious, Jack,' he said.

'And Judy? Is she not ambitious either?'

Lloyd had never really thought about it.

'Look, Lloyd. I don't know how serious it is – I'm just saying watch your step, that's all. You've all but got your promotion – they'll come down on her harder than they will on you.'

'It's not against the bloody law!' It wasn't even happening at the moment. He'd barely even seen Judy out of working hours since Michael became desk-bound.

'If her husband took it into his head to complain . . . ' Jack said, leaving the sentence unfinished.

'So what?' said Lloyd. 'What do you think they'd do, Jack? Break her on the wheel? She'd get shifted to another station, that's all.'

'As sergeant. No promotion – and it's hard enough for women to make inspector without having the reputation of—'

The car swerved slightly as Lloyd took his eyes off the road. 'She has *not* got a reputation!' he shouted.

'Sorry, sorry. I didn't mean it like that. It would be a black mark, that's all. One that a woman can't afford in this job.'

'When did you get Women's Lib?' Lloyd muttered, running the window down to check for traffic.

'She's a nice girl – and she's good. I'd like to see her get on.'

Lloyd pulled up outside Jack's house, and Jack undid his seatbelt, but he didn't get out. He turned to Lloyd. 'If it's just a fling, she's risking more than you. That's all I'm saying.'

Lloyd sighed. 'It's not really like that,' he said. 'Judy and I go way back. To before she was married.'

Jack raised his eyebrows. 'I didn't know that,' he said.

'No. You don't know everything, O Wise Grey-haired One.'

'Sorry. None of my business,' he said, as he got out.

'No. But I'll pass your message on.'

'Right.' Jack leant back into the car. 'Come whenever you like tomorrow,' he said. 'Lunch will be at about two-thirty.'

'Smashing. Thanks, Jack – oh, and . . . ' He smiled. 'Thanks for the warning.'

It was after eleven by the time he got to the flat, and well past midnight by the time he had the little tree under control. He picked the pine-needles from his sweater, and strung the lights through the branches. Then he solemnly brought the little present from the bedroom, and took out the white nylon ribbon. With considerable lack of skill, he finally persuaded it into a bow, and snipped the ends until it looked more or less even. He swept the pieces of ribbon into the big empty ashtray that only Judy ever used, and switched on the tree lights.

Standing back to admire his handiwork, he wondered if Judy wanted to be a DI in Barton.

Michael's mouth brushed her neck, beginning its comfortably predictable quest, and Judy turned towards him, responding to the familiar overtures almost without conscious thought. She frowned, puzzled, as he drew away from her.

'What's the point?' he said.

'Michael?'

'It's no good.'

'How do you know? We haven't done anything yet.'

He swung his legs out of bed, and sat with his back to her. 'Would you have noticed if we had?' he asked.

47

'Michael! That's not fair.'

'No?' His shoulders hunched slightly. 'It's all so—' he began, and abandoned it. 'You were on automatic bloody pilot,' he said.

The protest died on her lips as she acknowledged the truth of his complaint. 'Sorry,' she said, touching his shoulder. He didn't respond, and she took her hand away. 'Come on, Michael,' she said. 'What do you expect? We've been married too long for—'

'For what? A simulation of some interest in the proceedings?'

'I wish you'd get back into bed,' Judy complained. 'It's freezing.'

'I don't expect passion,' he went on.

'We were hardly at the passionate stage, were we?' Judy said.

'We never have been,' he said, turning to look at her. 'But there used to be some enthusiasm. Not now.' He looked at her for a moment. 'Now, it's a way of passing the time. Like doing a crossword, but without the emotional involvement.'

'Are you saying that's just me?' she asked hotly.

'Keep your voice down,' he said urgently. 'They're just across the landing!'

'I will not keep my voice down! Our marriage may not be anything to write home about – but lack of emotional involvement is your speciality, not mine!'

He looked away again. 'I'm sorry if I bore you,' he said.

Judy frowned. 'You don't bore me,' she said. 'Are you bored? Is that what it is?' She sat up, and smiled. 'Is it unnatural practices time?' she asked.

'Don't be silly.'

She lay back on the pillow. 'What's all this leading up to, Michael?' she asked.

Did he know about her and Lloyd? She was surprised to find a cold pool of dread beginning to form. Not guilt, she noted dispassionately. Just panic at being found out before she was ready. But it couldn't be that. Michael must have decided long ago to push any suspicions about her and Lloyd to the back of his mind, and leave them there. So why would it bother him now, when she wasn't even seeing Lloyd?

'*Do* you want to do something?' she asked. 'Tell me. The worst I can do is say no.'

'There is something I'd like us to do,' he muttered, only just loudly enough for her to hear. He looked over his shoulder at her.

Judy waited, ready for anything.

'I'd like us to have a baby.'

Almost anything. She felt as though the world had stopped, as she stared back at him, at the eyes no longer bleak now that he had unburdened himself.

'It's not such an unnatural practice,' he said.

A baby had no place in Judy's scheme of things, if she had a scheme of things. Life was complicated enough without that. 'Why?' was all she could ask, when she found her voice.

'Why not?'

Why not? My God, she could give him a dozen reasons.

'You like babies, don't you?' he asked, the words incongruous coming from him, from Michael, from room-at-the-top Michael.

'I have a marginally higher opinion of them than Herod,' she said.

'Oh, for—' He flopped on to his back. 'You agreed we'd talk about it one day,' he said.

'Did I?' She couldn't imagine under what circumstances. 'So, we're talking about it.' Now, she really was on automatic pilot. Suitable words were filling up the spaces, while her mind raced through the impossibility of it all.

'I'm talking about it,' Michael said. 'You're doing one-liners.'

'When did I?' she asked, suddenly galvanised into life. 'You've never shown the slightest interest in starting a family.' Her eyes widened as she realised. 'It's your mother, isn't it?' she said angrily. 'It's your mother who wants us to have a baby!'

'Not so loud,' he said again. 'Yes, all right, she's mentioned it. She wants a grandchild – that's not unnatural either.'

'Well, tell her I'm sorry, but it just isn't convenient.'

'We can't wait for ever.'

'What's this *wait*? I'm not waiting for anything.'

Michael sat up. 'But this is when we should start a family,' he said. 'I'm not flying half-way round the world any more. We've got this house. It's time we put down roots.'

Judy's mouth fell open. 'You and me?' she said. *'Roots?'*

'Why not you and me?'

'Because we live separate lives,' she said.

'But we've been apart,' Michael argued. 'We're not apart now.' He lay back. 'People expect someone in my position to be a family man,' he said.

'I thought I'd heard it all, Michael,' Judy said wearily.

'Will you think about it?'

She shook her head.

'But that's what marriage is for,' he protested.

'Not our marriage.'

'What's *wrong* with our marriage? We've stayed together ten years,' Michael persisted.

Judy sat back. 'We've stayed together,' she said, 'because it's convenient. You married me because I had a career of my own, and I wouldn't be hanging on to your coat-tails. Because I wouldn't complain about your being away half the year, and I wouldn't ask too many questions when you got back. Because being married was a desirable plus on your CV – like children, presumably. That's why you married me.'

He didn't deny it. 'Why did you marry me, Judy?' he asked.

Because she couldn't have Lloyd. 'For all the wrong reasons,' she said.

The bedside phone rang, making them both jump.

'Half past one,' Michael said. 'I expect it's for you.'

Judy picked it up.

'Judy?' Lloyd said. 'Sorry, but you're needed. We've got a murder.'

50

Chapter Three

Lloyd waved back as Judy appeared at the window. A few moments later she came down the path, stopping at her own car and taking something out. Then she joined him, bringing with her a blast of freezing air.

'Happy Christmas,' he said.

'Very funny.'

'I wasn't being funny.'

She looked apologetic. 'Happy Christmas,' she responded belatedly, handing him a heavy, rectangular parcel. 'I was going to come in this morning,' she said. 'But I couldn't.'

He smiled, and put it on the back seat. 'Yours is at home,' he said, as the car bumped over snow already freezing now that the wind had dropped.

'Where are we going?' Judy asked, her voice flat and uninterested.

'Byford village.'

'I thought the road was still blocked,' she said.

He smiled. 'We've got our own personal snow-plough.' Judy didn't seem as impressed as he had been.

'Are we going to be first there?' she asked, with a sigh in her voice.

'No,' he said. 'There's a village bobby these days. I expect he's coping.' He glanced at her, but it was too dark to see.

'What's up?' he asked.

'What sort of murder is it?' she asked, ignoring him.

'Domestic.'

She groaned.

'They have their advantages,' he pointed out. 'No incident rooms, no house-to-house – no breaking it to the relatives since they were probably all there at the time.' Still no reaction. 'That's why I had to get you,' he said wickedly. 'Domestics need a woman's touch.'

But not even that elicited a response from Judy. There was something wrong. But then, he thought, she had been dragged out at two o'clock on Christmas morning. 'Sorry,' he said.

She hadn't even asked for details, and he had been looking forward to imparting them.

'One man dead,' he said. 'That's all I know. But you'll never guess where it happened.'

No response. Not even irritation. He soldiered on. 'The vicarage, would you believe? Our very own *Murder at the Vicarage*.'

'Sorry?'

'*Murder at the Vic*—' He sighed. 'Of course, you're not an Agatha Christie fan, are you?'

'No.'

'Vicarages, snow-bound villages,' he said, with a grin. 'With any luck we'll find a retired Indian Army colonel, a gigolo, a faintly sinister Austrian professor, and an old lady who'll sort it all out for us.'

'Mm.'

'Are you listening to anything I'm saying?'

'I didn't think you were saying anything important,' she said, then immediately repented. 'I'm sorry,' she said. 'Don't take any notice of me.'

Ahead, Lloyd could see the yellow flashes from the snow-plough. 'We'd better let him get further away,' he said, pulling the car up. He waited to see if she would talk to him, but she didn't.

'Someone is head-hunting you, if my little bird's got it right,' he said.

She turned to look at him, at least. 'What do you mean?'

'Moves afoot in Barton. Coming up in the new year, I'm told. But – there's a but.'

'But what?'

'But your relationship with me could rock the boat.'

'Why?' she asked. 'What's it got to do with anyone else? We wouldn't even be working together any more.'

'It shouldn't matter,' he said. 'Unless Michael complains about me.' Despite his dismissal of the consequences, Lloyd knew that Jack was right.

'Michael doesn't know,' she said.

'Can you be sure?' Lloyd asked.

'Yes,' she said. 'If he did, he'd have packed his bags by now.' She gave a sigh. 'Or mine,' she added.

'Suppose he finds out?'

'Michael won't complain,' she said. 'That would be regarded as making an exhibition of himself. Michael doesn't do that.'

'So you'll go after it?'

'Let's wait until it's officially there to be gone after, shall we?' she said.

The yellow light had slowly moved over Lloyd's horizon, and he set off again, through the moonscape. Following yonder star. He smiled, remembering how he used to long for it to snow at Christmas, and it never did. Christmas used to be fun. *'I can never remember,'* he quoted, *'if it snowed for six days and six nights when I was twelve, or twelve days and twelve nights when I was six.'*

'Dylan Thomas,' she said.

'See?' he said. 'I've taught you something.' Judy's lack of soul was something about which he complained, but which pleased him, really. It gave him something to work on. 'Unless it was a guess,' he added.

'A Child's Christmas in Wales,' she said, and he could tell that she was smiling at last.

He wound down the window as they approached the all-conquering snow-plough.

'All clear ahead,' a voice shouted. 'For now. You might not get out again, though.'

'And a merry Christmas to you,' Lloyd shouted back, and his voice sounded dead, in all that high-piled insulation.

A chorus of unsuspected voices called season's greetings. Judy behaved as though they weren't there. Lloyd frowned. No point in asking what was wrong, not while she was in this mood.

A lone police car sat outside the vicarage, and a young constable approached as they got out of the car.

'Chief Inspector Lloyd?'

'Yes – this is Sergeant Hill,' he said, waving a hand at Judy.

The constable nodded. 'Parks, sir,' he said. He stamped his feet.

Lloyd smiled. 'Parky by name . . . ?' he said.

The constable smiled, and Lloyd was truly grateful to him, after the hard time Judy was giving him. 'So,' he said. 'What's gone on here, then?'

Constable Parks led them up on to the porch steps, where he seemed to regard it as warmer. 'The dead man's called Graham Elstow,' he said. 'He's been battered to death with a poker.'

Lloyd groaned, and exchanged glances with Judy, who looked a little apprehensive.

'It's not too bad,' said Parks, sympathetically. 'There are three other people in the house. George Wheeler – he's the vicar, sir. His wife Marian, and daughter Joanna – that's Elstow's wife. She identified the body, sir.' He rubbed cold hands together. 'They reckon it happened while they were out, and Elstow was in the house on his own.'

'But you don't?' Lloyd asked, hearing the disparagement.

'The daughter's been beaten quite badly, sir. By her husband, I believe.'

'Wonderful,' said Judy.

'It's not my fault, Sergeant.' His breath streamed out as he turned to her, the vapour caught in the light from the door.

'Right, thanks. Let's go and have a look,' Lloyd said. 'Do you know the family?'

'I've passed the time of day with Mr Wheeler,' he said. 'And I know Mrs Wheeler and the daughter by sight – but I've not been here long.' He pulled the door to, in case he was overheard. 'The daughter's been staying with them since October,' he said. 'I didn't know she was married until tonight.'

Lloyd nodded, and pushed open the door again.

They trooped into a long, wide, Christmas-decorated hallway, where there was a tree surrounded by presents.

'The body's upstairs in one of the bedrooms,' the constable said. 'The family are in the kitchen, and no one's been in the other rooms since I arrived. They say it must have been an intruder, so I thought you would probably want to check the rest of the house, just in case.'

'Quite right,' Lloyd said. 'Good lad.' As he spoke, another car appeared in the driveway. 'Freddie,' said Lloyd to Judy. 'It's the doctor, constable – show him upstairs, and ID the body. OK?'

'Sir.'

Lloyd briefly introduced himself and Judy to the family, who sat round the kitchen table, rather as though they were at a board meeting. A big, well-built man who looked slightly out of place in a clerical collar. A pretty wife – wearing a trouser suit, which rather surprised Lloyd. He still expected the wives of clergy to wear twinsets and pearls, but it had been about thirty years since he'd had anything to do with that sort of thing. A daughter who was probably pretty when she hadn't been beaten up. No tears, no hysterics. Mr Wheeler stood up to shake hands.

The courtesies completed, Lloyd apologised. 'I'm afraid the snow's caught us all on the hop,' he said. 'We're a bit short-handed here. We'll be back in a few moments, if you'd excuse us.'

'You'd better go and say hello to Freddie,' he said to Judy, once they were out in the hallway. 'Send Parks down, will you?'

So it wasn't straightforward, and he would have to bring forensic in. Lloyd glanced up as Parks came downstairs. 'What's it like up there?' he asked.

'Well,' said the constable, 'I wouldn't want my mum to see it.'

Poor Judy. Lloyd left Parks phoning for back-up, and went back in to the silent group in the kitchen.

'Are you all right, Mrs Elstow?' he asked. 'Do you want a doctor?'

'No,' she said. 'I'm all right, thank you.'

Her face, pale beneath the discoloured skin, belied the polite answer.

'Well,' he said gently. 'Let's start with what happened to you.'

She glanced quickly at her mother, who took a preparatory breath.

'I'd rather hear it from Mrs Elstow herself,' said Lloyd quickly.

'I – that is . . . ' the girl began, then stopped. 'Graham – that's my husband – he . . . '

Lloyd sat down at the table. 'You'd left him,' he said, hoping his guess was right.

She nodded.

'And why was he here?' asked Lloyd.

'He came to ask me to go back with him,' she said, dully. 'I wouldn't.'

Lloyd put his chin on his hands and looked at her. 'And that was how he hoped to persuade you?' he said.

Her eyes met his defiantly. 'He got angry,' she said, and it was said in her husband's defence.

Lloyd sat back, and nodded slowly. 'And when was this, Mrs Elstow?'

Again, a glance at her mother, who looked down at her hands.

'This afternoon. Evening. I don't know.' Then she added, in a low voice, 'About five.'

'Mr – Lloyd, is it?' said Wheeler. 'I don't quite see what this has to do with what happened.'

Lloyd raised his eyebrows at him.

'We were all out,' he said. 'Someone must have—'

'So when was he found?' asked Lloyd, talking through him.

'Just before one o'clock,' said Mrs Wheeler. 'I found him. We'd been to the midnight service.'

'Thank you,' said Lloyd. 'Which of you saw him last?'

They all looked at one another; no one looked at him.

'I did,' said Joanna Elstow. 'At five.'

Slowly, painfully, the story emerged. Lloyd didn't ask for detail, or for clarification. He made a mental note of the points that puzzled him, but he didn't ask about them. He just listened. George Wheeler and his daughter had left the house at seven. Mrs Wheeler had gone out at about ten to eight. Wheeler and his daughter had returned first, to find themselves locked out. Mrs Wheeler had let them in when she got home, and they had all left again at eleven for the midnight service.

Lloyd had heard the others arrive during his patient questioning of the family. When Marian Wheeler completed the story with her account of finding Elstow, he thanked them, giving every indication that he accepted their story as gospel. Which was appropriate, he thought, as he stood up. 'Excuse me again, please,' he said, and went upstairs, where Judy was directing the activities of the photographer. The fingerprint lad was whistling quietly, as he carefully stepped over the body; the photographer impassively snapped away, the doctor was making interested noises, and Judy looked green.

'What do you think?' Lloyd said.

'I think I want to go home and let Miss Marple get on with it,' she said.

So she had been listening to his one-sided conversation in the car, he thought. She was just being bloody-minded, which at least was in character. 'You go down and see what you can get,' he said, having given her the bare bones.

Judy escaped, and Lloyd looked round the room. The poker lay on the floor by the body; he peered at it before it was bagged up, then squatted down beside the doctor. 'Well?' he said. 'How long?'

'Under twelve hours. Anything between five and eleven hours. That's very rough – I'll be able to narrow it down.'

Lloyd checked the time. 'Between four-thirty and ten-thirty p.m.?'

'Well – my *guess* is eight to ten hours. The PM will probably confirm that.'

'Could a woman have done it?' Lloyd asked.

'Oh, yes. They're heavy blows, but a woman with a good double-handed backhand could have done it.' He grinned, altering his thin, serious face. 'Judging from that,' he said, nodding at the decanter which was being dusted for prints, 'and the smell, I'd say he made it easy for whoever did it. I'll confirm that at the lab.'

'His wife says he'd had a lot to drink before he got here.'

Freddie nodded. 'I expect so,' he said. 'And he'd been hitting someone.' He smiled broadly again. 'If that's any help.'

'His wife,' said Lloyd.

'Ah. The Case of the Turning Worm?' asked Freddie.

'They were all out when it happened,' said Lloyd, his eyes wide, his hands held out in helpless innocence.

'Of course they were,' said Freddie. 'Can you give me a photograph from this angle, please?' he asked the photographer, indicating what he meant. 'Looks like a woman's prints on the poker.'

The flash made Lloyd blink. 'How long between the attack and death?' he asked.

'Not long. Look.'

Lloyd didn't really. He'd developed a trick of making his eyes blur.

'Not all that much blood.'

'What?' Lloyd looked at the bed.

'Oh, there's a lot splashed about,' Freddie said. 'But he didn't lie bleeding on the floor for long. I'll know better when I've had the chance to make a proper examination. I can do it today, if you want to arrange for someone to be present,' he said. 'Spoil someone's Christmas dinner.'

'It had better be mine,' said Lloyd.

'Pity,' said the doctor. 'I thought I might get a couple of hours in Sergeant Hill's company.'

Lloyd smiled. 'I'm not that cruel,' he said.

'Is it the blood, or me?' asked Freddie.

'Sir!'

Lloyd went to the fireplace, where it was just possible to see the charred remains of clothing.

Freddie bent down to take a closer look. 'Oh, yes,' he said. 'Enough left to identify it, I'm sure.' He straightened up. 'You're home and dry this time, Lloyd.'

Joanna sat at the table, her mother on one side, and Sergeant Hill on the other. Her father was over by the fire.

Sergeant Hill was very attractive, Joanna thought absently. Good clothes.

'Can you tell me why he hit you?' she was asking.

'He came to see if I would go back with him, and I wouldn't,' Joanna said, her voice light. She wasn't going to cry.

'I'm sorry,' the sergeant said. 'I know this must be very difficult for you, and I won't keep you long, I promise. But I do have to know what went on in here tonight.'

'That wasn't tonight,' her father said. 'It was this afternoon. It had nothing to do with what happened tonight.'

The sergeant looked over her shoulder. 'Were you here, Mr Wheeler?' she asked. She was simply requesting information, but Joanna saw her father's colour rise a little.

'No, I was not!'

'George,' said her mother, 'the sergeant has to ask questions.'

'Sorry.'

'Don't worry about me, Mr Wheeler,' Sergeant Hill said. She turned back to Joanna. 'When did it happen?' she asked.

'I told the inspector,' Joanna said. 'Five o'clock.' She could still hear the clock chiming as Graham advanced on her. Her head ached, and she wanted to close the eyes that it was so painful to keep open. She wanted to be alone, to assess her position, to work out what it all meant, how she felt. Graham was gone. And with his going, the ever-present fear had slipped away from her. But that wasn't all she was going to feel. She needed the chance to find out.

'He only stopped because he heard us coming home,' her father said.

'You and Mrs Wheeler?'

'Yes.'

'What time was that?' asked the sergeant.

'Let's see,' said her father. 'I stayed at the church for a while. I must have left at about quarter-past five, I think. Is it important?'

Sergeant Hill smiled apologetically. 'You never really know at this stage in an investigation,' she said.

'There were other people there until just before I left,' he said. 'You could check with them.'

'I picked you up at about twenty past,' said her mother. She turned to Sergeant Hill. 'We came straight here,' she said.

'And is that right, Joanna?' the sergeant asked. 'He stopped because he heard your parents coming in?'

'When he heard their car,' Joanna said miserably. 'He went upstairs.'

The inspector came back in then, and apologised for all the disruption, as if it was his fault.

'I'm afraid we'll be here for some time,' he said. 'There's a great deal of difficulty getting vehicles here. And there's—' He waved a hand. 'A lot to see to,' he said.

He meant that they couldn't get Graham out yet, Joanna thought grimly.

'Especially,' he went on, 'since you say it happened while you were out.'

'Say?'

Joanna flinched, hearing the danger signals in her father's voice.

Inspector Lloyd came over to the table, and leant both hands on it, bending down almost conspiratorially. 'We've had to get the lab boys in,' he said, and Joanna noticed his Welsh accent for the first time. 'To tell us what went on in there.' There was a pause. 'And they can,' he said, straightening up. 'Make no mistake. Everything in that room's got a story to tell.' He looked directly at Joanna when he spoke again. 'So if any of you could save us some time and trouble . . . ' He waited.

Joanna looked steadily back at him. He had blue eyes.

'Mrs Elstow?' he said.

'I've told you all I know.'

He stepped back from the table, and went over to stand by the door, as though she might make a break for it.

'Joanna,' Sergeant Hill said. 'You said just now that Graham ran upstairs? Where did you have the fight with him?'

'It wasn't a fight,' Joanna said helplessly. Then again, almost to herself, 'It wasn't a fight.'

'I'm sorry. Where were you when he hit you?'

'The sitting room.'

'Where's that, love?' the inspector asked.

'The last door on the left,' she said.

He opened the kitchen door, and looked down the hall. 'You weren't upstairs with him at any point?' he asked.

'No.'

The sergeant glanced at him, and Joanna saw him give a tiny nod.

'Are you sure, Joanna?' the sergeant asked.

'Of course I'm sure.'

'Did you try to defend yourself?'

Defend herself. Joanna shook her head. 'I just tried to get away,' she said.

'How?'

'I ran to the door, but he slammed it.'

The inspector got up and went out; for some reason that she couldn't fathom, Joanna felt safer with him there.

'Didn't you try to fight back?'

Joanna looked at her, at the clear brown eyes that watched her so closely. 'You *can't* fight back,' she explained, to this woman who had never been in that position. For all Joanna knew, Sergeant Hill regularly waded into pub brawls and mad axe-men. But she had never been knocked off her feet by her own husband.

'You must have been angry, Joanna.'

'Angry?' Joanna repeated, genuinely puzzled.

The sergeant frowned. 'Weren't you?' she asked.

'No. I was frightened,' she said. 'Frightened.'

The sergeant wrote that down. She wrote everything down. It was beginning to irritate Joanna.

'What did you do after he'd gone upstairs?' she asked.

'Nothing.'

'But your parents had come home,' she said. 'Didn't you see them?'

'No. I didn't leave the sitting room. I heard them come in, and then they went upstairs.'

'And you stayed where you were?'

'Yes.'

'For how long?'

Joanna shook her head. 'I don't know,' she said.

'It would be about a quarter of an hour, twenty minutes,' her father supplied. 'We didn't know any of this had happened, and we just went up to change. We thought—' He broke off. 'We thought Joanna was in her room,' he said. 'We didn't want to disturb her.'

The sergeant looked back at Joanna. 'But you were downstairs all the time?' she asked.

'Yes. Until Daddy came in and found me.'

'Why, Joanna?'

'Look – is this really necessary?' her father demanded.

'Why?' asked Sergeant Hill again.

Joanna swallowed.

'Why didn't you come out when your parents came home? Why didn't you tell them what had happened?'

'Because—' Joanna could feel her skin redden, as she tried to explain. 'Because you feel ashamed,' she said.

Eleanor quietly placed the pedal-car at the foot of the bed. The pale moonlight lit the room, with assistance from the snow, and for a second, she recalled exactly the moment of waking to find her stocking bulging and lumpy with presents.

Tessa would be awake in a couple of hours, she told herself. It wasn't sensible to stay up half the night worrying about something she couldn't alter.

She cried, as she watched Tessa sleep. If only Tessa had known him; if only he could have seen her. But the tears weren't for Richard. He was beyond tears, and had been from the moment the car hit him. For a while, during the long evening, she had thought that she had been released from the crushing loneliness. George had needed her, and it had been so long since anyone at all had needed her.

Tessa needed her, she reminded herself, as she watched her turn, and sigh contentedly. But that was dependence, and that wasn't the same. A two-year-old takes love where she finds it; she was as happy with her grandmother as she was with Eleanor. But George had needed *her*. Not someone who would feed him and clothe him, and keep him safe. He could do that for himself. He had needed her, and she had helped him. She hadn't been able to help Richard, and that had been the worst part. It had been a long time since she had been able to offer rather than ask for help. It had been a step towards the open door, the light from which now paled the edges of her darkness.

Today had been a turning point. But she shouldn't have done what she did; she knew that even at the time, though she couldn't have stopped herself. She had waited so long. So perhaps the tears were remorse. A brief moment of satisfaction, followed by the reckoning. The tears were for herself.

She tucked the quilt round Tessa's sleeping figure. Perhaps it hadn't been the release she had longed for, but it had been a moment's respite; she deserved that.

And the tears were drying.

They were taking the tumble-dried clothes out of the washing-machine. They had asked politely enough, and George had given his permission with a co-operative readiness that he did not feel. George watched the two constables who were carefully listing the clothes, then dragged his attention back to the inspector.

'When did you and your daughter get back from the pub?' he asked.

'Just before ten,' said George quickly, not looking at Joanna. 'Joanna was tired, so we left a little earlier than usual.'

'And you came straight home?'

'Yes,' said George. 'But as Joanna said, we were locked out. Surely that's important?' he asked. The inspector hadn't seemed terribly interested. 'It wasn't accidental,' he said. 'We never lock the doors.'

'Never? the sergeant asked.

'No,' he said. 'There's still no need to lock doors in Byford. Not the vicarage doors, at any rate. We've nothing here worth stealing.'

'But you still think someone came in to steal tonight?' the inspector asked.

'I think we had an intruder,' George said carefully. 'When whoever it was went into Joanna's room, Elstow presumably startled him. And for some reason, he must have locked the doors when he left.'

Joanna buried her face in her hands, and Marian put her arm round her shoulders.

'Whoever it was would have needed a key for the back

door,' said the inspector.

'The key's kept in the door,' said George.

'I thought Graham had done it,' Joanna said, not taking her hands from her face. 'I thought he was just—'

'And the front door's a Yale lock,' said the inspector, almost to himself. 'But why would anyone want to lock the doors?'

George wasn't sure if a reply was needed. He shook his head.

'Well,' said Lloyd. 'We'll see what prints we can get. Lucky you had a key, Mrs Wheeler.'

'There's one on the ring with the car-keys,' she said.

'Before you left for the pub,' asked Sergeant Hill, 'did anyone check on Mr Elstow?'

'No,' George said heavily. 'Marian asked me to let him sober up first.'

'After you came back?'

'We thought he'd locked us out. We left him to stew.'

'So from five o'clock, nobody saw Mr Elstow at all?'

'No.'

'Mrs Elstow?' asked Lloyd.

Joanna, her face still buried in her hands, shook her head.

'The front door,' Marian said. 'I pushed the catch up again as we left for the midnight service. I've probably spoiled any fingerprints.'

'What about the back door?' asked the sergeant.

'I unlocked it,' said George. 'It annoyed me – I thought Elstow . . . ' He ran his hands over his face. 'It has to have been a burglar,' he said.

'But nothing was taken,' Sergeant Hill said quietly. 'You've got presents under the tree in the hall – why would he go upstairs?'

'I've no idea. Evidently he did.'

'Why would he come in and go straight to the one room that had someone in it?' she asked.

He looked from her to the inspector. 'I don't know,' he said. 'But that's what must have happened.'

'That's it,' said the policewoman who was making out the

65

laundry list. 'Would you sign it, please, Mrs Wheeler?'

Marian signed it, and was given a copy.

'We'll try not to hang on to them too long,' said the inspector. 'But what with Christmas and everything, I can't promise. We really do appreciate your co-operation.'

'We understand,' George said. 'You're welcome to take anything you think will help.'

'I suppose you've got your job to do,' Marian said, and the inspector looked a little uncomfortable.

'Well,' he said. 'It's just that whoever did do it must have changed his clothes. We have to eliminate possibilities as well as investigate them.'

Marian stood up. 'If there's nothing else you want Joanna for,' she said, 'I think it's time she got some sleep.'

'Of course,' said Lloyd.

'I know you're taking these clothes away because you think I did it,' Joanna said.

'We're trying to establish what happened,' Lloyd said. 'That's all.'

George almost believed him. He kissed Joanna, and Marian took her off. He turned back to face Lloyd, his shoulders sagging. 'You do think Joanna killed him,' he said.

'It's a possibility,' said Lloyd. 'Isn't it?'

George got up and filled the kettle. 'I think I'd like a cup of tea,' he said. 'Good old English stand-by. Will you join me? I'm very aware that we are ruining your Christmas.'

The sergeant frowned a little. 'I don't suppose,' she said slowly, 'that your own Christmas has been improved.'

He filled the kettle, and switched it on. 'Sergeant Hill,' he said, turning to face her, 'my Christmas was ruined when that young man came here this afternoon. The fact that he will hopefully soon be leaving my house, albeit feet first, is a source of considerable satisfaction to me.'

Sergeant Hill's eyes widened.

'You think a man of the cloth should be showing more compassion,' he said.

66

'Or more discretion,' she said, with a smile.

He laughed. Really laughed. He liked this lady with the shrewd brown eyes and quick tongue.

'All I know is that Joanna won't suffer at his hands any more,' he said. 'And quite frankly, I don't *care* who killed him. But it wasn't Joanna.'

'You seem very protective of your daughter, Mr Wheeler,' Lloyd said.

'Do I?' he asked. 'No more than any other parent.'

The sergeant wandered over to the window wall, where Marian had begun pinning up the photographs of Joanna when she was three weeks old. George watched her as she perused them.

'My wife had two miscarriages before Joanna was born,' he said. 'We were told she shouldn't have any more children after Joanna.'

'She's very pretty,' said Sergeant Hill.

'But you have to find that out from a photograph,' George said. 'She isn't very pretty tonight.' He stood up, and walked over to where the sergeant stood. 'She's twenty-one years old,' he said, and tapped the wall. 'That's all twenty-one years of her.' He looked at the photographs. 'Two months ago, I had to bring her home from hospital, Sergeant.'

'Hospital?'

'Oh, yes,' said George. 'Cracked ribs. A broken collar-bone. Battered – that's the word, isn't it?'

'Did she bring charges against him?' she asked.

George shook his head. 'I thought you'd understand about battered wives, Sergeant,' he said. 'They're too ashamed – too scared. Too—' He shrugged, and walked away. 'I don't know,' he said. 'Do you have children, Sergeant?'

'No.'

'Inspector?'

'Two,' Lloyd said. 'A boy and a girl.'

'How would *you* feel?' George asked. 'How would you feel, if you found your daughter in the state that mine is in tonight?'

67

Lloyd's blue eyes looked at him steadily. 'Angry,' he said.

George nodded. 'That's how I feel,' he said.

'And,' Lloyd carried on, 'I'd think he'd deserved all he'd got.'

George sat down heavily.

'And if I came in,' said Lloyd in measured tones, 'and found her laying into him with a poker, I might feel inclined to . . . fix it?' he suggested. 'Fix it so that she didn't get the blame.'

'So might I,' said George. 'So might I. But, fortunately, it wasn't necessary.'

Lloyd didn't believe him, he could see that.

Marian sat with Joanna until she fell asleep, her poor battered face almost peaceful. Upstairs, people still moved about, rattling up and down the stairs, going in and out of the door. Using the telephone. Talking in low voices. Across the hall, they were even in the sitting room. She bent down and kissed Joanna as she had when she was a child, and said a prayer for her. Then she straightened up, and went back to the kitchen.

'Mrs Wheeler,' Inspector Lloyd said, getting to his feet. 'I think I'm in your seat.'

'Oh, no. Please. Sit down again. I'll sit here.' She sat at the table with the sergeant.

'We'll be out of your hair soon, Mrs Wheeler,' she said.

Marian looked across at George, who smiled quietly at her. 'What time is it?' she asked him.

He looked at his watch. 'Twenty-five to five,' he said.

Marian had thought it must be much later. 'Why are they in the sitting room?' she asked the inspector.

He cleared his throat before he spoke. 'Your daughter says that she and her husband were in there when he lost his temper,' he said. 'She was pretty badly knocked about, Mrs Wheeler. The room isn't.'

'I tidied it,' Marian said. 'Before all this. After we found her in there.'

She watched realisation dawn in the inspector's eyes. 'Of course,' he said. 'I didn't think – I must be tired.'

Marian was surprised that she wasn't. She ought to be. But somehow it just felt as if this was happening to someone else. 'Are you accusing Joanna of killing him?' she asked.

'We're not accusing anyone,' said the inspector. 'Not yet.'

'Mrs Wheeler?' the sergeant said. 'No one at all saw Mr Elstow between five o'clock, when he left your daughter, and just before one, when you found him. That's right?'

'Yes,' said Marian, a little worried.

'No one went to check on him, or try to talk to him?'

'No.'

'So what made you go up when you did, Mrs Wheeler?'

She looked at George. It must be agony for him, sitting there, putting up with all these questions, hardly answering back at all. He'd called it pretending to be a vicar, earlier on. He'd been in such a funny mood all day. And that sermon was odd, too. As she watched, George pulled out his handkerchief and mopped his brow. And there, hanging out of his pocket, was his tie.

Marian stared at it, transfixed by it for the second time. Oh, my God. My *God*. He'd said he'd been with Joanna all evening. Oh, my God.

'Mrs Wheeler?'

She blinked at the sergeant. 'Sorry?' she said.

'What made you go up to him when you did?'

'Joanna,' Marian said, trying to drag her thoughts away from the tie. 'She said she wanted to see if he was all right. It was Christmas Day, that sort of thing.'

'Joanna felt sorry for him!' George said angrily, interrupting her. 'So I told her that if anyone was going to see

69

him, it would be me, and that I would talk to him in language that he understood.' He turned to the sergeant. 'I'm sorry, Sergeant Hill, if I'm failing to live up to your expectations of the clergy. Clearly, I disappoint my daughter – even my son-in-law, I was told tonight. But that's how I felt.'

'He'd got Joanna and George at each other's throats,' Marian said. 'So I went up. Just to let him know what he was doing to us. And I found him,' she finished.

'Did you touch anything, Mrs Wheeler?' Inspector Lloyd asked.

She shook her head. 'I just called George,' she said, still barely aware of what she was saying. George had been with Eleanor Langton.

'Then I phoned the police,' George said.

'Just one more thing,' said the inspector. 'Where did you go when you went out, Mrs Wheeler?'

'I checked up on the older people in the village. Because the weather was so bad. To make sure they were all right.'

'Could I possibly have a list of the people you saw?' he asked. 'Not now, of course. Perhaps tomorrow?'

'Yes. Yes, of course.'

Marian acknowledged their leave-taking with half of her brain. She wasn't sure she could cope with this.

George came back in. 'You could go to Diana's,' he said. 'You don't have to stay here.'

Marian shook her head, getting up slowly from the table. She looked across at her husband, her face sad.

'How many commandments have you broken today, George?' she asked.

'Well, Watson?' said Lloyd, starting the engine. 'What do you think?'

Judy leant back and closed her eyes. 'I think it's all very

depressing,' she said. 'And he's a very odd sort of vicar.'

'Is he? I don't know much about vicars,' Lloyd said.

'He's not like any one I've ever known,' Judy said, and yawned. 'But then, I haven't known very many.'

'Someone tried to burn some clothing,' Lloyd said. 'Can't tell what yet. But we'll find out, as I told Mrs Elstow.'

Judy frowned. 'Why the business with the washing-machine?' she asked. 'If you'd already found the clothes?'

Lloyd smiled. 'Confuse the enemy,' he said. 'And never take anything at its face value. What's your verdict?'

'That Joanna got hit once too often, and got her own back when he fell asleep,' Judy said. 'And they're covering up for her.'

'Then what about the doors?' Lloyd said. 'Why mention that at all? It just buggers up their own intruder theory.'

Judy was too tired, too confused, to listen to one of Lloyd's flights of fancy. 'You don't seriously think it was an intruder, do you?' she said sharply.

'No.'

'Then can we leave it until we know what we're talking about?'

'Yes, miss.'

She rubbed her forehead, where an incipient headache was forming.

'Do you fancy taking on young Mrs Elstow in single combat?' he asked.

'Poor kid. Yes, I think that might work.' She yawned again. 'When?'

'Tomorrow afternoon, I suppose,' he said.

'By tomorrow, I take it you mean today?'

'I'm afraid so.' He smiled. 'You should worry. I've got the post mortem.'

Judy closed her eyes again. 'Michael will go through the roof,' she said. 'He already thinks it's the height of bad manners to get yourself murdered at Christmas time.'

71

'Just go to Byford when you're ready,' Lloyd said, obviously none too interested in Michael's problems. 'No need to let them know you're coming.'

The car bumped over the snow, as a new fall came floating down.

'I should be back at the station at about four,' Lloyd said. 'You can let me know how you've got on.'

'Eleven hours from now,' Judy said gloomily, her eyelids heavy.

'Let Michael cook the dinner,' Lloyd said.

'Looks like I'll have to,' said Judy.

Lloyd lapsed into an unnatural silence then. Lloyd loved speaking. Judy sometimes loved to listen. But this time she was grateful for the silence, as he concentrated on his driving, through conditions which had worsened still further.

'At least the road's not blocked,' she murmured, closing her eyes again. Just for a moment.

'We're here,' Lloyd said, and she was startled to find herself in the police station car park. 'Oh, Lloyd, I'm sorry,' she said.

The heating had, of course, broken down, and Judy began writing up her notebook until her hands became too numb. Lloyd left instructions for the day-shift, and at last decreed that they could leave.

She flopped into the car. 'Home, driver,' she said.

'Come to the flat first.'

Judy turned to him. 'Lloyd, I've got Michael and his parents expecting a jolly Christmas Day, and it's almost six in the morning!'

'That's why you need to unwind. Come to the flat.'

Unwinding would be nice, she thought.

'Just for a cup of coffee,' he persisted.

Lloyd's quiet, restful flat, or Mrs Hill banging on about Christmas being for the kiddies, really. 'All right,' she said. Though even Mrs Hill would not be banging on about Christmas at six o'clock in the morning, she reflected, as Lloyd drove off. She curled into a cold, uncomfortable heap, until at last she was in Lloyd's flat, in the exquisite, centrally-heated warmth. She took off her coat for the first time since she'd left home.

'I'll get the coffee on,' he said, stopping at the kitchen door. 'You go through.'

She opened the door to find the living room in darkness, except for a tiny tree, its coloured lights filling the room with exotic shadows. She smiled. 'It's lovely,' she said, going in.

Lloyd came in after her, and her present to him joined the one under the tree. 'I thought it was pretty good,' he said, catching her hands. 'Happy Christmas, Sergeant Hill.'

He was kissing her, holding her close, and it was so peaceful, so good to have him to herself. Too good. 'Put the light on,' she said.

'Why?'

'Because you said just a cup of coffee, not kisses by coloured lights.'

He smiled, and reached over to a table lamp, which filled the room with a soft glow.

'That isn't much better,' Judy complained, her hands still clasped behind his neck.

'What do you expect in a bachelor flat?' he said. 'I've only got seduction lighting.'

Judy laughed. 'It would take more than lighting,' she said. 'A few pep-pills and some rhinoceros horn, maybe.' She kissed him. 'When did you get the new lamp?' she asked.

'About six weeks ago,' he said.

Now Judy felt guilty. 'It's ages since I've been here,' she said.

He nodded. 'I'll go and really put the coffee on.'

Judy loved Lloyd's flat, which bit by bit was being made the way he wanted it. It was quiet, and tranquil, and not at all like him.

He came back in. 'Five minutes,' he said. 'And Santa's been.'

He sat on the sofa; she sat on the floor, and opened her present to find the little ebony cat that she'd seen months ago, and told Lloyd about. 'Lloyd,' she said. 'I didn't mean you to *buy* it.'

'I know you can't take it home,' he said. 'Before you tell me. But you can keep it here, can't you? Or at work, I suppose.'

She smiled. 'Where do I need the most luck?' she asked.

He didn't reply, but picked up his present.

'It isn't as romantic as yours,' she warned him.

'I'd be disappointed if it was,' he said. 'One romantic is enough in any relationship.'

She watched anxiously as he opened it, and his smile seemed genuine. 'The new one,' he said. 'I've been waiting for this.' He opened it. 'It's *signed!* How did you manage that?'

'I queued for two hours,' she said.

'That's romantic,' he pointed out. 'What was he like?'

'Like someone who'd been signing books for two hours.'

She joined him on the sofa for the rest of the five minutes, which stretched to ten. 'Coffee,' she said, pushing him away.

'Coffee.'

He came back with a tray on which were set two mugs, the coffee jug, cream, and a bottle of brandy. 'Right out of pep-pills and rhinoceros horn,' he said.

They drank the coffee with liberal helpings of brandy, which seemed to have the opposite effect to pep-pills, and this rather counteracted any similarities it may have had to rhinoceros horn. They sat on the sofa, arms round one another, eyes half-closed. Judy squinted at her watch. 'It's after seven,' she said. 'I have to go.' But she didn't move.

'What's wrong, Judy?' Lloyd asked.

'Oh, nothing. Everything. I don't know.'

'Michael's parents getting you down?'

'Yes. And Michael's getting me down. And the weather. It took almost an hour just to get here from Byford.'

'I know,' he said. 'I was driving.'

'Sorry I fell asleep on you.'

'Well,' he said, squeezing her. 'It was better than being ignored.' He looked at her. 'Have you had a row with Michael?' he asked.

'Yes.'

'What about?'

'Nothing.'

'Tell me.'

'No – it doesn't matter.'

'Come on,' he said. 'It might help if you get it off your chest.'

She sighed. 'He said he wanted us to have a baby,' she said, her eyes closed. She felt Lloyd pull away from her.

'What did you say to him?' he demanded.

'Oh, Lloyd! What do you think I said?'

He sat for a long time without speaking. Just looking at her.

'Lloyd – I've got no intention—'

'Judy,' he said, talking through her. 'Judy, I don't think I can go on sharing you.'

Oh, God. She felt like one of those rubber dolls that bounced back to get knocked over again. 'Not now, Lloyd,' she said. 'Please, not now.'

'It's how I feel now,' he said.

'I've already had one row with Michael,' she said, running a hand through her hair. 'I've been up all night, I've had to look at a man with his brains bashed in, I've got my in-laws expecting Christmas dinner – I don't *need* this, Lloyd!'

'No,' he said, getting to his feet. 'And it's what you need that matters, isn't it? Always.'

'I don't want a row,' she said, wearily.

'It's not a row. It's just the truth. I can't bear thinking of you and him—'

'Then *don't* think about it!' she shouted.

'I can't ignore it any longer – don't you see? That's the whole problem!'

She stared at him. 'I've been straight with you from the

start,' she said, almost in tears. 'I've never pretended it would be any other way.'

Lloyd poured brandy into his empty cup. 'Things change,' he said. 'I don't want it to be like that. Not now.'

'If you're driving me home, you can leave that until you come back,' she said hotly.

He put the cup down. 'You're afraid to leave him,' he said. 'Because he asks nothing of you, and I would.'

Judy's head was spinning. 'This isn't fair,' she said. 'It isn't how this is meant to be.'

'No. You were meant to carry on with your nice safe marriage, and I was meant to sit around like a bottle of bloody aspirin, waiting for you to have a headache.'

Judy didn't know if this was an unprovoked attack, or simple home-truths. She'd have to sort it out later, when she'd had some sleep. It seemed like an unprovoked attack.

'I don't want that any more,' Lloyd said.

'Will you take me home, please?'

He drove her home in silence, and this time she didn't enjoy it. She had always been aware that she was walking a tightrope between triumph and disaster. And now she had fallen off.

'You'd better stop here,' she said, as she saw the side road, worse than it had been when they left. She got out of the car, and took a deep breath of sharp, cold air before looking back in. 'Is it all over?' she asked.

Lloyd reached over to the open door. 'No, you silly bitch! I want to marry you!' And he slammed the door and drove off, his back wheel spinning in the deep snow at the edge of the road.

She'd fallen off the tightrope all right. But she was damned if she knew which way.

Chapter Four

Eleanor opened the door, and let out a sigh. 'Thank God,' she said. 'The radio just said—' She stepped out into the frosty courtyard.

'You've heard, then,' said George.

'My mother-in-law did. I didn't know what to do – thank God you're all right.'

'It's Elstow,' George said. 'Elstow's dead.'

She nodded. 'How? What on earth happened?'

George licked dry lips. 'Someone battered him to death,' he said.

'Someone?' The wind that had once again begun to bluster across the fields suddenly swirled round the courtyard, lifting a stinging flurry of hard snow. Eleanor stood like a statue, just staring at him, blinking as her hair blew across her eyes.

'Eleanor?' Her mother-in-law, George presumed, appeared at the door, an Instamatic in her hand. 'Is it all right if I take photographs? The castle looks lovely with the snow.' Mrs Langton senior smiled at George expectantly, but Eleanor was too preoccupied to satisfy the curiosity that had prompted the photographic urge.

'Yes,' she said. 'Help yourself.'

'Oh, my goodness.' Mrs Langton shivered. 'Don't stay out

here too long, will you? You'll catch your death.' Then, perhaps just a little reluctant to begin her quest, she set off with her camera.

Eleanor waited until she had disappeared round the thick castle wall. 'Come in,' she said.

He followed her into the living room, and saw Tessa, engrossed in a cartoon.

'Is it good?' he asked, crouching down beside her.

She nodded, laughing delightedly as Bugs Bunny emerged unscathed from a crippling fall.

George smiled. 'At least that's all she's got to worry about,' he said.

'Look!' Tessa demanded. 'Look, Mummy, look!'

'I can see,' Eleanor said.

George stood up straight. 'I thought you ought to know,' he said, plunging in at the deep end. 'I've told the police that I was with Joanna all evening.'

Eleanor, still obediently watching Bugs Bunny, looked slowly away from the screen, towards him. 'Was that wise?' she asked.

'I don't know,' he said wearily. 'Wisdom didn't seem to come into it.' He looked away from her. 'It's entirely up to you what you do about it,' he said.

'*Watch*, look! He's *flat*!'

'Do about it?' Eleanor asked. 'Why should I do anything about it?'

George sat down. 'We think it was an intruder,' he said. 'But the police aren't inclined to believe us.'

Eleanor sank down on to the sofa, her worried eyes not leaving his. 'What are they doing?' she asked. 'The police?'

'The usual things,' he said. 'They're asking questions. All over the place – checking up on where we were, what we were doing. Even what we were wearing.'

Tessa's laughter made George look at the screen. It was easy there. If you got bent out of shape you just shook yourself, and everything was all right again.

'They'll find out,' Eleanor said. 'If they're asking questions they'll find out that you—' She glanced at Tessa, obviously trying to think of words that would mean nothing to her, but she clearly wasn't listening anyway. 'That you weren't entirely straight with them,' she said.

'Perhaps not,' George said. 'The pub was very busy – they wouldn't necessarily know how long we were there. But yes,' he sighed. 'They'll probably find out.'

'More?' Tessa enquired as the credits came up.

'I don't know, Tess,' said Eleanor. 'Wait and see.'

There was more, and Tessa turned her attention once more to the television.

'What do you want me to do?' Eleanor asked.

'Whatever you think is right,' he said. 'I had no right to lie. So if you want to tell them the truth, then you must.'

Eleanor shook her head. 'I won't go to them,' she said. 'But if they ask – I don't know, George. Why did you lie?'

'Are they going to ask you?' he said. He hadn't answered her question, and she didn't answer his.

There were good reasons for his lie, but he didn't offer them to Eleanor.

'George,' she said quietly, 'do you know what really happened?'

Judy was having Christmas dinner with the Hills. That's what it felt like – not like her own house at all. She hadn't even produced the meal.

She had arrived home, tip-toeing upstairs to find Michael getting dressed.

'I couldn't sleep,' he had said.

Judy, cross and confused, had tried hard not to take it out on Michael, whose fault it certainly wasn't. The realisation that the whole mess was entirely her own fault had made her slightly less confused, but even more cross. So when Michael had touched on the subject of Christmas dinner, she had bitten his head off.

'Oh, for God's sake, Michael! Everything's *done* – you've

79

only got to put it *on*. I'm sure your mother wouldn't mind doing it anyway.'

He had listened, maddeningly patient, until she'd finished.

'I just meant should we leave it until evening so that you can get some sleep?' Mild, solicitous, and calculated to make her feel guilty for jumping down his throat.

'Sorry,' she had said. 'No – no, I'll just need a couple of hours. I'm sorry, Michael,' she had said again, but there had still been an edge of irritation in her voice. Unwarranted. Unfair. Unkind. 'I've had a bad night,' she had said. 'I'm sorry. I really am.'

Michael had looked a little puzzled at her reaction to what had been an entirely routine skirmish. 'Was it a nasty one?' he asked.

A brief nod of confirmation, and he hadn't asked any more questions. 'And I have to go out again this afternoon,' she had warned him.

'Oh.' He had turned to leave, then turned back. 'I take it that it is really necessary?' he had said.

'Yes.'

'Well. You'd better get some sleep, then.'

'I want a bath. You haven't used all the hot water, have you?'

A cool bath, and an uneasy sleep punctuated by the sounds of the neighbours' children having a snowball fight, doubtless having abandoned all the batteries-not-included goodies laid before them in favour of playing with the weather, were to be her lot. And it seemed she had barely closed her eyes when it was time to get up again, time to drink a sherry and open presents with the Hills. Time to eat with the Hills.

She tried to enjoy the meal, which was, of course, delicious. Mrs Hill never forgot to warm the plates, or allowed the vegetables to overcook. Her turkey was never too dry. Michael must have sorely missed his mother's cooking, but he had never said so. Lloyd would have done, she thought. But then Lloyd didn't automatically assume that women did the cooking.

There was no point in weighing up advantages and disadvantages; there was no comparison between Lloyd and Michael.

Mr and Mrs Hill and their son Michael spoke a language that Judy didn't understand. They spoke about things in which she had no interest. She watched Michael, so engrossed in his conversation with his father that he was quite unaware of her scrutiny.

The sound of their voices faded and merged, just a confused background jumble, as she studied Michael as though he were a close-up on a cinema screen. His thin face was animated, even when he was listening rather than talking. His eyes went from his father to his mother when she spoke. He drank some wine, and poured more for everyone, including Judy. But he was in a world where she didn't really exist; a world of property chains and loft conversions, of the mileage you could get from Austin Princesses compared to Rovers, neither of which any of them owned. A world of small investments, of tax concessions and pension funds.

She had seen a man who had been battered to death.

What sort of masochism was it that she was so intent on practising? Why cling to something alien, instead of to someone who understood? Someone she could understand? What was it that Michael got from this fake marriage that he was prepared to introduce a baby to it? She knew the answer. Independence. The mere fact that they *were* married to one another meant that no one else could own them. It was why they had thought it would work. It hadn't, but they wouldn't let go.

She got through the rest of the meal, as she always had before, on these rare family occasions. Michael must feel like this when they visited her family. Making no contribution, not expecting to be included.

After lunch, she went to see Joanna again.

Joanna didn't want to speak to Sergeant Hill, but she didn't seem to have much option. They were in the back bedroom,

81

with the fire burning brightly, reminding Joanna of childhood ailments, when the bed in here would be made up so that her mother didn't have to run up and down stairs all day. No matter how itchy the spots, how sore the throat, being ill had been almost fun, in this cosy little room, with the fire going. It made her feel secure, and she wasn't at all sure that she should, with Sergeant Hill's watchful brown eyes on her. She had been aware of the danger with Graham, when she had relegated her interview with him to the sitting room. She must still be aware of it now, she reminded herself, as the sergeant waited for an answer with infinite, unbearable patience.

'I tried to *protect* myself,' Joanna said, when she couldn't stand it any longer, and looked away. 'Not defend myself.'

'All right,' said Sergeant Hill. 'I'll ask you something else.'

Joanna's eyes slid unwillingly back.

'You said that the row with your husband—'

'It *wasn't* a row,' Joanna said stubbornly. A row. That was twice she'd called it that. She had simply no idea. No idea at all.

'You said that your husband became violent at about five o'clock,' she said.

Joanna nodded, hearing the chimes, seeing Graham's face.

'And that he stopped when he heard your parents' car,' said the sergeant.

Joanna stiffened. She'd thought that this bit was over. 'You've asked me all this,' she said. 'It's in your note-book.'

Sergeant Hill nodded, and pointed to the notebook. 'It says that your parents came home at half-past five,' she said.

'Yes.'

Sergeant Hill looked at her for a moment without speaking, then carefully turned to a clean page in her note-book.

'That wasn't going on for half an hour,' she said, pointing

to the bruises. 'Or you'd have been in hospital again.'

Joanna blushed. She didn't know they knew about that.

'So let's start again,' said Sergeant Hill.

'I don't see what it's got to do with it,' Joanna said. 'It's private.'

'He stopped long before your parents got here,' she said, as if Joanna hadn't spoken. 'Why?'

Joanna didn't answer.

'Were you upstairs with him, Joanna?'

'No.'

The sergeant looked thoughtful. 'Something stopped him hitting you,' she said. 'And it wasn't your parents' car driving up, was it?'

Joanna didn't speak, didn't look at her. It was no one else's business. No one's.

'People will understand,' Sergeant Hill was saying. 'If you picked up something to defend yourself.'

'I didn't. I've *told* you what happened.'

'But you haven't told me the truth.' She reached over and touched her hand. 'You said yesterday that it made you feel ashamed when he hit you,' she said.

Joanna looked down.

'I know you think I don't understand any of this,' she went on. 'But I can understand that.' She sat back again. 'Now, something made him stop hitting you,' she said. 'At the moment, it looks as though you fought back.'

'I didn't.'

'I don't think you did,' said the sergeant. 'So what did happen? You've nothing to be ashamed *of*, Joanna.'

'Ashamed?' Joanna repeated, puzzled. 'Oh,' she said. 'Sex? Is that what you're talking about?'

'It's not an unusual pattern,' said the sergeant. 'Some men get—'

'Get turned on by it? Perhaps they do, but that isn't how it was.'

'I'm sorry if I've offended you.'

83

'It would help if you called a spade a spade!' Joanna said angrily.

Sergeant Hill smiled. 'I expect it would,' she said. 'All right. Something stopped him, Joanna. And if it wasn't being battered to death, then what was it?'

Joanna's eyes filled with tears. 'The baby,' she said, in a low voice. 'I'm going to have a baby. I thought Graham had hurt it, and that's why he stopped.'

'Did he know you were pregnant?'

Joanna shook her head. 'Not until then,' she said. 'I was so frightened – I screamed at him, and he stopped.'

'Why in God's name didn't you tell me that in the first place?' the sergeant shouted, angry with her.

'Because I didn't want anyone to—' But she had suddenly and uncontrollably burst into tears. 'I didn't want to tell them,' she sobbed, as Sergeant Hill put her arms round her. 'That's why I stayed in the sitting room. I didn't want to see them.' But the words were incoherent. She couldn't speak, couldn't even breathe, for the convulsive sobs. She tried desperately to control them.

'It's just reaction,' said the sergeant. 'You cry.'

But it wasn't reaction. Joanna knew what it was, and it would be so easy to tell her, just tell her and get it over with. But she couldn't. She gulped in air with the sobs, her face buried in the sergeant's shoulder, until the shuddering stopped.

And then she tried to explain. She wanted Sergeant Hill to understand. But the words she could find didn't really describe her near-hysteria, and Graham's remorse; the tears, the gentleness, the closeness. The common fear that the baby had been hurt in a battle that Joanna was only just beginning to understand.

She looked up, expecting scepticism, but not finding it. 'I wanted to go home,' she said. 'I wanted to go home, and start again. With Graham and the baby. I wanted to do it *right*. But we heard the car, and I made him go

84

upstairs and stay there, or my father would have killed him.'

Sergeant Hill's arms were still round her; Joanna felt the slight reaction to her words, and pulled away. 'It's an expression,' she said. 'It's just an expression.' But oh God, why had she used it?

'I know,' said the sergeant.

'I was so scared,' Joanna said again. 'I was scared about the baby.' Tears ran down her face again. 'I knew I'd tell them if I saw them,' she said. 'I didn't want to tell them.'

The sergeant took some tissues from her bag, and handed them to her. 'Do they still not know?' she asked.

'No.' Joanna took a deep, difficult breath. 'It's not their baby,' she said. 'And it's not going to be.'

A nod; understanding, perhaps, a little. 'Have you seen a doctor?' she asked.

'Yes. She's made an appointment for me to have tests. But she says there's nothing to worry about.'

'Good.'

'Sergeant Hill? You won't tell them, will you?'

She shook her head. 'But they'll have to know sooner or later,' she said.

'I know. It's silly, I know, but just not yet.'

'That I *can* understand,' said the sergeant, with a little laugh. 'Believe me.'

Everyone had their problems. Joanna wondered what Sergeant Hill's were.

'How long were you married?' she asked.

'Eighteen months,' said Joanna. Eighteen months, she thought. A June bride.

'Was he always violent?'

'Not really. Not to start with. He'd get angry with me— He didn't like . . . ' She looked away. 'He didn't like my parents very much,' she said. 'And it just somehow started.'

'You said he'd been drinking – was he often drunk?'

85

'No – he didn't really drink. He said he'd met someone. I suppose they just—' She shrugged. 'It's Christmas,' she said. 'People drink too much.'

She looked round the safe, secure, comfortable room. 'He hated this place,' she said. 'He said I'd never come out of the womb.'

It was when Freddie was cheerfully removing bits of Graham Elstow that he dropped his unintentional bombshell.

'Between seven o'clock and nine o'clock,' he said. 'That's right, isn't it, Kathy?' The question was thrown over his shoulder at his assistant, who seemed equally happy in her work as she industriously checked samples.

Lloyd's face fell. 'What?' he said. 'What about five?'

'Five? No. Definitely still alive and digesting at five. He ate at two o'clock, according to the barmaid.'

The barmaid had had good reason to remember Elstow, who had refused to leave at closing time. In the end, she had brought in reinforcements, and Elstow had left, protesting that no, he hadn't got a home to go to, no one could call that a home . . .

'Still alive at five,' Freddie went on. 'And at six – almost certainly still at seven.' He flashed a wide smile at Lloyd. 'And definitely dead by nine,' he said.

'Don't *do* this to me, Freddie! We've got a theory.'

Freddie sucked in his breath. 'Tricky things, theories,' he said.

'Our theory,' Lloyd went on, 'says that Elstow arrived in the afternoon to make things up with his wife. He's successful, and they go up to her room. But Elstow has to knock her about to get in the mood – and when he's sleeping it off, she gets her own back with the poker.' He raised his hands. 'Simple,' he said.

'Simple is the word,' said Freddie. 'Simple, neat, tidy – what a pity it doesn't fit the facts.'

He didn't sound too cut up about it, Lloyd thought sourly.

'He didn't die until Mrs Elstow was safely in the pub,' he went on, then picked up some papers. 'Preliminary report from forensic,' he said. 'Have you got yours?'

'No.' Lloyd glared at him.

'It's probably on your desk now. They don't have much to go on yet – they're working with a skeleton staff, and half of them couldn't get in. But it does say that Elstow's full handprint was on the inside of the sitting room door – as it would be, if he'd slammed it shut, like Mrs Elstow said. And there were scuff marks on the polished floorboards, consistent with two people struggling.'

'All right, all right,' Lloyd said. 'Stop being so smug.'

Freddie laughed. 'He was lying on the bed when he was attacked,' he said. 'Probably asleep.' He looked up. 'That fits in with your theory,' he said. 'If only he'd died a couple of hours earlier.'

Joanna had been a fairly conspicuous visitor to the pub, with her black eyes. They had all seen her arrive with her father, at about ten past seven. Still, Lloyd thought, Freddie said he could have died *at* seven.

'Could she have killed him before the pub?' he asked.

'And ten minutes later she's sipping cider?' Freddie said. 'No, Lloyd. I think he was alive at seven, anyway.'

'But it's possible? In theory?'

'Theoretically, he could have died at seven. But for Wheeler and his daughter to be in the pub by ten past – which several witnesses say they *were* – they have to have left the house by seven. The weather precluded speeding – if we assume they travelled at a reasonable speed, it would certainly take ten minutes from the vicarage to the pub.'

'Are you saying he couldn't have died even a few minutes before seven?' asked Lloyd.

'I am. Seven and nine are the absolute outside times, Lloyd. Between seven-thirty and eight-thirty would be my guess.'

'So I have no leeway?'

'No,' said Freddie. 'Not on the time. But there are two other interesting points,' he said, brightening up.

Lloyd shook his head. 'Other people would object to their Christmas Day being broken into in this fashion, Freddie. Why don't you?'

'I'm happy in my work,' he said, with a shrug.

Lloyd looked at Freddie's work, and shook his head again.

'This has *made* my day,' he went on enthusiastically. 'It's a puzzle, Lloyd. If you look at the—'

'I'll take your word for it, Freddie, whatever it is.'

'Right. Two of the blows occurred after death. They're not particularly heavy – nothing like as heavy as the others.'

'Whoever did it expended a lot of energy,' said Lloyd.

'Sure, sure. The last blows wouldn't be as strong,' Freddie said. 'But if you were that tired – why hit him again?'

'She just kept going until she was certain,' said Lloyd. He couldn't see what there was to get excited about.

And he didn't miss Freddie's raised eyebrows at his use of gender, but it was Freddie who had said that he thought the prints on the poker were a woman's.

And Lloyd thought they were Joanna Elstow's, and would continue to do so until he was proved wrong. But God knew when that would be. It was Christmas Day, and it was snowing; that apparently meant that the system ground to a halt.

'Elstow died almost immediately,' said Freddie. 'But he got hit again, twice, some considerable time after he had died.'

Lloyd frowned. 'Why would anyone want to do that?'

'You're the detective,' said Freddie. He grinned.

Lloyd regarded him sourly. 'When you haven't got your hands in a corpse, you're nice and miserable like the rest of us,' he said. 'You're only really happy round death. That's weird, Freddie.'

'So I've been told. I like dead bodies.' He smiled. 'I like some live bodies, too. Has Sergeant Hill recovered?'

'Yes, thank you,' said Lloyd. 'You said two points. What's the other?'

'The prints on the poker – oh, I forgot. You haven't seen the report yet.'

'What about them?'

'They agree with me that they're probably a woman's,' said Freddie. 'Of course, since we haven't got the comparison with the family's prints yet . . . '

'The Wheelers' prints were taken as soon as possible,' Lloyd said with exaggerated patience. 'Don't blame me because they've got stuck in some bureaucratic snowdrift.'

Freddie laughed. 'It's lonely at the top, Acting Chief Inspector.'

'Is that it?' Lloyd said. 'That they're a woman's prints?'

'*Could* be a woman's prints. And yes, in a way, that is it, because the poker was held with one hand. Now, it's not impossible, but I'd have said that to inflict blows like that, the average woman would have needed both hands.'

Lloyd nodded. 'A good double-handed backhand, you said this morning.'

'That's still what I think,' said Freddie. 'So there you are. You go away and puzzle that lot out, and I'll get busy on the details. If and when we can get any,' he added.

Lloyd groaned. 'It only happened today,' he said. 'And it's Christmas Day, Freddie – a day we simple folk celebrate.'

'Until we've got them, you don't know if you're looking for an intruder or not,' Freddie said.

'Intruder!' Lloyd snorted. 'It's a domestic, Freddie. Pure and simple.'

'Like your theory?'

Lloyd sighed. 'Don't remind me,' he said. 'I've just sent Sergeant Hill to lean on someone that you tell me was in a pub with a hundred witnesses when the deceased met his maker.'

Freddie bristled slightly. 'Let's hope she left her rubber truncheon at home then,' he said. 'Look – you shouldn't have gone on my estimate at the scene. I told you it was rough – I even told you it could be down to eight hours.'

Lloyd held up a conciliatory hand. 'I know,' he said. 'I know. But young Mrs Elstow is not telling the truth about what went on, wherever she was when he was killed,' he added.

'When did he stop beating his wife?' Freddie said.

'Quite.' Lloyd shook his head. 'How you can make jokes in a morgue is beyond me,' he said, looking at his watch. Four forty-three. Surely Judy would have been and gone by the time he got to the station. 'I'm off,' he said. 'Enjoy yourself with the rest of Mr Elstow.'

'I shall,' said Freddie cheerfully. 'I shall.'

'It's Graham's father,' said Marian to Joanna. 'On the phone. I didn't say you were here.'

She had almost gone in when she'd heard Joanna crying. She *had* gone in as soon as Sergeant Hill had left. But Joanna had said that everything was fine. It had just caught up with her, she had said. Sergeant Hill had comforted her, she'd said. She hadn't made her cry. So all that worrying had been in vain.

'I'll talk to him,' said Joanna. 'I think it'll be about the funeral arrangements. I called him, but he wasn't there.'

The funeral. Marian hadn't given it a thought. It was as if once they had removed his body from the house, that was that. But it wasn't, of course. It was very far from being that.

'No one can do anything until the police say so, anyway,' said Joanna. 'I ought to go and see him, really.'

'Yes,' said Marian absently. 'Perhaps you ought.'

She could hear the rise and fall of Joanna's voice on the phone. It would be over, she told herself. One day, it would

90

all be over, and they could get back to normal.

'The vicar,' Eleanor said, in answer to the inevitable question that had been an unnaturally long time coming.

Penny's smile faded. 'The *vicar*?' she repeated. 'You didn't tell me you *knew* them.'

'I don't really.' Eleanor was very fond of her mother-in-law, who had been everything to her for the last two years: her mother, her friend, her adviser, a shoulder to cry on, a baby-sitter. But she was incurably interested in other people's business.

'Why was he here?'

Eleanor pushed her chair away from the table, and eyed the remains of the Christmas dinner. Tessa's plate, abandoned in favour of Dumbo in the other room, was particularly uninviting. Two-year-olds had no preconceived notions about what you could eat with what.

'We'll get this done in no time,' Penny said reassuringly, standing up. She hesitated. 'You're not—' she began, then obviously decided that even she couldn't continue that particular line of enquiry. 'Why *was* he here?' she asked, taking the direct approach.

'They'd invited us over,' Eleanor said. 'He came to explain what had happened.'

'Oh.' Penny began to pile up plates. 'Are you going to finish your pudding?' she asked.

Eleanor shook her head.

'I thought you were worried this morning. Why didn't you tell me you knew them?' She made a hideous pile of left-overs.

'I didn't want to worry you,' Eleanor said. 'One of us worrying was enough.'

'Who was killed?' Penny asked, her voice low.

'I'm not sure,' said Eleanor, departing from the truth. 'He didn't go into details. Someone who was visiting them.'

Penny tutted. 'How did it happen?' she asked.

91

'They think it was a burglar.'

'You mean someone just got in and *killed* someone?' Penny pushed open the kitchen door. 'Haven't they caught anyone?' she asked, alarmed.

'No, I don't think so.' Eleanor picked up the cream jug and the barely-touched pudding. She didn't know how much of this third-degree she could take.

'I don't like the idea of your being here alone,' Penny said. 'Why don't you and Tessa come back with me? Spend the rest of the holiday in Stansfield?'

Eleanor managed a smile. 'I'm not really on holiday except for today and tomorrow,' she said.

'It seems so lonely here,' Penny persisted. 'Tessa's all on her own.'

'Not usually. There's the play-group – there are lots of children in the village.'

'But for Christmas, I mean. The people next door to me have got a little boy a few months older than Tessa – that would be company for her, wouldn't it?'

'We're perfectly all right here, Penny. We won't be murdered in our beds, I promise.'

Penny sighed, and went into the kitchen. For a moment, all that could be heard was water running into the dish basin. Then it was turned off, and there was a little silence.

'Someone was,' she called through. 'Don't forget that.'

Chapter Five

'Something odd,' Jack Woodford said, as his head appeared round Lloyd's door. 'Got a minute?'

'All the time you want,' Lloyd said. 'Something odd means we're getting there.'

Jack looked less certain of that than Lloyd, as he came in, a sheet of paper in his hand.

Judy arrived before Jack had closed the door. 'I thought I'd better report in,' she said.

Lloyd had indeed successfully avoided her the day before, after his visit to the morgue; he had rather hoped that she wouldn't come in today.

'You thought you'd get away from your in-laws,' said Jack.

'That too,' she confessed with a smile, taking off the new leather coat that she was wearing.

'Jack's about to give us something to go on,' said Lloyd, glad that Jack was there. Their row had been yesterday; it seemed like a year ago. But it was still only Boxing Day, and this interminable festive season ground on around them, with no shops open and no proper programmes on the telly, even if he'd had the energy to watch.

Jack laid the sheet of paper on Lloyd's desk. 'My lads have been checking up on the people Mrs Wheeler visited,' he said. 'On Christmas Eve.'

Lloyd glanced down at the list. Beside the names, Jack had jotted down times.

'They're only approximate,' Jack said, as Lloyd opened his mouth to ask. 'People didn't think to look at their watches in case the vicar's wife needed an alibi for murder.'

'No,' said Lloyd.

'But she says she left the vicarage at about ten to eight – right?' He didn't wait for the unnecessary confirmation. 'And the earliest visit we can find is . . . ' He leant over, reading the sheet upside down. 'Mrs Anthony,' he said, running his finger down the list of names. 'And that was at eight twenty-five. The thing is – Mrs Anthony's house is in a row of cottages right beside the drive up to the vicarage.'

Lloyd remembered passing them just after they had spoken to the snow-plough crew.

'If Mrs W. had gone on her hands and knees into a force eight,' Jack went on, 'she'd have taken no more than five minutes getting there. Which seems to my untrained eye to leave half an hour unaccounted for.'

'Well, well, well,' said Lloyd briskly, looking over at Judy. 'I think we'd better go and talk to this Mrs Anthony – don't you?'

On the way, Judy expanded a little on the notes she'd left him on her interview with Joanna. She had obviously believed her; Lloyd trusted Judy's instincts, but he had a question.

'If she'd made it up with him,' he asked, 'why didn't she go up to see him?' He slowed down to let Judy read the numbers on the cottages.

'Eleven, thirteen – seventeen must be that one with the yellow door,' she said. 'I don't know. That is a bit odd.'

'It's not like you to miss a trick,' he said.

She got out of the car without replying. He'd said it to annoy her. She had said nothing at all about their row, or about his parting shot. In fact, she was behaving as though nothing had happened, obeying Lloyd's own rule that their private relationship mustn't affect their work. But she was much more of a professional than he would ever be, and the ease with which she donned her policeman's helmet irritated him. Irrationally, he conceded. But it did.

Mrs Anthony took some time to come to the door; when it opened, they saw a frail old lady backing her wheelchair away. Lloyd introduced himself and Judy, and they were shown into a small, neat living room.

'Do you remember Mrs Wheeler coming to see you on Christmas Eve?' Judy asked, raising her voice slightly, enunciating clearly.

Lloyd suppressed a smile as Mrs Anthony regarded Judy with a bleak eye. 'I am almost eighty years old,' she said. 'I sometimes have to use this wheelchair. I would prefer to be thirty-five and walking about, like you, but I do assure you that neither of these disadvantages affects my hearing, my acumen, or my memory.'

Judy's face grew pink. 'Oh – I do apologise if I gave the impression—'

'You did,' said Mrs Anthony sharply.

It gave Lloyd just a little perverse pleasure to see the efficient Sergeant Hill so firmly on the carpet.

'I'm sorry,' Judy said.

'And now that we have established that I can remember all the way back to the day before yesterday, what did you want to know?'

'We'd like to know what time she got here,' Lloyd asked.

'Eight twenty-five. Between then and half past, that is,' said Mrs Anthony, without hesitation.

'Can you be sure about that?' Judy asked.

'What was the point of asking me if you don't think I can tell the time?' demanded Mrs Anthony.

Judy looked uncomfortable. 'I just wondered how you could be so precise,' she said.

'Because the programme I was watching had just got to the end of part one,' said Mrs Anthony, relenting slightly. 'The advertisements were on when the doorbell rang, and I

95

hoped that whoever it was wouldn't stay. She did, though,' she added.

'How did she seem?' Lloyd asked.

'Not her usual self,' said Mrs Anthony.

'You know her quite well?' asked Judy.

'If I didn't I wouldn't know what her usual self was, would I?' snapped the old lady. 'I've known her all her life.'

Lloyd decided that he didn't really like witnessing Judy being eaten for breakfast after all. 'And what was her usual self?' he asked.

The world-weary eyes regarded him. 'She was always a very determined girl,' she said, thoughtfully.

'Oh?' Lloyd, who had been standing by the radiator, came over and sat near to Mrs Anthony. 'What makes you say that?' he asked.

'Poor George Wheeler,' she said, smiling softly, as though at some memory. 'I don't imagine he'd still be a vicar if he hadn't married Marian.'

A silence fell, and Judy jotted something down. She looked up, frowning slightly. 'What do you mean, Mrs Anthony?' she asked. 'Why wouldn't he still be a vicar?'

Mrs Anthony smiled her soft smile again, but the eyes remained lack-lustre. 'Lack of faith,' she said. 'But Marian thought it was right to encourage George's scepticism; she thought it made him more accessible. One of the boys. And Marian always thinks she's right,' she added.

'And you don't think she was right?'

Mrs Anthony raised her eyebrows. 'I think a leaning toward religion is preferable in a vicar,' she said. 'I think if George had married someone else, he would have realised that a lot sooner than he has.'

'You think he has realised now?' asked Lloyd.

'Oh yes,' she said. 'His sermon at the midnight service made that obvious. To me, at any rate.'

'And what was his sermon?'

'Being true to yourself,' she said.

Judy and Lloyd exchanged glances as Mrs Anthony wheeled herself closer to the radiator. 'Marian just wants people to be true to her,' she said. 'That's all she asks. But she couldn't protect George from his own thoughts,' she said, turning up the temperature control. 'She had a damn good try, though. I'll give her that.'

Judy, perhaps a little apprehensively, looked up. 'Do you think this has got something to do with what happened at the vicarage?' she asked.

'Let's just say it doesn't surprise me that you're asking about Marian Wheeler,' she said. 'It doesn't surprise me in the least.'

She wheeled herself back to where Lloyd and Judy sat. 'And I'll tell you how she seemed,' she said to Lloyd. 'She seemed upset. Nervous.'

Judy's face assumed an expression Lloyd knew well. 'How did this manifest itself?' she asked, her tone matching the disbelieving look.

'For one thing,' said Mrs Anthony, her eyes suddenly alive, 'her hands were shaking so much that she spilled coffee on her dress.'

And Judy, overmatched, took refuge in her note-taking.

'Fortunately,' continued Mrs Anthony, 'most of it went in the saucer.'

'Did she say what was upsetting her?' asked Lloyd.

'She'd hardly do that, would she, Mr Lloyd?'

It wasn't a crime to be upset, as Lloyd pointed out to Judy on their way up to the vicarage.

Marian Wheeler opened the door, and gave a short sigh when she saw them.

'Joanna's resting,' she said. 'Unless it's really important, I'd rather you didn't talk to her just now.'

Lloyd smiled. 'I quite understand,' he said. 'But it's you we've really come to see, Mrs Wheeler.'

'Oh.' There was a strange mixture of apprehension and relief on her face. 'You'd better come in.'

They followed her through to the kitchen, where George Wheeler was drying dishes.

'It's the police,' said Mrs Wheeler.

'Any further forward?' asked Wheeler, turning round.

'Things are moving,' said Lloyd smoothly. 'Slowly, I'm afraid. But they are moving.'

'Good.'

'Why we're here, Mrs Wheeler, is to clear up a small . . . inconsistency, I suppose.'

He explained the nature of the small inconsistency, while Wheeler dried the cup that he held in his hand until he had almost worn it away.

'Are you certain that you left the house at ten to eight?' Lloyd concluded.

Marian Wheeler frowned. 'Yes,' she said. 'I must have missed someone off the list.'

Judy handed her a copy of the list, and Mrs Wheeler took glasses from her handbag. 'I can't think who,' she said as she looked at it. 'But I was a bit shaken up when I wrote it out. I can't honestly remember.'

'Perhaps you wouldn't mind thinking about it?' asked Lloyd. 'Let me know if you remember.'

'Certainly I will.' She handed the list back.

'Mrs Anthony said you seemed upset,' said Judy.

'Did she?' Marian Wheeler took off her glasses. 'Yes – yes, I suppose I was. Of course I was, after what had happened to Joanna.'

Wheeler at last put down the cup. 'What are you suggesting?' he asked quietly.

'Nothing at all,' said Lloyd. 'But we have to try to account for half an hour that has somehow got itself lost.' He turned to Marian Wheeler. 'I'm sure it'll come back to you,' he said. 'You've got the number to reach me, haven't you?'

'Yes, thank you.'

'Well – thank you for your time. Don't worry – we'll see ourselves out.'

They didn't stay long at the station, and Judy left before Lloyd did. He decided that now was as good a time as any to make his duty visit to Barbara and the kids.

Two hours later, he went back to his flat, none the better for seeing his family, who had merely added to his worries and irritations. He consoled himself with a large glass of the Woodfords' present, and a few chapters of Judy's.

And by the next morning, the things that had been moving slowly started moving fast, now that the world had got itself over the twin difficulties of snow and holidays. Late Saturday afternoon found him reading the first detailed forensic report.

The fingerprints on the poker were Marian Wheeler's; another set of her prints had been found beside an attempt to clean a bloodstain off the landing floor. One of her shoes bore traces of blood. Lloyd looked up thoughtfully from the report.

He wondered about Freddie's belief that a woman would have had to hold the poker in both hands. Any woman, according to him. So – what would he think of Marian Wheeler, small and slim, wielding the poker one-handed? Not a lot. Much more likely that she had interfered with the scene once she'd found Elstow. She had run into the room, picked up the poker – got blood on her shoe. Then what? Why not just say that that was what she had done?

And yet, Lloyd knew, people reacted oddly under stress. TV and books had done a wonderful job in instilling into the public the vital importance of leaving murder scenes untouched; if only they could direct this talent to pointing out the beneficial effects of not murdering anyone in the first place, he thought irrelevantly.

But it was possible that she thought she shouldn't have touched anything, and so denied going into the room at all. But she'd hardly have given Elstow a couple of thumps with

99

the poker, he thought, and shrugged, giving his attention once more to the report.

No traces of an intruder, inside or out. No fingerprints other than those of the deceased, Mrs Elstow, and Mr and Mrs Wheeler. Nothing disturbed, nothing taken, nothing vandalised. Just one dead body.

The clothing. Forensic said it was a woman's dress, probably size 12, in a pink or peach-coloured unpatterned material, judging by the reinforced collar and cuffs which had failed to burn up as well as the rest of it had. There were traces of blood on one cuff. Type B, similar to the deceased's.

Size 12. Judy was a 14; so was Barbara, and so, if he was any judge, was young Mrs Elstow. Mrs Wheeler would be a 12. Things did not look good for Marian Wheeler.

He felt that there was probably something a little suspect about a man who could sum up a woman's dress size at a glance, but there it was. Gigolos and detectives were supposed to notice things like that.

Marian Wheeler would have to be brought in.

He dialled Judy's number, which barely rang out at all before she picked it up.

'We've got work to do,' he said.

'Thank God for that.'

He smiled at the dialling tone, and replaced the receiver.

'A man-made material,' the inspector said. 'Plain – probably pink or peach-coloured.' He looked from Joanna to Marian. 'Do either of you own such a dress?'

Marian saw George's head turn involuntarily towards her as the inspector spoke. She heard Joanna try to smother the confirmation that had escaped, despite her efforts.

Christmas was over; the waiting was over. The police, suspicious from the start, had taken away clothes and shoes, had come every day, politely and courteously making them

100

tell their stories over and over again. They had been all over the village, asking questions.

'If it was an intruder' – slight accent on the 'was' – 'then someone must have seen him. He would be badly blood-stained.'

That had been the explanation offered for their checking-up on the comings and goings from the vicarage, when Marian had demanded one. It had been given to her by the crisp, concise Sergeant Hill.

Now she was here again, with the inspector. They looked a little stern, a little sad. And they were looking at her.

'Was it your dress, Mrs Wheeler?' The sergeant.

They had taken away the ashes from the fires in Joanna's bedroom and the kitchen, and Marian had endured Christmas somehow. Though it wasn't really Christmas, not with all that had happened. The house always seemed to have some figure of authority in it. If it wasn't police, it was clergy. There had been a lot of work to take her mind off it.

'Mrs Wheeler?' The sergeant again, not impatiently.

She took almost as much on herself as Chief Inspector Lloyd. Marian found herself inconsequentially wondering if that annoyed him. She decided it couldn't, or presumably he would have stopped her doing it. Whereas often he would almost melt into the background while she did the asking.

The sergeant came over to her. 'Mrs Wheeler,' she said. 'Was it your dress?'

'Yes.'

Inspector Lloyd cleared his throat. 'Mrs Wheeler, I'd be grateful if you could come with us to the police station,' he said. 'There are questions we would like to put to you concerning the murder of Graham Elstow.'

'This is outrageous!' George roared.

'George,' said Marian. 'It's their job – they're only doing their job.'

George gaped at her, then shook his head.

101

'Mrs Wheeler,' said the sergeant briskly, 'if you could get your coat—'

'No!' Joanna shouted. 'I don't understand – what are you doing?'

Inspector Lloyd looked far from happy. 'Mrs Wheeler has simply agreed to help us with our—'

'Agreed?' George said. 'I didn't hear her agree.'

Lloyd glanced at Marian. 'Mrs Wheeler?' he said.

'George is right,' she said. 'I haven't actually agreed to come.'

'Are you going to force me to arrest you?' asked Lloyd.

'Yes!' shouted George. 'If you want my wife to go with you, you're going to have to arrest her.' He took a step towards the inspector. 'So you had better be very sure of your ground, Chief Inspector Lloyd,' he said.

Marian saw the inspector shrug slightly at the sergeant, and she was being arrested.

They were telling her she didn't have to say anything. She knew that. She knew the wording of the caution. She wondered when the British police would feel obliged to alter their simple, direct sentence into whole paragraphs of statutory advice, like the Americans. Or was that just New York? America was funny, with all the states having different laws.

They were taking her out to their car. George was white, and Joanna walked with her arm round his waist, holding on to him like a child. George was saying something about a solicitor. The sergeant got into the back of the car with her, the leather coat she wore creaking slightly, smelling new. There was a constable at the wheel of the car, and he closed the passenger door as George kept the inspector talking.

Joanna had gone back into the house, obviously on George's instructions, and re-emerged, carrying coats. She got into her car as George at last walked away from the inspector, turning twice on his way to call something angrily over his shoulder.

The inspector got in then, slamming the door. Marian could see the tension in the back of his neck, as the car moved off through the new fall of snow. Five days of it, Marian thought, and it still hadn't given up. Not constant, or the vicarage would have disappeared under it. But snow, every day, and the driveway was deep again now. The incessant cars had churned it up into slush, and it might freeze. Someone could break their neck. They said you were responsible, if someone did. If they were there for a reasonable purpose. Postmen, newspaper boys. Policemen.

The sergeant was speaking to her, but she hadn't been listening.

'Mrs Wheeler?'

Marian turned to face her. She had a nice face, Marian realised. Not just nice-looking – which she was – but something more. People could have beautiful faces that weren't attractive. Sergeant Hill wasn't beautiful; she had a good face, the kind photographers like. Warm brown eyes, and an open friendliness that was there even when she was briskly arresting you.

'Are you all right, Mrs Wheeler?'

'Oh – yes. Thank you.'

On, through white-banked roads, into Stansfield, with no one speaking at all. Skirting round the now pedestrianised centre of the town to the police station at the other side. Marian had sat on the Young Offenders Committee in there, in her time. It had folded, not through any lack of young offenders, but because it hadn't really helped.

The sergeant was opening the door as the driver pulled round to park. She was out of the car as it stopped moving, her hand held out to assist Marian, who was then taken – no doubt about it – *taken*, the sergeant's hand lightly holding her elbow, into the building. She was taken to the desk, where another sergeant began filling in forms. He repeated that she didn't have to say anything, but if she did . . . She signed a form. Then she was taken into a room with a formica table and chairs, like the one the YO committee had used. A woman police officer came in, and the sergeant told Marian to sit down. Told her.

It was odd, for someone who was used to being shown and asked, to be taken and told.

'Just leave it here,' said George, as Joanna pulled up at the police station.

'I can't,' she said. 'It's double yellow lines.'

Double yellow lines. Marian had just been arrested, and she was worrying about double yellow lines. But that was just like Marian would have been, George thought, if the positions had been reversed.

'You go in. I'll take it round to the car park,' she said.

George strode into the station, and saw Inspector Lloyd talking to Sergeant Hill. Ignoring the desk sergeant, he walked purposefully up to them. 'Where's my wife?' he demanded.

Lloyd broke off his conversation and turned. 'Mr Wheeler, you can't see your wife at the moment. I'm sorry.'

'She has the right to have a solicitor present,' George said.

'Of course she has,' said Lloyd.

'But how do I get hold of one?' George found himself asking. Pleading. 'It's Saturday afternoon!'

Lloyd pointed back down towards the entrance. 'Go to the desk sergeant,' he said. 'He'll help you.'

'Will he?' George felt bewildered. In the last few days, the police had altered their image for George. They had gone from being symbols of security and order to being invaders of privacy. Now, they just seemed like the enemy. Why would they help?

But help they did, and the solicitor said he would come right away. George looked round helplessly as he finished his call, but he couldn't see the inspector. He went out the front door, and walked round to the back, where he found the car park, and Joanna's car.

'Why would she burn her *dress*?' Joanna asked, as he got in.

'I don't know.'

'But why?' she said again. 'What possible reason could she have for doing something like that?'

'I don't *know*!' George shouted, but he wasn't angry with Joanna. 'No,' he said. 'Perhaps I do.'

'What?'

Eleanor. It had to be Eleanor. 'Perhaps,' he said, hitting the flat of his hand against the dashboard as he spoke. 'Perhaps I do. She could have burned it because she was angry with me.'

Joanna turned, her eyes wide. 'What have you done that would have made her angry enough to burn your Christmas present?' she asked.

George closed his eyes. 'It doesn't matter,' he said. 'A misunderstanding. It's possible, that's all.'

Joanna frowned, but she didn't ask again.

They waited in the police station car park, not knowing what to say or do. The solicitor was taking his time, thought George. He'd said he'd come right away.

There had to be a simple explanation. There *had* to be. But she hadn't given them one. And he had thought that they were just trying to alarm her into producing an explanation, when they'd asked her to go with them. That was why he'd said they would have to arrest her. Because he thought they couldn't, not just on that. But they *had* arrested her, as though confirmation about the dress had been all that they had needed. What else could they possibly have found to link Marian to it? And so what if she *had* burned the dress? It was her dress. She could do what she liked with it.

At the back of his mind, a doubt was creeping in. He'd told her she was wrong about Eleanor. Surely, *surely*, she would have told him about having burned the dress then? Or was she ashamed of having done it? He'd asked her why she wasn't wearing it, once he'd noticed. She had said it wasn't a good fit. Why hadn't she just told him the truth? Or had

105

she just hoped that he would forget about it? Hadn't she realised the consequences of failing to mention it to the police?
Hadn't it occurred to her what the police would think when
they discovered it? Or did she think that the fire would have
destroyed it completely?

Anyway, his mind asked him, despite his conscious effort to
make it stop, *when* did she burn it? Elstow was in the room
all the time . . .

George's eyes were tight shut. 'I need some air,' he said,
scrambling out of the car. He ran to the bushy hedge that ran
along one side of the car park, and was violently sick.

Joanna watched impassively as her father bent over in the
bushes, his shoulders heaving. She couldn't help him.

Whatever nonsensical idea the' police had got would be
disproved; if her mother had burned the dress in a fit of
pique – though that was hardly like her, but if she *had* –
then she would tell them, and they would let her go. But she
obviously hadn't told them, doubtless in a misguided attempt
to shield her father from embarrassment. And if that was the
case, then he should go in now, and tell them why he thought
she'd burned the dress.

It was ridiculous, her mother being in there, under arrest.
Almost laughable. She supposed her father thought that eventually they would realise what a ludicrous mistake they were
making, without his intervention. And they would, of course,
in time.

Joanna was rather looking forward to the moment when
the sharp-eyed, sharp-tongued Sergeant Hill would have to
climb down and apologise. Because she would have to; there
was no possibility of their continuing to imagine her mother
guilty. None. It was a combination of circumstances, that was
all. It would get sorted out. It probably took them hours to
unarrest someone. It *would* get sorted out. It had to. Tears
rolled down her face, unchecked. But crying wouldn't help.
Throwing up in the bushes wouldn't help.

She dried her eyes, and got out of the car. Up some steps to a door, slightly ajar. Joanna took a deep breath, and went in.

She was in a corridor, with doors off it, all closed. There must be someone somewhere, she thought, as she walked along. She heard footsteps behind her, and turned to see a young constable.

'Can I help you?'

'I want to see Sergeant Hill,' she said.

'If you'll come with me,' he said, 'I'll see if we can find her for you.'

She followed him round into the main entrance, where he asked her to wait.

A few minutes later, he came back, and she followed him once again, through a room full of people, into an ante-room. Sergeant Hill stood up when she came in.

'Joanna,' she said, her face concerned. 'Have a seat.'

'No, thank you.' Joanna didn't know what to say now that she was here. Screaming abuse at her would hardly help, but that was all she really wanted to do.

'We were given no option but to do what we did,' Sergeant Hill said.

'No option?' Joanna shouted. 'You can't seriously believe my mother killed Graham!'

'We just wanted to ask her some questions, Joanna. It needn't have been like that.'

Somewhere, at the back of her mind, behind her desire to call her names, Joanna knew that she was right. Her father had forced them into a corner.

'But why?' she demanded. 'Why did you want to question her? Because of the dress? My father thinks she did it because she was angry with him – it was his Christmas present to her.'

'Oh?' said Sergeant Hill. 'Why was she angry with him?'

'I don't know! You'll have to ask him that.'

'Where is he?' she asked.

'Being sick!'

'I'm sorry,' she said. 'Please sit down, Joanna.'

Joanna felt some of the anger drain away, to be replaced by hopelessness. She sat down. 'Why have you arrested my mother?' she said again.

'I can't discuss it with you,' Sergeant Hill said. 'But in view of what you've said about the dress, I would like to talk to your father.'

Joanna went to find her father; he was angry with her for telling the sergeant.

'If you think she had a good reason for burning the dress, you have to tell them!' Joanna said.

'I didn't say she had a—' He sighed. 'Sorry,' he said. 'It's not your fault.'

Joanna waited for him by the desk. It would get sorted out.

'Yes,' Eleanor said, as brightly as she could, 'I will think about it. I promise.' And she waved as her visitor drove out of the courtyard, then closed the door with a sigh.

'You should go,' said Penny, as she went back in.

'I can't see myself at a New Year party,' said Eleanor.

Penny shook her head. 'You've got to start some time,' she said. 'And the sooner the better. You don't have to stay long. But you should start going out.'

Eleanor knew all that. But how could she start going out now, for God's sake? Penny didn't understand. And she wouldn't, for as long as Eleanor could keep it that way.

'I'd look after Tessa,' Penny went on. 'You know that.'

Eleanor smiled. 'I know,' she said. 'You're right. But I just don't think I could face it.'

'At least do what you said you'd do,' Penny said. 'Think about it.'

'I will.'

'I was wondering,' said Penny. 'I know you won't come – but would you mind if I took Tessa back with me when I go tomorrow night? There's nothing much for her to do here, is there – and you'll be working. It would be more fun for her.

108

There's a little boy next door that she could play with.'

'You told me,' said Eleanor, with a smile.

'Well? It would be a few days rest for you, and I'd love to have her.'

'Yes, of course,' said Eleanor.

'If she wants to come, that is,' said Penny.

Tessa would want to go. There was only one thing she liked better than visiting anyone, and that was visiting her grandmother. They couldn't ask her then and there because she was off visiting the Brewsters, who had three of the children that Penny kept insisting were non-existent in Byford.

'Thank you,' Eleanor said. 'It would be nice to have a break.'

George Wheeler hadn't been very forthcoming as to why his wife should have been angry with him. He had just sat there, looking like death, saying that it was a misunderstanding, until Judy had told him he could go.

Lloyd raised his eyebrows when she told him. 'Sounds a bit desperate to me,' he said. 'The best excuse he could come up with.'

'I know.'

'All the same,' said Lloyd. 'I don't think Freddie's going to go much for Mrs Wheeler as a likely candidate.'

'Has she said anything yet?'

'No,' said Lloyd. 'Do you want to come and have a go?'

Judy got up. 'Is her solicitor here?'

'No. I suppose Wheeler did ring one,' he said. 'Every time I see him, he's rushing into the loo.'

Judy went to the door. 'Are you coming?' she asked.

'Yes,' he said wearily. 'Why not?'

Marian Wheeler sat at the table in the interview room, looking entirely unperturbed.

Judy sat down. 'Have you remembered where you were on Christmas Eve?' she asked.

'No.'

'Can you give us an explanation for your fingerprints being on the poker?'

'No.'

Judy clasped her hands, and thought for a moment. 'Did you go into the room when you found Elstow's body?'

'No.'

'Were you in that room at all on Christmas Eve?'

'I was in and out during the day,' she said. 'The last time would have been at about two, I think. Just before I went out in the afternoon. I made up the fire.'

'You're sure that was the last time you were in there?'

'Yes.'

'Oh, come on, Mrs Wheeler!' Lloyd suddenly spun round to face her from having his back to her.

His voice startled Judy, but Mrs Wheeler looked as calm as ever.

'Your fingerprints were on the poker. There had been an attempt to burn a dress – *your* dress, which had blood on it. Type B, Mrs Wheeler. Elstow's type.'

Marian Wheeler didn't speak.

'You must give us some explanation for these facts, Mrs Wheeler,' Judy said, her voice as calm as Mrs Wheeler's.

'I understood I didn't have to speak to you at all.'

Judy sighed. 'You'll have to give an explanation to someone, some time,' she said. 'You will have to defend the charges, won't you?'

'You haven't charged me, have you?' Mrs Wheeler looked eager; interested. Not as though it was happening to her at all.

'No,' said Judy. 'We haven't. But we will, Mrs Wheeler, unless you have an explanation. Do you?'

'No,' said Mrs Wheeler.

'No?' Lloyd said. 'You mean you don't *know* how the blood got on your dress? You don't know how your fingerprints got on the poker?'

He leant over the table, and Mrs Wheeler pulled back a little.

'You say you were never in the room, Mrs Wheeler. So how come blood got walked out of that room on to the landing on the sole of *your* shoe?'

'I don't know. I'm sorry.'

'You don't know,' he said, his voice menacingly low and Welsh. 'Someone tried to clean up the blood on the landing – did you know that? Someone who left their fingerprints by the stain.' His own hand, fingers spread, thumped down on the table. '*Your* fingerprints, Mrs Wheeler. You don't know how that happened?'

She was getting to Lloyd. Judy could tell when simulated anger was turning to real frustration. 'I've just been talking to Joanna,' she said, conversationally.

Mrs Wheeler stiffened.

'She suggests that you burned the dress because you were angry with her father.'

'Does she?' A frown crossed the serene face.

'Were you angry with him?'

'No.'

'So that isn't why you burned the dress?'

'No, of course it isn't.'

A silence fell, and Lloyd sat down, leaning back, relaxed.

'But you did burn it, didn't you, Mrs Wheeler?' Judy asked quietly.

Mrs Wheeler nodded, and Judy felt her heart skip a little.

'I wanted him to leave,' Marian Wheeler said. 'I wanted him out of the house just as much as George did. I just wanted to ask him to leave. To go away, and stop hurting Joanna. So I went up. But – but when I spoke to him, he just . . . *came* at me. He was drunk, I suppose. I told him to stop, but he was threatening me. I picked up the poker. I told him to stop. I *told* him I'd hit him.'

Judy glanced at Lloyd, whose eyebrows twitched a little.

'Are you saying it was self-defence?' she asked Mrs Wheeler.

111

'Yes,' she replied. 'I was frightened. I warned him. But he kept coming. Then he lunged at me, and I hit him. He fell,' she said. 'I realised he was dead.'

'We don't think it was self-defence,' Judy said carefully. 'Our evidence suggests that he was lying on the bed when he was attacked.'

Marian Wheeler's eyes widened and for a moment she said nothing. Then she shook her head.

'He wasn't lying on the bed?'

'No. He was coming at me.'

'Where was he when you hit him?' Lloyd asked.

'Near the fireplace,' said Mrs Wheeler. 'That's why I could pick up the poker.'

'And that's where you're saying you struck the first blow?'

'Yes,' she said.

Lloyd looked at her for a long time, without speaking. Mrs Wheeler looked back, wide-eyed. Judy stayed out of it. After a while, Lloyd sighed heavily, and rubbed his face. 'I told you that everything in that room had a story to tell, Mrs Wheeler.'

Mrs Wheeler looked away from both of them, as though something had caught her attention.

'Blood stains,' Lloyd went on. 'They talk, Mrs Wheeler. Elstow was nowhere near the fireplace.'

She looked back then, her eyes defiant. 'Yes,' she said. 'He was.'

'Then what?' said Lloyd, abandoning the topic.

'There was blood on my dress. I took it off, and put it on the fire. It wouldn't burn properly, because the fire was almost out. So I used matches, and firelighters. Then when I left, I could see I'd made marks on the landing. I cleaned my shoe, and then I cleaned up the stain.'

She paused. 'I washed, and went into my own room. I put on different clothes, and different shoes, and then I went out to check up on the old people, since that was what I had been going to do in the first place. And I *did* lock the doors,' she said. 'So that no one would find him.'

Judy noted the emphasis – 'I *did* lock the doors' – but its significance escaped her.

Mrs Wheeler's statement was being typed when her solicitor arrived, full of apologies to his client for the long delay, occasioned by his car breaking down in the middle of nowhere. He couldn't even find a phone; he had had to walk to a garage through the snow. He advised her against signing the statement, but she did anyway. Lloyd still didn't charge her; her solicitor wasn't happy about that either, but Judy understood his reluctance.

Back in the office, Judy tidied up her desk. They had informed Mr Wheeler of the course of events, and he'd gone rushing outside. Joanna Elstow had stared uncomprehendingly at them, then followed him. The solicitor had sighed, and gone after both of them.

'Let's go and talk to Freddie,' said Lloyd.

Judy looked at her watch. 'At the hospital?' she said. 'Will he be there this late on a Saturday?'

'Of course he will. He practically lives there.'

Judy drove them in her car; Lloyd's had been left at home in favour of the front-wheel drive of official vehicles. Her car might not be in the first flush of youth, she pointed out, but it didn't get the vapours at a little snow and ice.

Freddie was, as predicted, at the path lab, as joyful as ever with his choice of profession. 'Confessed?' he beamed. 'Well, there you are. You do win some.'

'Do we?' Lloyd said. 'By the time it gets to court, she may well have changed her mind.'

Judy hated the smell of the place. She didn't want to be there, and she wasn't sure why she was. But Freddie was always pleased to see her, so that cheered her slightly.

Lloyd continued. 'She's either going to plead self-defence or not guilty,' he said. 'How good a case have I got?'

'She won't plead self-defence,' Freddie said decidedly. 'If she brings in her own pathologist, he can't not agree with me. The man was lying on the bed when the first blow was struck.'

113

'She says he was by the fireplace,' said Lloyd.

'Well, you know he wasn't.'

'Could he have fallen on to the bed? From being hit?'

Freddie shook his head. 'He was on the bed,' he said. 'There's no argument – look at the bedclothes, man!'

'I'd rather not,' said Lloyd.

'All right,' sighed Freddie. 'Let's suppose we get given an argument. Wherever he was, he wasn't standing up. Or if he was, then his attacker was standing on a step-ladder. There is no way a blow of that force could have been delivered except from someone with a considerable height advantage – so if you've got someone nine feet tall on your list, that's your man.'

Lloyd smiled. 'So what will the defence do with a not guilty plea?' he asked. 'Apart from produce a nine-foot tall suspect?'

'Well,' said Freddie, 'if I was defending, I *would* go on build. I wouldn't produce the giant theory, but I would point out how small and slim Mrs Wheeler is.'

'You said a woman could have done it,' Lloyd said in injured tones.

'Certainly. But Mrs Wheeler's height and weight would suggest that she'd need two hands to produce blows that strong.' He warmed to his task. 'She only used one hand on the poker. So if I can produce a good reason for her prints being there, and ram home her diminutive stature . . . ' He left the rest of the sentence eloquently unfinished.

'Are you saying she'll get off?'

'No,' he said. 'Because she *could* have done it. If she was frightened enough. Or angry enough.'

'So what *are* you saying?' Lloyd asked testily.

Freddie smiled. 'If she sticks to self-defence, she's got no chance,' he said. 'If she simply says she didn't do it, well – you've got her confession, her prints, and the burnt dress on your side. She's got the fact that she's small, pretty, female and a vicar's wife on hers.'

'And the fact that she was alone with him in the house at the material time,' Lloyd said. 'I've got that on my side,

114

too.' He thought for a moment. 'Suppose she *did* hit him by the fireplace?' he said. 'Ineffectually. Making him dizzy – he grabs hold of her as he falls. So she's only got one hand free, and she's terrified. What then?'

'Is that what she says?' asked Freddie.

'No,' Lloyd said. 'But could that produce what you've found?'

'If he happened to fall on to the bed,' said Freddie. 'Which I suppose he could have done. It's highly unlikely.'

'But self-defence might work?'

Freddie shook his head slowly. 'No,' he said. 'That could just conceivably have been what happened. But he must have let go. And she didn't stop hitting him. Two blows were after he was dead, remember.'

'Yes, I know,' said Lloyd. 'That's what puzzles me.' He got up. 'Thanks, Freddie,' he said. 'See you in court.'

'Are you going to charge her?' Judy asked, as they got back to the car.

'Not tonight,' he said. 'I'm not happy with any of this. Why would she hit him twice after he was dead? And why wouldn't she tell us that she had?'

'Do you still think she just tried to tidy up after someone else?'

Lloyd looked tired, as he shook his head. 'I can't see *when*,' he said.

Judy frowned. 'So what do you think?' she asked, puzzled.

Lloyd smiled. 'You'll give me one of your looks if I tell you,' he said.

'Try me.'

'Well,' he began a little sheepishly. 'I'm beginning to think she wasn't there at all.'

Judy stared at him, giving him one of her looks. 'Someone else burned her dress?' she said incredulously. 'Someone *else* put blood on her shoe?'

He nodded.

'And she's *letting* them?' Judy shook her head. 'What about the prints on the poker?' she said.

'Ah, yes. There are those.'

Judy smiled, and started the car, and there was silence then, as though leaving the lab was a signal that the working day had ended, and now she and Lloyd were back to being just two people who didn't know what to say to one another.

The headlights lit the snow-covered verges as the car sped along a country road now dry and cold, and it was the first time they had been alone together, out of working hours, since Christmas morning. It seemed to Judy that Lloyd had engineered their lack of privacy; perhaps it was because she hadn't responded to what she assumed had been a proposal of marriage, or perhaps because he was regretting it already, and wanted to avoid any discussion on the matter.

Judy thought of several things she should be saying, but she didn't voice them. A minute and painful examination of her position had forced her to see things from Lloyd's point of view. She did want everything her own way. She did want to run back to the safety of her marriage, and it wasn't a marriage, not really. It never had been. But where she and Michael bickered and complained at one another, she and Lloyd had rows. Real rows, where feelings were involved. Lloyd, with his quick Celtic temper, could forget them five minutes later. Judy couldn't. It was all too raw and emotional for her, and the rows would haunt her for days. But this one, despite having ended in the odd way that it had, seemed to have left its mark on Lloyd too, and she knew why.

'I didn't know I was hurting you,' she said.

'You're not,' Lloyd said, his voice surprised. But Lloyd could do that. Surprise, sorrow, anger. Whatever was needed.

'You said you felt like a bottle of aspirin,' she said.

'That's irritating,' he said, as she slowed the car down, and signalled left. 'It doesn't hurt.'

'Then why have you been avoiding me?'

He didn't answer for a moment, and Judy affected deep

116

concentration on her negotiation of the turn into the old village, where Lloyd had his flat. Stansfield, town of supermarkets and light industrial estates, of civic theatres and car showrooms like the one she was passing, had once just been a farming village, like Byford.

She could abandon the decision she had come to in the path lab; she could drop Lloyd off by the alleyway. But she drove on, turning through the entrance to the garages, parking beside Lloyd's car.

'I had no right to say these things,' Lloyd almost muttered.

'But they're true,' Judy said gloomily, stopping the engine. She looked out at the blackness of the garage area, only marginally relieved by stray beams from a failing street-lamp, and not at all in the shadow of the ornamental wall. She was surprised as always that the place wasn't littered with the unconscious bodies of muggees. But throwing empty bottles at the garage doors seemed to be the most popular pastime in this particular back alley.

'No,' Lloyd protested. 'I knew the position all along. You were right.'

This wasn't helping, thought Judy. Trust Lloyd, who could always be relied upon to defend himself, to turn sweetly reasonable on her.

'I am being selfish,' she said. 'I know I am. But—' She stopped. How could she explain it to Lloyd? She and Michael didn't need one another; they needed the marriage. That was why Michael had thought up his ridiculous notion of starting a family – it was one way to keep the marriage going. A marriage they both needed because it was safe, and predictable, and pleasantly boring, like a cricket match which will inevitably end in a draw.

'So what if you are?' said Lloyd. He gave a short, unamused laugh. 'If you'd given in to my lustful advances in the first place, you'd have the bachelor flat, and I'd be the one hanging on to my marriage.'

It was a joke, of sorts. But it wasn't true.

117

'No,' she said. 'You're braver than me.'

'Why won't you tell him about us, Judy?' he asked.

She didn't reply.

'I can't believe he hasn't guessed,' Lloyd went on.

He may have guessed, thought Judy. But she didn't think so. And guessing wasn't the same as finding out for certain. And it certainly wasn't the same as being *told*.

'Why?' he asked again.

Judy tried to explain. 'There's only ever been Michael and you,' she said. 'And you could come from different planets.'

'The trouble is,' said Lloyd, 'we're on the same planet.'

'Yes,' she said. Worse; they were in the same town. But she had to run some risks for Lloyd, or it was all too selfish for words. 'I'm here now,' she said. 'But I can't stay long – you do understand that.'

It had been a hard decision to make; she hadn't reckoned on Lloyd's reaction.

'What?' he said, taking his arm away.

'What's wrong?' she asked. It was an innocent question.

'What's wrong? What's wrong?' His voice grew louder. 'You can't see, can you? You still don't understand!'

He was shouting so loudly that Judy glanced fearfully up at the flats in case someone might hear.

'I told you what was wrong on Christmas morning,' he said. 'I don't want to share you any more, Judy. Do you understand? I don't want to share you *any more*!' And he got out and slammed the door so hard that the car rocked.

Chapter Six

Marian Wheeler had been awake when they brought her breakfast. The girl, an uncompromising young woman with sensible legs – though, Marian supposed, you didn't have much option but to have sensible legs in uniform – seemed almost apologetic. But there was nothing wrong with the food. She had sampled the canteen cooking in her YOC days; she had never imagined she would be eating it in a cell. She was by herself, because the others being detained were men. It gave her time to think.

By the time lunch had arrived, she had worked out what she was going to do. The solicitor had come, but she had refused to see him. Once she knew he was gone, she told the policewoman that she wanted to change her statement.

And now a sergeant was here; not the desk sergeant from last night, but it wouldn't be. He'd be on a different shift. This one had grey hair, and a kind, bored expression. Last night's had been a little surly, she thought. This one said his name was Woodford. Did she want someone to take down her new statement?

'No,' she said. 'I'll write it myself, if that's all right.'

'Yes,' he said. 'That's fine.'

The girl gave her a form, and the sergeant told her what to write at the beginning.

I make this statement of my own free will. I have been told that I need not say anything unless I wish to do so and that whatever I say may be given in evidence.

She signed that, and the sergeant left, leaving the girl with her. That inhibited her a little, like the invigilator in an exam, when he walks between the desks. But in the end, it was finished.

'Read it through,' said the girl. 'Make sure it says what you want it to say. Then sign it.'

Marian read it through.

In my statement dated 27th December, I said that I had killed my son-in-law Graham Elstow in self-defence. This was untrue. I was about to leave the house at about ten minutes to eight, but I did not want to leave him alone in the house, and I decided to try making him leave. I only intended speaking to him, but when I went up and told him to leave, he wouldn't answer, and he wouldn't turn round. He pretended to be asleep, and that made me angry. I suppose I just wanted to hurt him because he had hurt Joanna. I picked up the poker, and hit him. He sort of sat up, and fell off the bed. I kept on hitting him. I knew I had killed him. I had blood on my dress, and I burned it. I left the house at approximately eight twenty-five.

Marian signed it.

'I thought you didn't believe in it?'

Eleanor's voice, quiet, as befitted someone speaking in church, made George start.

'I'm used to doing my thinking in here,' he said.

He had behaved like someone about to steal the poor-box when he had arrived to do his thinking, making sure that his emergency stand-in had gone.

'What did Marian say?' she asked.

120

'What?'

'About your decision?'

She didn't know. Of course she didn't. How could she? It had only happened yesterday evening, and Eleanor, up in the castle, wasn't on the village grapevine. He tried to tell her. It was simple. The words were simple. *They've arrested Marian.* But he couldn't say them. He stuck on 'they' as if he had a stammer.

'They what? What's wrong?' She made an impatient noise at her own lack of tact. 'Sorry. But you know what I mean – has something else happened?'

George stood up, and walked into the aisle, where the stained-glass sunlight cast colours on to the floor. 'When I got engaged to Marian,' he said, 'Rosalind Anthony – do you know her?' He carried on as Eleanor shook her head. 'Rosalind Anthony told me that since she didn't know who gave vicars good advice when they were about to marry, she'd do it. She'd been married three times,' he told Eleanor. 'She'd be about . . . about Marian's age then, I suppose. She'd divorced two and buried one.'

Eleanor looked puzzled, and sat down.

'She was quite a girl in her youth, I believe,' he said. He paced along a few feet, turned and paced back, as he spoke. 'She said Marian would never let me down, and that I might find that hard to take.'

He looked across at Eleanor, who sat still, her hair touched by the soft colours from the window. She frowned slightly, not understanding.

'And I said something pompous about that being what marriage was about,' he went on. 'But she said that I might not want to be protected and shielded all my life.' He sank down on to a pew. 'She was right,' he said. 'She was right.'

'Has something happened with you and Marian?' Eleanor asked. 'Was it when you told her?'

'Told her?' He blinked. 'Oh – no.' He ran his hand over his face. He hadn't shaved. He hadn't slept. He must look awful.

121

'Rosalind said that if I married Marian, I'd have to go on pretending to be a vicar. She was right about that, too.'

Eleanor made sense of one thing. 'You *haven't* told Marian you're leaving the Church, have you?' she said.

'No.'

'Who have you told?'

'Only you.'

'And now you're not going to do it?'

George shook his head. 'I can't,' he said. 'I can't leave.' How could he leave? He was in prison. A prison that Marian had knitted for him. He dropped his eyes from Eleanor's. 'And now—'

'Now?' she asked, when he didn't continue.

'She's told the police that she killed Elstow,' he said, and he could practically hear the snowflakes fall outside. He looked up. 'She *didn't*!' he shouted. 'She didn't – don't you see?'

Eleanor shook her head, as if to rid it of confusion. 'But you said everyone was out all evening,' she said.

'We were. But – but Marian . . . ' He sighed, and tried to tell her rationally. 'At first, she said she left the house at ten to eight, but now she says she didn't. And then, well – there was the dress, and I don't know – there must have been more. But she's *confessed* – don't you see?' He buried his head in his hands.

'Dress?' said Eleanor, uncomprehendingly. 'What dress? What has a—?' She broke off. 'George?' she said. 'What did you say? What time did Marian say she'd left the house?'

He lifted his hands away, and held them up helplessly. 'She says she didn't leave until later,' he said. 'I don't know. What difference does it make?'

'It's important, George.' She sounded impatient, almost angry. 'She's made up some story to protect you, hasn't she?'

George looked up slowly. 'Me?' he said.

'I thought that's what you meant. When you told me about this Rosalind person. That Marian thought *you'd* done it.'

'What?' he said. Did she? No. Perhaps. He didn't know.

'Whatever her reason,' Eleanor said. 'Did you say eight?'

He frowned. 'Ten to,' he said. 'She said she left at ten to eight. They say she couldn't have, and it's got something to do with Ros Anthony. *That's* why I was telling you. She's always had a down on Marian – I wouldn't put it past her—'

'George.' Eleanor broke into his illogical accusations. 'George. We have to go to the police,' she said.

'You shouldn't have *let* her make statements!' Joanna said firmly.

Mr Barrington, a young, dark man with a worried expression, pulled papers from his briefcase, and laid them out on the kitchen table. 'I've made some notes,' he said. 'Some odds and ends that might help us.'

'Why didn't you stop her?'

'I can't tell your mother what to do, Mrs Elstow,' he said. 'I can only give advice.'

'Once you get there!'

'I have apologised for that – I couldn't get to a phone. And I did advise Mrs Wheeler not to sign the first statement, but she did. She wouldn't see me either of the times I called there today. And I wasn't there when she made the second statement.'

Joanna was making coffee for her visitor; it was like saying thank you to an automatic door, or apologising for bumping into a lamp-post. Making coffee for vicarage visitors was second nature, even if they'd come to tell you that your mother had confessed to the deliberate murder of your husband.

'But she *can't* have said she did it deliberately!' Joanna filled the coffee pot with water, and banged the kettle down.

'I'm afraid she has,' said Mr Barrington. 'And it ties in with the medical evidence.'

'I don't *care*!' Joanna tried to calm down. Deep breaths. 'Of course it does,' she said. 'Maybe they dictated it for all I know – maybe they made her sign it!'

Mr Barrington coughed. 'I doubt that very much, Mrs Elstow,' he said.

'Oh – I suppose you think the police are whiter than white?'

'No,' he said, his reasonable tones beginning to strain just a little. 'I'm sure some police officers are not above bullying known criminals, or convincing teenage boys that it'll be better if they confess. But I don't think they'd be likely to do it to someone like your mother.'

'It would be easier with her,' Joanna said, noisily removing mugs from the cupboard. 'She's not used to being arrested – being questioned.'

'She could certainly have been confused,' said Mr Barrington, clearing away some papers for her to put the coffee things down. 'That is one of the points I've made.' He pointed to his hand-written notes. 'She must have been alarmed, and tired – and perhaps she just told them what they wanted to hear. It does happen. But I know the inspector, and I'm sure that he would do nothing . . . nothing *underhand*.'

'You're chums with the inspector. Great.'

'I didn't *say* that, Mrs Elstow. I—'

But Joanna felt the tears coming again.

'Oh – Mrs Elstow. Er – please. Look – have some coffee, a glass of water?' He searched his pockets fruitlessly, and then pulled some kitchen paper from the roll. 'Mrs Elstow?' he said, pushing the wad of paper into her hands. 'I'm sorry. But I—'

This time, at least, she was under control. She blew her nose. 'Graham's *dead*,' she said. 'And they're accusing my mother, and I don't know what to *do*.'

'There isn't a great deal you can do at the moment, Mrs Elstow,' he said. 'But there are things I can do – look. I've made notes on them. I really came to talk to your father – I should have waited for him. I shouldn't have bothered you.'

Her father. Whose answer to the situation last night had been to disappear into his study until it was time to go to bed. Who had spent most of the night in the loo, and stayed in his room all morning. Who had eaten lunch in silence, and left without a word.

'No,' she said. 'He's not very well. I'm all right now,' she assured him, sitting up straight. 'What happens next?'

'Well,' he said helplessly, 'I take it you mean what happens to your mother?'

'Yes.'

'She'll be charged, and go before the magistrates. That doesn't take more than a few minutes. I can't promise anything, but there's a possibility that she'll be released on bail.'

'And if she isn't?' Joanna couldn't take it all in.

'Once she's been committed for trial,' Mr Barrington went on briskly, as though she hadn't spoken, 'I'll be able to brief counsel.'

Joanna pulled at the screwed-up paper towel in her hands. 'And he'll have all the answers?' she asked bleakly.

'She,' Mr Barrington said. 'She may have some. It's what she's paid for. It does rather depend on your mother.'

'My mother didn't kill Graham.' There was no response to her words, and she looked up to find Mr Barrington watching her closely.

'Then someone else did,' he said. 'So she must be protecting someone.'

Of course she was, thought Joanna, as she shredded the paper towel. 'It was someone who came in,' she said obstinately. 'A burglar.'

'There's no evidence of a burglar,' he said gently. 'And your mother – if she *is* protecting someone – doesn't believe it was a burglar.' He looked away from her. 'Mrs Elstow,' he said. 'It is a very serious situation.'

Joanna frowned. 'Do you think I don't know that?' she asked, and then her brow cleared. 'You think she's protecting me, don't you?'

'Is she?'

'Probably,' said Joanna. 'But she's wrong.'

125

He wasn't convinced. Or perhaps he just believed her mother's confession. Joanna didn't know, but she wished her father had found someone older, more experienced.

'Mrs Elstow – is there anyone else who might have felt that violently about your husband?'

Joanna didn't answer.

'I mean someone he might have admitted to the house.'

Joanna shook her head. 'I don't think so,' she said.

'You see—' He cleared his throat, a little embarrassed. 'It's possible that – in view of the fact that you had left him – your husband took up with someone else. It's just possible, since there is no evidence of an actual intruder, that someone was invited into the house, and subsequently—' He opened and shut his mouth a few times.

'Up to my bedroom?' Joanna supplied.

'That's where it happened,' he said, almost defensively. 'Whoever did it was in the bedroom with him.'

Joanna wiped the tears away. 'You think Graham could have had another woman? But why should she be here?'

Mr Barrington sighed. 'It isn't at all likely,' he said. 'But I understand that he may have met someone here – at the pub, I think your father said.'

'Yes,' said Joanna doubtfully.

'It's worth investigation,' he said. 'If there was someone else, she may be the person he met in the pub. It's a very long shot,' he stressed. 'But I'll put an enquiry agent on to it, if you think it's worth it. In my experience, men who show violence towards their wives do so towards other women with whom they have relationships. If someone else was here, it could have turned violent.'

'But he didn't have anyone else here, did he?' said Joanna. 'The police didn't find any other fingerprints, or anything. And Graham wouldn't have done that anyway,' she added.

'It's . . . well, I won't pretend I'm not clutching at straws, because unless your mother co-operates, that's all I can do, other than to set out the mitigating circumstances. And I gather your father doesn't want that. Not yet.' He began to put away the papers that Joanna hadn't even looked at. 'I could wait, and talk to him,' he said. 'When will he be back?'

'I don't know.'

'Well, then – I'll ring later. Do you think he'll agree to an enquiry agent?'

'Yes.'

'Good.'

Eleanor finished her story, and glanced at George, who sat tight-lipped, not looking at her. She looked back at the inspector.

He ran his hand over his hair, and drew in a slow breath. 'Well, well, well,' he said. 'An alibi.'

Eleanor frowned.

'Well, I mean,' he said, and he sounded much more Welsh than he had to start with. 'Convenient, isn't it?'

'Do you think I'm making it up?' she asked, startled.

He picked up the file that he had brought in with him, stood up and walked to the window.

Eleanor exchanged glances with George, but all George's bluster seemed to have gone. He looked almost furtively away again.

'Langton, Langton,' the inspector said, consulting the file, murmuring her name. 'No,' he said. 'No Langton on Mrs Wheeler's list of visits.' He looked out of the window, his back to her.

'Mrs Wheeler was at my house at five past eight on Christmas Eve,' Eleanor repeated, her voice firm.

'Was anyone else there?' He didn't turn round.

'Only my daughter. She's two and a half years old, and she was sound asleep.'

'Not much good, then,' he said.

He still hadn't turned round, which was beginning to irritate Eleanor.

'Friend of the family, are you?' he asked.

She said no, just as George said yes.

Then Lloyd turned. Of course he turned. 'Shall I go out?' he asked. 'Give you a bit more rehearsal time?'

'I help out with the church play-group,' Eleanor said, aware that she was going pink, as she did with unsophisticated ease. 'I know Mr Wheeler. I've only met Mrs Wheeler a couple of times.'

'One of those times being five past eight on Christmas Eve?'

'Yes.'

The door opened and Eleanor turned to see a young woman come in, glancing over at George, who just looked through her.

'Well, then, let's see,' said the inspector. 'If you saw her, perhaps you can give me some sort of proof. What was she wearing, for instance?'

'I never notice what people are wearing.'

Eleanor had only been aware of what she herself had been wearing. George's tie.

Inspector Lloyd sat down again. 'Definitely under-rehearsed,' he said.

Eleanor refused to take the bait. 'Someone like him could have had enemies,' she tried. 'Why don't you look for them?'

'Someone like what?'

'Like Graham Elstow. Someone who beats up women, for a start.'

'Wouldn't that make his wife's mother an enemy?'

'She was with *me*.'

He leant forward. 'And why do you suppose Mrs Wheeler didn't tell us that?' he asked.

'I don't know,' Eleanor said.

'Perhaps,' said Lloyd, 'it's because she doesn't know that that's suddenly where she was. She was out making certain that old people were keeping warm enough, according to her original story. Where do you fit in?'

'That isn't why she came to see me,' Eleanor said. 'She wanted to confirm Mr Wheeler's invitation for Christmas

128

lunch. And I'm not on the phone,' she added. 'So she had to call personally.'

'Why?' asked Lloyd. 'It was hardly necessary.'

Eleanor frowned. She had never thought about it.

'Going out on a night like that just to repeat an invitation?' He shook his head. 'That sounds very weak, Mrs Langton.' He leaned forward. 'Even weaker, if I may say so, with Mrs Wheeler's husband sitting beside you,' he added.

He thought they'd made it up. Or he wanted them to think that was what he thought.

'That's why she came,' she repeated stubbornly.

'How long would it take her to get from the vicarage to the castle?' Lloyd asked.

'About fifteen minutes,' Eleanor said. 'By road.'

'By road?'

'There's a shortcut,' she said. 'Across the fields. But Mrs Wheeler was in the car.'

'Quarter of an hour,' Lloyd said, and sat back tipping his chair up. 'Imagine you are Mrs Wheeler,' he said, then flicked his eyes at George and back to her. He raised an eyebrow.

Eleanor wished that George would at least *react*.

'And you are going to call on about half a dozen people in the village,' Lloyd went on. 'Would you start with someone who lived . . . what? Three miles away? Then go on to someone who lived at the bottom of the drive? Then off somewhere else altogether?' He opened the file again. 'No,' he said. 'You'd start or finish with the person closest, wouldn't you? Which is what Mrs Wheeler did, Mrs Langton.' He tapped the list of names. 'She started with Mrs Anthony. And she didn't call on you.'

'Why would I make it up?' she asked.

'Oh, I don't know,' Lloyd said. 'Misguided loyalty.' He looked at George again. 'Or perhaps it's just women sticking together. Women against this, that and the other. Especially the other. Wife-batterers deserve all they get.'

Eleanor refused to let him get to her. She stood up. 'Look, Inspector. I don't know what she was wearing, and I don't know

129

why she didn't tell you, but Mrs Wheeler was at my house at five past eight. I put Tessa to bed at seven. I decided to wait an hour before doing her stocking. I checked on her at eight, and I started to assemble the pedal car. About five minutes after that, Mrs Wheeler arrived. I want to make a formal statement to that effect.'

He sighed.

'If George—' She stopped, then decided that to amend it to Mr Wheeler would make things worse. 'If George and I had cooked it up, would we have come here together?'

'You'd have been better going to Mrs Wheeler's solicitor,' Lloyd said. 'But you can make a statement if you want.' He stood up. 'I notice George hasn't had much to say for himself,' he said.

George had gone pale, and Eleanor could see beads of sweat on his forehead. Lloyd had been deliberately trying to provoke him, all the time, and he still didn't say anything.

'And I must warn you,' Lloyd went on, 'that if you make a statement you can be prosecuted if you say anything knowing it to be false.' He opened his office door. 'Still want to make it?' he asked.

'Yes.'

He brought in a young man who took it down and read it back. Eleanor signed it with an angry flourish and handed it to Lloyd.

'Thank you for coming in,' he said.

She left, with George following behind her like a large dog. Outside, he sat down on the wall.

'You only said one word, and that made me look a liar,' Eleanor said angrily, then saw how he looked. 'Are you all right?' she asked.

'I will be,' he muttered. 'Once Marian's out of there.'

Eleanor sat down with him. 'Why didn't you ask to see her?' she said.

He shook his head, and they walked round to her car.

'He didn't believe a word,' George said. 'Not a word.'

'Oh – that was just theatre,' Eleanor said. 'I told him she had the car – someone's bound to have seen it.'

'Let's hope so.'

She looked at the pale, defeated face. 'Look, George, she *was* there! They can't make out in court that I've got some daft female solidarity reason for saying so.'

'What if she doesn't want you to give evidence?' he asked.

Eleanor's hand stopped in the act of unlocking the car door. 'Don't be silly,' she said, after a moment. 'She's bound to. You saw what he was like – no wonder she confessed. He was making me feel as if I was lying, and I'm not being accused of anything.'

They got into the car. 'Let's go and see her solicitor,' said Eleanor. 'He'll know what to do. Where does he live?'

George took a card from his wallet, and handed it to her in silence. She had to stop twice on the way to let him out to be sick.

'It'll be all right,' she said, arriving at the house. She squeezed his hand. 'You'll see. It'll be all right.'

'Do you really think she's making it up?' Judy asked, picking up Eleanor Langton's statement.

Lloyd shrugged. 'I don't know what to make of it,' he said. 'It sounds a bit unlikely. And George Wheeler didn't seem too keen on it himself.'

'No,' said Judy. George hadn't acknowledged her presence at all; she could have understood if he'd been resentful, like Joanna, and simply hadn't spoken to her. But it hadn't been like that. It was as though she hadn't been there. No, she amended. It was as if *he* hadn't been there.

'And there's this,' said Lloyd, putting a handwritten statement on her desk.

Judy read Marian Wheeler's new statement and looked up at Lloyd. So that was why he'd called her in.

'Now it makes a bit more sense,' she said.

But something didn't; she knew that even as she said it. She frowned at the statement. It seemed all right – it confirmed Freddie's findings.

'More sense,' Lloyd agreed. 'But we told her he was on the bed, didn't we? And she knows he ended up on the floor.'

Judy nodded. 'What does Freddie think?'

'Would you believe I haven't been able to get hold of him? He must take the last Sunday in the year off.'

'*I kept on hitting him,*' Judy quoted. 'Could that account for the blows after he was dead?'

Lloyd shrugged. 'Probably,' he said. 'That's what I wanted to ask Freddie. That, and—' He smiled. 'No,' he said. 'Forget it.'

Judy flicked through her already thick notes. It all seemed to fit, but there was something that wasn't right.

'What's up?' asked Lloyd.

'I'm not sure. Something doesn't fit.'

Lloyd came over, picking up the statement, and sitting on the corner of her desk. It usually irritated her, but this time she was glad.

'About this?' he asked, reading it through.

'No. I don't think so. It makes sense. It fits in with the forensic evidence – it maybe even explains the two extra whacks.'

'*Lizzie Borden took an axe, and gave her . . .*' mused Lloyd. 'But you don't believe it,' he said.

'I might,' said Judy. 'If I could find what I'm looking for.' She looked up at him. 'Because if you've got a piece left over after you've finished the jigsaw, it must belong to another puzzle – right?'

'There are quite a lot of puzzles,' Lloyd said. 'Little puzzles. What was Mrs Anthony hinting about George Wheeler, for instance?'

'What was Marian Wheeler angry with George about?' asked Judy.

'If she was,' said Lloyd. 'I'm inclined to think he made that up, like today's little pantomime.'

But Lloyd wasn't really dismissing Mrs Langton's statement just like that, Judy thought. It had set him thinking; he was

132

going to ask Freddie something, and he wouldn't say what. So he had to be back on his frame-up theory. No point in asking; he'd tell her when he felt like it.

'And why *didn't* Joanna go up to talk to Graham in all that time, if she'd made it up with him?' she asked. 'Eight hours, Lloyd.'

'Well,' he said. 'If this statement's true, none of that is any of our business.'

There was a knock, and Jack Woodford came in. 'Just going to the machine,' he said. 'Anyone want anything?'

'Coffee,' Lloyd said, digging in his pocket for a coin. He threw it. 'Thanks, Jack,' he said, as his phone rang, and he slid off Judy's desk. 'We'd better talk to Mrs W. again,' he said, as he picked up the phone. 'Lloyd.'

He listened.

'Right. Thanks. Tell them to wait – I want a word with them before they go.'

He hung up and turned to Judy a little sheepishly. 'Just something I have to talk to Bob Sandwell about,' he said.

Judy gave him one of her looks for good measure, for whatever he was up to, he clearly deserved one. She watched the door close behind him, and uncharacteristically put down her notes, thinking about Lloyd, and Michael, and the dreadful mess her life was in.

Next door, two typewriters clattered, one expertly, one inexpertly. There were voices, laughter, as someone was being teased. Outside, a bus churned through the slush to the bus-station. Someone walking past was whistling *Plaisir d'Amour*. She wished she could be in Lloyd's flat, quiet and peaceful. Their few snatched moments on Christmas morning had been shattered, and she was afraid that her life might be going the same way.

The last time she'd been there – really been there – had been how long ago? She looked at the calendar on the wall. Almost three months ago. My God, was it that long? No wonder Lloyd had had enough. She had known then about Michael's promotion, and she had wondered, as she and Lloyd had made love, what she was going to do. She had pushed the thought away, told herself that it would all resolve itself somehow. But it wouldn't. It couldn't. *She* had to resolve it.

The door opened suddenly, jerking Judy back to her surroundings with a heart-stopping jump.

'Lloyd's coffee,' Jack said. 'He's gone off somewhere – he said just to give it to you.'

'Thanks,' said Judy, taking the paper cup. Her hand trembled slightly from the start she had been given, making coffee spill over on to her desk.

'Don't worry – I've got it,' said Jack, mopping it up with blotting paper.

Judy stared as the brown stain spread over the paper.

'All right?' Jack asked.

'Yes,' she said absently. 'Yes. Thanks, Jack.'

He went out, and she picked up her notebook, leafing through to find the right page.

Her hand shook. Spilled coffee on dress.

Well, fancy that, Judy thought. She sat back, looking at the sentence for a moment. Then she put on her coat, scribbled a note to Lloyd, and left.

The phone was picked up this time.

'Freddie? Where the hell have you been?'

'Out,' said Freddie. 'Playing Trivial Pursuit, if you must know.'

'I didn't know dead bodies could play Trivial Pursuit,' said Lloyd.

'Neither did I, until my wife took it up.'

Lloyd smiled. 'How does your wife put up with you?' he asked.

'She's a saint, Lloyd, a veritable saint. What can I do for you?'

Lloyd read him Marian Wheeler's second statement.

'Mm.'

'Mm?'

134

'It fits.'

'But?'

There was a pause. 'Same buts as before, really. Still, she's admitted it, so that's that. Though—'

'Though – what?' Lloyd said eagerly.

'Two confessions seems like one too many to me,' he said. 'It's a funny one, Lloyd.'

'I know,' said Lloyd. 'And what I wanted to know was – does her second statement account for the two post-mortem thumps?' he asked.

'Not really. I don't know what to make of them.'

'Freddie?' Lloyd said, preparing him for the silly question. 'Is there any doubt about the murder weapon?'

He heard Freddie draw in a slow breath. 'No,' he said. 'But if you were to bring me something else that general size and shape, I'd certainly consider it.'

'Like another poker?' Lloyd said. 'The one from the kitchen?' He held his breath.

'The one we've got gives every indication of having been used,' said Freddie.

'Could it have been used just for the two extra blows?'

There was a long silence. 'It's improbable, but just possible,' Freddie said at last. 'You bring me the other poker, and the chances are I'll know if it was used.'

'Good,' said Lloyd. 'Because it's on its way here now, with any luck.' He had dispatched Bob Sandwell and one of the uniformed lads to the vicarage an hour ago.

Freddie laughed. 'What's your theory this time, Lloyd?' he asked.

Lloyd didn't know what sort of reception it would get. 'Marian Wheeler had been using the poker in Elstow's room,' he said. 'When she made up the fire earlier that day. Someone could have killed him with one poker, cleaned it, put it back – then bopped him a couple of times with the one that already had Marian Wheeler's fingerprints on it.'

'What about the fingerprints on the landing?' Freddie said.

'Coincidence. It's a polished floor. Chances are, her prints are all over it. From polishing.'

'Maybe,' said Freddie, unconvinced. 'I'd have thought that polishing was supposed to have the opposite effect. And are you saying she's just going along with all of this?'

He sounded just like Judy. Lloyd didn't answer, because he hadn't worked out that part of his theory.

'And what about the dress?'

'Someone else could have burned the dress, too,' Lloyd said, beginning to feel cornered.

'She was *wearing* it, Lloyd,' he said. 'But it's an interesting point about the poker. Send it to me anyway.'

'Don't worry,' said Lloyd, irritated. 'I will.'

He put down the phone, and there was a knock at the door.

'Sir?' Bob Sandwell came in. 'We've brought them both,' he said, handing him two pokers, in separate bags. 'Mrs Elstow told us about this one.' He held it up. 'It's from the back bedroom,' he said. 'She says her mother got a fire going in there on Christmas Eve, so her prints might still be on it. I checked the other rooms, but they've all got gas or electric fires. No other pokers, sir.'

'Thank you,' said Lloyd. 'Give them to Sergeant Woodford, will you? Tell him I want them taken to the lab first thing in the morning.'

Sandwell departed, ducking under the door, though he wasn't quite that tall. Lloyd sat forward. He was still lost in thought when Judy came in.

'I've tried my theory out on Freddie,' he said.

'Your frame-up theory?' she asked.

'Yes. Plus my poker theory.' He gave her a brief résumé. 'And all that Freddie could find to fault it was that she was wearing the dress,' he said. 'But she may not have been wearing it. She changed into it when she thought she was going to the pub – but she ended up doing a whole load of housework instead, didn't she? She did a washing, and made a bed up for Joanna – she even got a fire going in the back bedroom.

136

Heaving coal about? In a brand new dress that she wanted to wear to the midnight service?' He sat back. 'Perhaps she wasn't wearing the dress at all,' he said. 'Perhaps she laid it on the bed, ready to change into when she got back from visiting.'

'Except that she *was* wearing it,' Judy said again. 'When she went visiting.'

Lloyd smiled. 'All right,' he said. 'I suppose you can prove it.'

'Yes,' said Judy.

'Oh, well,' Lloyd said resignedly. 'Another theory gone west.'

Judy shook her head. 'No it hasn't,' she said.

Lloyd smiled. He loved it when Judy got on to something. She looked just like a gun-dog.

'The dress,' she said. 'When we saw Marian Wheeler on Christmas morning, she was wearing a trouser-suit. There wasn't a dress in the washing, and there wasn't one with coffee stains on it anywhere else. But according to Mrs Anthony, she spilled some coffee on her *dress*. I've been back to Mrs Anthony,' she said. 'I got a good description. Peach, full skirt . . . '

Lloyd frowned, as he realised what that meant. 'But if she was wearing it at half past eight,' he said, 'she couldn't very well have thrown it on the fire some time previously.'

'No,' said Judy. 'She couldn't.'

'She spilled coffee,' said Lloyd slowly. 'And went home to change yet again. Are you saying that someone burned the dress after that?'

'Not after,' said Judy, sitting forward. 'Lloyd – if someone frames you for murder, I imagine you don't usually just go along with it, do you?'

'Well, I normally protest my innocence, I must agree,' said Lloyd.

'Make fun of my grammar if you like,' she said. 'But there is one circumstance in which you *wouldn't* protest your innocence.'

'Is there?' Lloyd thought hard. 'You mean I'd want to be framed?' he asked. 'I'd have to have framed myself.' He hit his head when he finally saw the point. 'Let's talk to the lady,' he said. His eye caught Mrs Langton's statement as he stood up. 'You'd better take that,' he said to Judy.

Judy picked up Mrs Wheeler's statements too, and read all three while they waited in the interview room.

When she was brought in, Marian Wheeler looked as calm and composed as she had when they had arrested her, but the slightly far-away look had been replaced by watchfulness.

'Some more questions, Mrs Wheeler,' said Judy. 'You understand that you don't have to answer them, and you can have your solicitor present if you choose?'

'I understand.'

Judy laid Mrs Wheeler's two statements down in front of her. 'Do you want to make a third?' she asked.

'No,' she said. 'I've told you everything.'

'Except the truth.'

Mrs Wheeler didn't speak.

'Right,' said Judy. 'Where were you at five past eight on Christmas Eve?'

'I've told you in my statement,' she said.

'Where were you at five past eight on Christmas Eve?' Judy asked.

Lloyd watched Marian Wheeler. He'd never been able to perfect Judy's trick of asking the same question over again, just as though it was the first time. It was dreadfully irritating, and almost always produced a response.

'I've just told you.'

'You were in your daughter's bedroom?'

'Yes.'

'Laying into her husband with a poker?'

Marian Wheeler raised her eyebrows. 'Yes,' she said. 'If you want to put it like that, I suppose that is what I was doing.'

'And then you burned the dress, and went to see Mrs Anthony?'

Mrs Wheeler didn't reply, but the watchfulness became wariness, and she sat a little further back in her chair.

'Where were you at five past eight on Christmas Eve?' asked Judy, pleasantly.

'I – I was at home.'

'Battering your son-in-law to death?' enquired Judy.

Marian Wheeler looked shocked. 'Sergeant, I don't think there's any need to—'

'There isn't a gentle way to say it,' said Judy. 'Someone battered him to death.'

'I did,' said Mrs Wheeler. 'I've told you.' She picked up the statement.

'And then you burned your dress?'

'Yes.'

'No,' said Judy. 'You were wearing the dress when you saw Mrs Anthony.'

'No! No – Mrs Anthony's a very old lady—'

'We made that mistake,' Lloyd said, chiming in. 'She's old, but she's *sharp*. Right, Sergeant?'

'She's described it to me, Mrs Wheeler,' said Judy. 'Peach, full skirt, deep cuffs . . . ' She paused. 'You spilled coffee on it. You went home to change.'

'Yes,' said Mrs Wheeler. '*That's* when I did it – I got confused, that's all.'

'You didn't leave Mrs Anthony's house until ten past nine. Graham Elstow was already dead.'

Mrs Wheeler's eyes had lost their wariness, their defiance, and Lloyd knew that Judy had won.

'Where were you at five past eight on Christmas Eve, Mrs Wheeler?' asked Judy, in the same interested, polite tones.

'At the castle,' she said, her voice flat. 'I went to see a girl called Eleanor Langton. She's working there. A sort of archivist or something.'

Lloyd sat down. 'And *then* you went to see Mrs Anthony.'

She nodded. 'But while I was there I spilled some coffee on my dress. Well,' she said, 'she told you that, didn't she? I was still shaking. What if we hadn't come back, Mr Lloyd? What would have happened to Joanna if he hadn't stopped?'

'And yet despite how you felt – and despite the weather – you went all the way to the castle first?' said Lloyd. 'To confirm an invitation? I almost didn't believe Mrs Langton when she told me.'

'I wish you hadn't,' she sighed. 'Yes – that's what I told her. But I just wanted to . . . ' She gave a short laugh. 'See what I was up against,' she said. 'She's been taking up rather a lot of my husband's time lately.'

'I see,' said Lloyd.

'I wonder if you do,' said Mrs Wheeler. 'Anyway, I *did* want to confirm the invitation. I wanted to be sure she knew that it was from both of us, if you see what I mean. I went there first to get it over with.'

'And then you went to Mrs Anthony's, and from there you went home to change,' said Lloyd. 'Go on.'

'I went upstairs,' she said. 'And I looked along the landing. Joanna's bedroom door was open. I thought Graham had left. I went in, and . . . and found him,' she said. 'He was dead. I didn't know what to do. I thought—'

Lloyd stood up, and walked slowly round the room. 'You thought your daughter had killed him,' he said.

'Yes,' she said. 'He deserved it!' she shouted. 'He deserved it – he put her in hospital – did you know that?'

'Yes,' said Lloyd. 'So what did you do then, Mrs Wheeler?'

'I didn't know what to do,' she said. 'I knew Joanna must have done it. That was why she wouldn't let her father go up to him.'

She looked up at Lloyd. 'I wasn't going to let her suffer for him any more,' she said. 'So I . . . I made it look as if I'd done it.'

Lloyd sat down, feeling tired and old. 'What did you do?' he asked.

'I cleaned the handle of the poker,' she said. 'And I held it. But then I thought – they can tell, can't they? They can tell *how* you've held something. I've read it in books. So I hit him, to make sure I was holding it right. I hit him twice.'

140

Someone walked along the corridor outside. Lloyd leant on the table, his chin resting on his clasped hands. She hadn't switched pokers, he thought. Other than that, his theory was pretty good. 'And the dress?' he said.

'I burned it,' she said. 'I got blood on the sleeve, and I realised that if I burned it, you'd find it.' She looked at Lloyd. 'What difference does it make?' she said. 'You've got *me* – why don't you charge me? I'd have done it – if I'd seen him hitting Jo, I'd have done it!'

Lloyd was beginning to lose what little patience he'd had left. He counted off on his fingers. 'One, you have wasted police time. Two, you have tampered with evidence. Three, you have made false statements. And if I can think of any more, I will, Mrs Wheeler. You can be prosecuted for these offences – perhaps that will feed your desire for martyrdom.'

She looked at him with vague surprise. 'I wasn't being a martyr, Mr Lloyd. I was just—' She obviously decided that he would never understand, and gave up with a shrug.

Then, Lloyd realised what she had done. What she had really done, and he was assailed by something worse, much worse, than mere irritation. 'When you left the house in the first place,' Lloyd said, 'you left it unlocked, as usual?'

Marian Wheeler looked haunted for a second. 'Yes,' she said.

Lloyd closed his eyes. Between ten to eight and ten past nine, the doors were unlocked. And someone went in. How the hell were they supposed to find out who? Marian Wheeler was out visiting, Wheeler and his daughter were at the pub . . . Well, they could make more vigorous enquiries about all of that. But the other possibility loomed before him.

'Someone could have got in,' he said slowly, angrily. 'Just like you said.'

Marian Wheeler's mouth opened, but she closed it again.

'And you destroyed any evidence that there might have been,' he went on. 'You misdirected us, you obliterated possible fingerprints, you tampered with the scene of the crime. You have given him time to get away, to destroy his clothing

– in short, Mrs Wheeler, you have made our job practically impossible.'

He walked out of the room, resisting the temptation to slam the door. Bloody woman. Bloody stupid interfering woman. Who the hell could have got in and murdered the man? Why? Someone he knew? It had to be. Someone he didn't know? Lloyd's heart sank. Someone who might do it again. There had to be a coat, something, that the murderer had jettisoned. He'd get men looking tomorrow. Thank God they had taken the intruder suggestion seriously enough to issue a warning. But now an intruder wasn't just a desperate explanation thought up by the Wheelers. It was a real possibility. And they would have to start looking into Elstow's background.

He met someone in the pub. He'd ignored that. Now, he'd have to talk to the villagers, find out if they had seen a stranger hanging round. Oh, God, this should have been done days ago!

But some of it had, he reminded himself. Elstow had been alone in the pub, according to the barmaid. He had come in alone, and remained alone. And they only had his wife's word for it that he had ever mentioned meeting anyone. He calmed himself down, and walked back to the office. Joanna Elstow still seemed the likeliest candidate, even to her mother. Lloyd sighed. He'd taken her word for it that her row with her husband started at five. He was going to have to rub out anything that that damn family had told him, and start again.

Judy came in. 'I'm driving Mrs Wheeler home,' she said, then closed the door. 'Should I come back?' she asked him.

'No,' he said. 'There isn't much we can do tonight.' He looked up from the desk. 'Is there?' he asked, and he sounded bitter.

'I thought perhaps there might be,' she said quietly.

'No.'

Her direct brown gaze held his for a moment. 'Don't do this to me,' she said, almost under her breath.

'I'm not the one who's doing it,' he replied.

He watched as she slipped on the dark grey leather coat that Michael had given her for Christmas. He'd like to have given her something like that. As it was, they had to be content with the sort of thing that wouldn't be remarked on. Suddenly, he understood why long-standing mistresses would deliberately get pregnant. It wasn't vindictiveness. It was desperation of a sort.

He watched out of the window as she drove off with the would-be martyr, and darkly formulated the charges against Mrs Wheeler. Because he *would* prosecute, and Judy would tell him he was being uncharitable.

But maybe not, he thought, sitting down again. Not if she was busy being a DI in Barton, and he'd made it clear that she wasn't welcome. Damn it, she was more than welcome, she was *necessary*. He needed her, and his bloody pride would have to take a back seat. Sharing her might not be ideal, but it was better than feeling like this. He just hoped he hadn't blown his last chance.

He picked up Eleanor Langton's statement. He'd better apologise – he really had been a bit high-handed with her. Perhaps he should go now, he thought, glancing at his watch. Why not? It would keep him out of the flat for another hour or two. And apologising to her might rid him of this nagging notion that he ought to be apologising to *someone*.

He was getting heartily sick of the journey into Byford, rendered utterly monotonous by the snow. In spring, the fields would shade from pale yellow to dark green, relieved here and there by the dark brown of a ploughed acre. Crows would rise noisily from the treetops, flapping across the road, and rabbits would dart from the fields, bobbing along the verges, occasionally coming to grief. But the snow deadened everything; no colour, no sound.

Up Castle Road, reluctantly past the pub, and on to the top, where he turned into the castle gates, the car bumping over the cattle grids. In the unlit castle grounds, he drove cautiously, only knowing he was on a road by the regular 5 m.p.h. speed-limit signs. On his left, suddenly looming into the night sky, was the castle, a dark, forbidding fortress. A reminder that there had once been worse things to worry about than muggers and vandals. Or even the odd murderer. He'd brought the kids here once or twice, when they were younger.

It had never made him shiver before.

Through the huge gatehouse, into the protected heart of the castle, lit by the odd wall-light where there once had been flaming torches. Turn left as you come out of the gatehouse, and left again at the end of the gatehouse walls, he'd been told.

He turned left, into a large, moonlit courtyard. Stables, whatever their function now, ran along the whole of one side, and Lloyd could practically hear the horses' hooves on the frosted cobbles, now broken up here and there by flower-beds. He pulled up beside two other cars and got out, walking past the shop which sold books and bric-à-brac, looking for Eleanor Langton's door. Beside the souvenir shop, the ever-knowledgeable Constable Sandwell had told him, and beside the souvenir shop it was.

A black door, with a brass knocker shaped like a lion's head. Through the window at the side, a light showed faintly from the rear. He knocked.

Mrs Langton let him in with a courtesy that he felt he didn't deserve. He followed her down the hallway to find an older woman sitting at the table in the small dining room.

'Oh, I'm sorry,' he said. 'I'm interrupting—'

'We've finished,' Mrs Langton said, and the other woman smiled. 'This is Chief Inspector Lloyd, Penny,' she went on.

'Acting,' said Lloyd, conscientiously.

'Some might say over-acting,' said Eleanor Langton in a quiet aside, as she began clearing away.

Lloyd was surprised, and smiled, pleased to discover that at least he'd been picking on someone his own size.

'This is my mother-in-law, Inspector. Penny Langton.'

144

'How do you do, Mrs Langton,' he said, shaking hands. 'It's a bit confusing,' he added. 'Two Mrs Langtons.'

'Then you'd better stick to Eleanor and Penny,' said Eleanor.

'Right.' He felt a little awkward now that he was on Eleanor Langton's home ground. She was in command here. She was enjoying herself.

'I'll be back in a moment,' she said, and Lloyd leapt to open the door to the kitchen as she made for it with both hands full. 'Thank you,' she said, and he was relieved to be left alone with her mother-in-law.

'You'll be here about the business at the vicarage?' said Penny, her eyes worried.

'Connected with it,' Lloyd said. 'Mrs . . . er . . . Eleanor has been very helpful.'

'Have I?'

He hadn't heard her come back, and he turned to see her in the doorway, flicking her long blonde hair back from her face. She was very good-looking, in a Scandinavian way. But there was something about her that reminded Lloyd of the snow-scene outside.

'Yes,' he said. 'I'm here to thank you for coming in, and to confirm that I have no reason to doubt the accuracy of your statement.' He paused. 'And to apologise if I . . . ' He searched for the appropriate words. 'If I offended you in any way,' he said.

Her eyes held his, and there was a hint of amusement in them that he didn't like.

'Why the change of mind?' she asked.

Lloyd thought for a moment. 'Further evidence has come to light that . . . casts a new light on the incident,' he said, annoyed with himself as soon as the words were spoken, because they had been clumsy. She unnerved him.

'Thank you for the apology,' she said. 'Will you join us for coffee?'

He hesitated, because he wished he'd never come at all. But it was a tedious drive back, and if she was prepared to

145

offer him coffee, the least he could do was to accept it. 'Thank you,' he said.

Over the coffee, Mrs Langton senior did most of the talking. Lloyd learned that her son had died in a motor accident, that Eleanor had coped wonderfully, and that Tessa was the most delightful grandchild anyone could ever want.

'I'll just look in on her,' said Eleanor. 'Help yourselves to more coffee.'

Penny Langton waited until she closed the door. 'It's very difficult for her,' she said. 'Bringing up Tessa on her own.'

'It must be,' said Lloyd.

'It's not money – she got some compensation after the accident. She doesn't *need* to work here, if you know what I mean. It's more for something to do – but I wish she'd move back to Stansfield. It's lonely here, don't you think?'

Lloyd couldn't but agree.

'But she says she really likes the job, and of course, another kind of job might be difficult, with Tessa, but . . . '

Lloyd waited.

'But the thing is, I'm worried about her being here,' she said. 'Is she safe?'

'Sorry?' said Lloyd.

'I mean – is she in danger, Mr Lloyd? If she's got some sort of evidence . . . if she's mixed up in it somehow.'

'Oh,' said Lloyd. 'No – she isn't involved in it. She's in no danger. Eleanor just cleared up a small mystery for us.'

She looked slightly less anxious. 'I was so worried, you see. Because Eleanor rang on Christmas Eve to say that the snow would probably block the road into the village, and I'd better listen for the road reports before I set out. So I put on Radio Barton in the morning, and the first thing I heard was that someone had been murdered in the village. I just got into my car, and thank God, the road had been cleared.' She paused for breath.

146

Lloyd nodded. He wasn't sure what he was supposed to be saying.

'What's happening about it, Mr Lloyd? The radio didn't even say who was killed. A man, that's all.'

'I'm sure Inspector Lloyd has better things to do than gossip,' Eleanor said.

Lloyd wished the damn woman wouldn't creep about. 'We have advised people in the area to keep their doors and windows locked, of course,' he said, thankful that that was the truth. 'And not to open the door to anyone they're not sure about—'

'Did someone get in?' asked Penny Langton. 'I haven't even seen an evening paper since I've been here.' She looked accusingly at Eleanor.

'I've *told* you, Penny. I'm not in any more danger than anyone else. I just told the police something I thought they ought to know.'

'But you won't talk about it.' She turned to Lloyd. 'Have you caught anyone?' she asked.

Lloyd took a breath. 'Our enquiries are proceeding,' he said. 'And I'm sure there's no cause for general alarm.' He was sure, he told himself. He was *sure*.

He suddenly felt sorry for Penny, stuck in the middle of nowhere with her enigmatic daughter-in-law, frightened to leave her alone. 'The facts are that the vicar's son-in-law was the victim, and that we are following a number of lines of enquiry, including the possibility of a break-in of some sort. And that's about as much as it said in the paper.' He smiled. 'We have no reason to think that the incident was anything other than a one-off,' he said.

'Do you mean it was someone in the *vicarage*?' she asked.

Lloyd refrained from glancing over at Eleanor. She had obviously told her mother-in-law nothing at all.

'Our enquiries are proceeding,' he said again, and rose.

Eleanor came out with him, almost closing the door, so that the only light was from the ghostly moon, full and low in the misty sky. 'Have you let Mrs Wheeler go?' she asked.

'Yes,' he said. He pulled on his gloves. 'You haven't told your mother-in-law about it?'

'No. I've tried to play it down,' she explained. 'Penny gets very nervous.' She shivered slightly in the cold air.

'I'd have thought that a village this size would know every detail,' said Lloyd. 'She'd hardly need the evening paper.'

'It's a very large village,' Eleanor said, proprietorially.

'By area,' Lloyd agreed. 'But most of that's farmland. There aren't so many people, are there? It can't be easy to keep a secret.'

'Probably not,' said Eleanor.

And you probably have one to keep, thought Lloyd, thinking about George.

'But we're sort of cut off from the rest of the village here.' Eleanor smiled. 'And I'm a newcomer.'

Lloyd glanced round at the stone walls of the castle. 'Is the family here?' he asked.

'No. They winter somewhere exotic.'

He frowned. 'Are you alone?' he asked.

'For the moment,' she said. 'They do have a couple of staff who live in, but they're on holiday too, just now.' She smiled her cold smile. 'The place is riddled with burglar alarms connected to the police station,' she said. 'I'm perfectly safe. I just wish they'd hurry up with the phone.'

'Aren't there any pay-phones?'

'One, would you believe? In the café, which is closed until Easter.'

'Well,' said Lloyd, slightly diffidently. 'I know the telephone manager – do you want me to put in a word?'

'It's not British Telecom who are dragging their feet,' she said, and smiled suddenly. A real smile. 'You don't have to worry about me,' she said. 'This place has survived Cromwell, hasn't it? I'm as safe here as I could be.'

Lloyd said goodnight, and got back to the car. He glared back at the snow when he turned on his headlights, and regretted bringing his own car back into service as he steered it gently over the icy ground back to the untreated estate road. He wondered, as he slowly made his way out, why Eleanor Langton was so unwilling to share her knowledge with her mother-in-law. Because of George? But it was idle curiosity, more than anything else. It was none of his business.

And apologising hadn't made him feel better in the slightest degree.

Chapter Seven

'Did you manage to see the kids?' Judy asked.

They were in the lounge bar of the Duke's Arms in Castle Road, where the Reverend Mr Wheeler and his daughter had spent some time on Christmas Eve. That much had been established; what they wanted now was a clearer indication of when they left the pub, but so far all they had done was wait. Voices floated in from the public bar, but she and Lloyd were alone in the lounge, except for the landlady, who couldn't help. Some of the regulars might, she had said. But they wouldn't be in until lunch time, and what with people taking the whole week between Christmas and New Year, there might not be many of them.

Lloyd laughed. 'Kids?' he repeated. 'Yes, I managed to get over for a little while on Boxing Day.'

'How is everyone?'

'Fine,' he said. 'Except – Linda's got some ridiculous idea about going to London. She's far too young.'

Judy smiled. 'I hope you didn't tell her that,' she said.

'No. In fact, I wondered . . . '

Judy raised an eyebrow, recognising the wheedling tone.

'You were a single girl in London,' he said. 'You know how difficult it is – accommodation, that sort of thing. I thought you might talk to her.'

'There wouldn't be much point,' said Judy.

'Why not?'

'For one thing, I lived with my parents, which is hardly the same thing: I don't know any more than she does about flat-hunting and finding a job – probably a lot less.'

Lloyd looked glum.

'And for another – Linda can barely bring herself to speak to me.'

'Oh, no,' Lloyd assured her. 'She's over all that, I'm sure.'

'Is she?' said Judy, disbelievingly. 'All right – she says hello if we meet, but she still doesn't think much of the idea of you and me.' She sipped her drink. 'It must run in the family,' she said.

'Judy,' Lloyd began. 'I don't—'

'I know, I know. I'm breaking the rules. But since you won't see me in anything *other* than working hours, I—'

The door banged open, and a middle-aged woman breezed in.

'You got back then,' said the landlady, unnecessarily. 'Did you have a nice time?'

'Oh, you know,' said the other woman. 'So-so. It's nice to be back in my own house.' She hung things up on various pegs. 'But anyway—' she began, excitedly.

'You didn't have too much trouble getting there?' interrupted the landlady.

'What? Oh – it was past midnight before I arrived. You wouldn't *believe* the number of cars out at that time on Christmas Eve. But never mind that,' she said. 'I can't turn my back for five minutes, can I?'

Judy could see the landlady in the mirrored wall, as she mouthed 'police', nodding over to their table.

The barmaid, for such she proved to be, looked over at Judy. 'We can't go to jail for talking about it, can we?' she asked, with a laugh.

Judy smiled.

'I couldn't believe it,' she said, and turned back to the landlady. 'I felt awful when I heard,' she said. 'I mean, I'd made a joke about it – you know the way you do.'

'A joke?' queried Lloyd, twisting round.

'About her black eyes. She said she'd been to the dentist, and I said something about her husband getting funny looks. I never dreamed it *was* her husband. And now . . . '

Villages. Judy didn't know how people could bear to live in them, with everyone knowing everyone else's business. When she had been Joanna's age, she would have died if she had thought her private life was common knowledge.

And when she *had* been Joanna's age, she reflected, her private life had been Lloyd, just as it was now. A secret, guilt-ridden, unconsummated love affair. She glanced at Lloyd, who was joining in the gossip. What was it now, now that it had been consummated? There was no guilt; Barbara was no longer part of Lloyd's life, and Judy owed Michael nothing. But there was still secrecy, because once Michael found out, champion of Victorian values that he was, her bridges would be burned, and she wasn't sure she could face that. And because of that, she was right back where she had been, when she had been Joanna's age. Sitting opposite Lloyd in a pub, staring unhappily into a half pint of lager, trying to disguise her cowardice as principle, and failing.

'They say he put her in hospital,' finished the barmaid.

'I'd heard that that was why she'd left him,' said the landlady. 'I didn't believe it myself. A vicar's daughter.'

'You never told me!'

'No. Well. You shouldn't repeat gossip.'

'See what I have to put up with?' the barmaid demanded.

Judy laughed; Lloyd picked up his drink. 'So you were here on Christmas Eve, then?' he said. 'And you spoke to Mrs Elstow?'

'Who? Oh – is that her name? Only for a minute. She was with her father – they were talking about something. In fact,' she said, 'he was angry with her, I'm sure. I remember thinking that the poor little girl could do with some sympathy, not being glared at.'

'Did you notice when Mrs Elstow left?' Lloyd asked.

'No,' she said slowly. 'No, sorry. We were packed – well, you know what it's like on Christmas Eve.' She thought hard. 'No, I just don't remember,' she said. 'I know when he left, though. The vicar.'

Lloyd turned back, glancing at Judy. 'They didn't leave together?' he asked carelessly, finishing his beer. He stood up. 'I'll have another one in there, love,' he said.

She pulled another pint, and handed it to him. 'He left on his own,' she said. 'About half past eight. There's always carols on Christmas Eve, and the pianist came in just as Mr Wheeler was leaving. I thought it was funny, because he and his wife normally stay for that. I wondered if she wasn't well, because she's usually with him. I don't think that girl was well enough to be out, quite honestly . . . '

She chattered on, and Lloyd looked as though he wasn't really listening, as he sat at the bar, reflectively sipping the beer Judy knew he didn't want. But he was paying much more careful attention than the barmaid suspected, for through her he was learning the habits of the Wheelers on Christmas Eve.

Habits which had, for one reason or another, been broken.

'Why did you do it?' Joanna was asking, her face sad and cross at the same time. It was the first time she had mentioned it; Marian had thought that she had escaped interrogation.

'The inspector thinks I wanted to be a martyr,' she said. 'But that wasn't it.'

'You can't really blame him,' said Joanna.

Marian considered her motives, now that she had been asked. 'I just think,' she said, after a few moments, 'that if you love someone, you should be prepared to help them.'

Joanna's eyes widened. 'But it was crazy!' she said. 'And unnecessary. You didn't *have* to do something like that.'

'People don't think it odd if someone dies saving their child from a fire,' Marian said. 'They don't call them martyrs.'

153

'But I didn't *do* it!' Joanna shouted suddenly. 'Everyone thinks I did – but I didn't, I swear I didn't.'

The front door banged, and George came back from wherever he had been. Marian could hazard a guess.

'It's very slippery at the top here,' he said. 'I almost broke my neck.'

'I'll put some ash down, shall I?' Joanna said, getting up.

Marian didn't think that was at all a good idea. 'No, dear,' she said. 'I don't think you—' She stopped. 'It's a very dirty job,' she said.

'I'll wear the overalls,' said Joanna.

'I'll do it,' said George.

'But you're not well,' protested Joanna.

George sighed. 'I'm all right,' he said. 'Doing something physical might help.'

Marian rather thought that was just what he had been doing. It didn't seem to help at all.

'It's just all this business,' he said.

Marian saw Joanna's eyes flash. Joanna was sometimes so like George.

'You're sick because you think I killed Graham,' she shouted. 'That's why you told the police you were with me all evening!'

Well, thought Marian, it was the reason advanced, at any rate. But unlike Joanna, she knew the real reason for the lie.

'I *don't* think you did it. I just thought it would clear you of any suspicion. It was stupid, I know. But it's done now.'

'You lied to them. Either you think I did it, or—'

'You think I killed him? I wish I had, Joanna. Believe me, I wish I had.'

Marian didn't want to hear this. She didn't want to know.

'Yes! Because then you could take the blame. You think I did it – you both do! The police do – and now they'll be convinced,' she added, with a flash of something less than gratitude

154

at Marian. 'You don't have to *lie* for me, do you understand? I can take care of myself.'

'Oh, can you? Then perhaps you'll enlighten us—'

'That's enough!' Marian's voice, rarely raised, brought the shouting to a halt. Normality. Ever since Graham Elstow had turned up, she had got by on normality, and so would they.

'Sorry,' muttered George. 'We're all a bit on edge.'

'Me too,' said Joanna, sitting down.

Marian relaxed. That was better.

Joanna frowned slightly. 'Where are the overalls?' she asked.

'*I'm* doing the path,' said George firmly.

'No – I mean where *are* they?'

Lloyd relieved himself of some of his liquid intake, and sighed. So, he thought, George and Marian always stayed for the carol-singing, which went on until ten-thirty. But this year, everything was different. It probably meant nothing, he told himself. But George must have gone somewhere.

He came out of the gents, and stopped at the door of the lounge bar, as he saw Judy. She looked a little sad, sitting there on her own, he thought, and he wished that things were different.

It still looked odd to him, a woman alone in a pub, but he was doubtless a male chauvinist. He breezed in. 'Right?' he said.

'Right.' She finished her drink and stood up.

'I've a good mind to charge the lot of them,' he said, as they left.

'You don't have enough evidence.'

'We know they've all lied to us.' He unlocked the car angrily, dropping the keys in the snow. He swore, and picked them up. 'We know Marian Wheeler interfered with the scene of the crime.'

'All that proves is that they've protected Joanna from the cradle,' said Judy briskly.

He opened her door, and she got in beside him. 'I think that's why Elstow got so violent,' she added.

Lloyd grunted.

'Did you look at those photographs of Joanna on the kitchen wall?' she asked. 'Joanna crawling, Joanna walking, Joanna's first tooth, first day at school – no wedding photographs. No photograph of Graham Elstow at all.'

'Are you surprised?' asked Lloyd.

Judy nodded. 'Yes,' she said.

'Well,' said Lloyd, reversing gingerly on to Castle Road. 'They'd hardly have Joanna's first black eye, would they?'

'But there's never *been* any,' Judy persisted. 'They're all written up – there haven't been any removed. They're in date order,' she said. 'And her wedding's been ignored.'

Lloyd got the car pointing the right way, and stopped.

'And George Wheeler was angry with her,' Judy went on. 'About Elstow. He wasn't frightened for her, like her mother. Joanna makes him *angry*.'

'What does that prove? She makes me angry too. Why the hell did she put up with it?'

Judy sighed. 'I think,' she said slowly, 'because she knew, really, *why* Elstow behaved like that. Imagine it, Lloyd. Coming up against all that jealousy. It was as if he didn't exist.' She turned to him. 'Elstow was frustrated,' she said. 'And no wonder. How would you feel?'

He smiled at the worried brown eyes that looked into his. 'Well, I wouldn't start knocking you about,' he said. 'I'd probably buy a twelve-year-old malt, sit down, and have a long heart to heart with your father.'

'Not everyone has your way with words, Inspector Lloyd,' Judy said, smiling. 'And not everyone is a push-over for expensive whisky.'

'Your father is,' said Lloyd.

Her face grew serious again. 'My father isn't in love with me.'

Lloyd started the engine again. 'Wheeler and his daughter?' he said. 'Is that what you think?'

'It's a possibility,' said Judy.

156

Lloyd pulled out on to the main road, and headed for the vicarage. 'Spiritual or physical?' he asked.

'Who knows? Behind closed doors, and all that.'

Lloyd settled in behind a lorry. 'Reciprocated?' He glanced at her.

'Oh, I don't know,' she said. 'I'm not even sure I really believe that. But why *didn't* she go up to Graham?'

'I asked you that,' said Lloyd.

'I'm not sure she knew what she wanted,' Judy said.

'I think she did,' said Lloyd grimly. 'She wanted rid of Elstow.'

'I don't think she had anything to do with killing him,' Judy said. 'It's Wheeler who left the pub, remember.'

So Wheeler killed him? It was possible, Lloyd thought, in theory. But there was a practical side to murder, particularly this murder, where the Wheeler solution just didn't fit. Clothes. They'd found nothing. No clothing of any sort. And Wheeler was wearing the clothes he'd worn in the pub when he and Judy arrived at the vicarage on Christmas morning. He smiled at his next thought. Surely the congregation would have noticed if his clerical robes had been covered in blood? His smile vanished. Had anyone checked the vestry?

'We are dealing with a family of pathological liars,' he reminded her.

'I think Joanna's telling the truth?' she said.

'The whole truth?' he asked, and she didn't answer.

He did trust Judy's instincts. But perhaps Elstow had trusted his, and look how he ended up.

For the next few minutes, he formulated several ways of telling Judy that he was quite prepared to share her with Michael. He didn't utter any of them, partly because they were in working hours, and he ought to obey his own rule, partly because it wasn't really true, and partly because she might tell him the offer was closed.

The castle's pale stone walls were just visible through the naked trees as they drove up to the Wheelers' drive. It was no more than a ten-minute walk over the fields, sharing the hilltop with the vicarage. Lloyd could even see the stables, but only because they had cleared the land for farming. In the Civil War, the castle had been totally camouflaged; it had commanded views of all comers from all sides, and couldn't be seen itself. It had succumbed to the Roundheads' gunpowder in the end, but as Eleanor had pointed out, it had survived. In daylight, it looked settled, peaceful. Pretty, even, in the winter light. But at night . . . He shivered again.

George Wheeler was waving a dustbin about. Lloyd frowned, but as they got closer, he could see what he was doing. They got out of the car.

'Good morning,' Lloyd said.

Wheeler scattered more ash. 'Doesn't look very pretty,' he said. 'But it works. This is something you can't do in centrally heated houses, now I come to think of it. Perhaps we're not so badly off, after all.'

'I'd like a word, Mr Wheeler.'

'Oh?' he said, shaking out dark gritty ash as he walked along. 'What about? Have you come to arrest my wife for cleaning her own landing? She tells me you intend to prosecute. Don't you think you'd be better employed looking for who really did it?'

Lloyd, who had never had the least desire to use his fists, knew how Elstow must have felt. But he recognised bravado when he heard it. This was George fighting his desire to throw up. This was George thinking that attack was the best method of defence.

Wheeler had stopped blustering, and stood waiting for a reply. So Lloyd didn't speak at all. And he could stand there in silence all day, if he had to. Judy affected a deep interest in her notebook. For a long time, all three of them stood, saying nothing at all.

The disintegration of George, thought Lloyd, as he watched Wheeler's eyes begin to move furtively from him to Judy, and back. He wiped his upper lip. 'Well?' he said.

'Well what, Mr Wheeler?' asked Lloyd, politely.

Wheeler didn't speak, and Lloyd looked down at the grey ash on the white snow, a fair approximation of Wheeler's complexion.

'Look,' said Wheeler. 'Marian went out, someone came in – and you haven't lifted a finger to find out who, or why. You're tearing this family apart, do you know that?'

Lloyd looked up from his contemplation of the black-speckled ash at his feet, stung into a reaction.

'We have carried out extensive enquiries in the village,' he said. 'We have been searching for days for any trace at all of someone gaining entry to your house. We're looking in six-foot high snow-drifts for abandoned clothing.' His feet crunched on the ash as he moved toward Wheeler, having to look up at the taller man. 'Your wife destroyed evidence, and misled us quite deliberately,' he said. 'So don't blame me for what's happening to your family, Mr Wheeler!'

George Wheeler looked down for a moment, then picked up the dustbin again.

'If you really want to help,' Judy said, stepping out of the way of a cloud of dust, 'you'll tell us where you were on Christmas Eve.'

'I was at the pub with my daughter,' he said. 'I've told you a dozen times.' He tapped the last of the gritty ash from the bin, and put it down.

'Let's go somewhere we can talk,' said Lloyd quietly.

Wheeler hesitated. 'My study,' he said, in the end, and led the way to the house, where Marian Wheeler and Joanna met them in the hallway.

'Joanna,' said Judy. 'Could we have a word, do you think?'

The girl looked apprehensively at her mother.

'You can come into the kitchen,' said Mrs Wheeler.

'Oh, I don't want to put you out of your own kitchen, Mrs Wheeler,' said Judy.

Marian Wheeler, tight-lipped at being thus dismissed, turned and went back into the kitchen by herself.

'We can use the back bedroom,' Joanna volunteered.

'What's going on, Inspector?' asked Wheeler.

Lloyd held out a hand, ushering Wheeler into his own study. 'I'll tell you, Mr Wheeler,' he said, looking at Joanna as he spoke. 'We don't like being lied to. That's what's going on.'

Joanna closed the bedroom door. 'What does he mean?' she asked.

Sergeant Hill raised her eyebrows. 'I think you know what he means,' she replied, turning to look out of the window.

'No,' Joanna said warily, sitting down on the bed.

The sergeant turned, sunlight suddenly breaking through the grey clouds, lighting her as though she were on stage. Dramatic light and shade; Joanna felt as if she were an actor in a drama. Guiltily, she was finding that she rather enjoyed it. Like long ago, when the room they were in had been the sick-bay. She had been the centre of attention then, too.

'I thought we had a bit more trust going for us than this,' the sergeant said.

'Trust?' repeated Joanna. 'You arrested my *mother*, and you expect me to trust you?'

Sergeant Hill gave a short sigh, and looked at her reflectively. After a moment, she turned away, looking out into the strong sunlight. 'People pay taxes,' she said slowly. 'Good money. For a police force. Who are supposed to prevent crime, and investigate the ones they've failed to prevent.'

You never knew where you *were* with her, Joanna thought worriedly. Now, she was to be given a lecture on police-work? She sat back, her elbow on the pillow, in a studied attitude of detached interest.

'The thing is,' the sergeant said, turning back again. 'The bobby on the beat might prevent ten shops being broken into, but nobody knows that. All they know about is the eleventh shop, which does get broken into. And they want results.'

Joanna looked back at her. 'So?' she said.

160

'So that's where I come in,' she said. 'I have to find out who broke in to the shop – and prove it.' She came over to the foot of the bed, and sat down. 'And the only way I can do that is if people trust me enough to tell me the truth.'

'Why should they?' Joanna sat up. 'You hear all the time about policemen on the take, planting evidence—'

She nodded. 'Just like you hear about the eleventh shop,' she said. 'But the rest of us are just doing our jobs. And the whole system depends on people telling the truth. On both sides.'

Joanna looked away from her.

'Where were you on Christmas Eve?' she asked.

'At the pub,' Joanna said. 'With my father.'

'And did you stay there after he'd left?' she asked.

Joanna froze. 'What?' she said, when she could say anything at all. But the sergeant didn't speak, and Joanna turned her head slowly to look at her.

'Your father left the pub alone at eight-thirty,' she said. 'And I want to know what you did. Did you stay there? What did you do, Joanna?'

'You think I killed Graham,' she said, almost inaudibly.

'I don't.'

Joanna's eyes widened with surprise.

'But your lies make it hard for me to justify my position,' she went on. 'What did you do after your father left the pub?'

Joanna's mind raced. 'I went to see Dr Lomax,' she said truthfully.

The sergeant opened her inevitable notebook.

'She's our doctor,' Joanna said. 'A friend of the family.'

Our doctor, she thought. Her doctor, her parents' doctor. Poor Graham.

'Were you seeing her as a friend or a patient?'

'I was worried about the baby. I told you I'd seen a doctor. I stayed there for a while. We talked about Graham – she told me where he could get help. And then I came home, but I couldn't get in because the house was locked up.' The words

161

were coming fast now. 'I knocked and knocked, and I thought Graham was just being stupid.'

'What time was this?'

'I got here at about half past nine, I suppose. I sat in the car to keep warm. And then my father came home.'

'When?'

'Half an hour after that,' she said.

'Did he have his car?'

'No. Mummy had it. He was on foot – he came over the field.'

'The field?' queried the sergeant.

'It's a short cut to Castle Road,' said Joanna, and with the words, she realised where her father had been. 'He waited with me until my mother came home. She was only a few minutes after that.'

'Why did you lie to us, Joanna?'

'I *didn't*,' she said indignantly, before she could stop herself.

The sergeant slowly turned back the pages. 'No,' she said quietly, looking up. 'I'm sorry. You just went along with a lie.'

And if she hadn't initiated the lie, then her father had, and the implication was obvious: Joanna could have bitten her tongue off.

'Joanna,' said the sergeant, apparently unconcerned about that. 'You told me you'd made it up with Graham – you'd decided to go home with him.'

'I had,' she said, puzzled.

'Didn't you want to talk to him?'

This was getting worse and worse. Joanna shook her head.

'All that time,' said Sergeant Hill. 'From five o'clock. Didn't you want to see him?'

'Yes! Yes, of course I did,' Joanna said. 'But it would have caused trouble, and that would have upset my mother.'

The sergeant nodded, looking a little baffled.

'When I did say I was going up to see him, it caused a row,' she said. 'Just before Mummy found him.' The tears threatened again.

Sergeant Hill closed her notebook. 'Thank you,' she said.

162

'The solicitor that my father got for my mother,' Joanna said. 'He said that Graham might have been seeing someone else – she might have come here that night.'

Her heart sank when she saw the look in Sergeant Hill's eye. But she had to try. Try to get them to look somewhere else for the murderer.

'Please,' she said. 'He was going to check up – get a private detective. But he won't now, and I can't afford to – *please*.'

'We already are looking into it,' said the sergeant. 'Graham said he'd met someone at the pub, didn't he? We're trying to find out about that.' She stood up. 'You didn't go to the house when our people checked it, did you?'

Joanna shook her head.

'You should,' she said. 'You're more likely to spot any indication of another woman than we are.'

Joanna hadn't thought of that.

'But Joanna,' she said, in the warning voice that Joanna had come to recognise. 'We have found nothing to suggest another woman, and there is simply no evidence at all that anyone else was in here that night. You do understand that, don't you?'

Yes, Joanna understood.

'And I hope you do think you can trust me,' she said. 'Because you can, you know.'

As she made to leave, Joanna made up her mind. Because she did trust her. 'Sergeant Hill,' she said. 'There's – there's something else. Something you ought to know.'

George had reiterated that he'd been in the pub with Joanna all evening, and said that the barmaid must have been mistaken. Then the inspector had chosen to take him through the whole evening again, and George was beginning to feel sick.

'Look, I've told you this three times! Why aren't you out looking for whoever came in here? I'll tell you why! Because you're convinced that my daughter killed him, that's why!'

Lloyd looked faintly surprised at the sudden outburst. '*We're* not convinced,' he said. 'I don't know so much about you.'

'You have already suggested that I am somehow covering up for my daughter, Inspector.'

'Her mother did,' Lloyd said imperturbably.

'I am not her mother! What her mother did was—'

'Extremely foolish,' said Lloyd. 'If there ever was an intruder, she carefully wiped away any traces of the fact.' He stood up, and toured the room. 'But she wouldn't have been that thorough,' he said. 'There would have been something. Fingerprints we couldn't identify. He came in from all that snow – there would have been footprints. Someone would have seen *something*. How could he have left here in that state without someone noticing him?'

George clamped his teeth together. He had to see this through; he couldn't let his stomach be the boss. 'I don't know,' he said, releasing his breath, and turning to look out of the study window at the frozen, still landscape. There was ice on the inside again. 'You know what I keep thinking?' he said.

'What's that, Mr Wheeler?'

'That if we'd had central heating, it would never have happened,' George said slowly, touching the ice, watching it melt and dribble down the glass. 'Silly, isn't it?'

'Not really,' Lloyd said. 'You get more shotgun murders in farmhouses than you do in penthouse flats, for instance. You can't pick something up if it isn't there to *be* picked up. And not too many people get bludgeoned to death with thermostats.'

A shotgun, George thought. He had a shotgun. His father's shotgun. He put the back of his hand to his mouth. The fields. Look at the fields. White, clean, fresh. Cold. Sweat trickled down the back of his neck. He turned, his stomach lurching. 'If that's all you wanted, Inspector,' he said, as civilly as he could, 'I do have some things to be getting on with.'

'No, it isn't all,' said Lloyd. 'I want the truth.'

George fought the nausea. His legs were shaking. He sat down, and tried desperately to get control. They *knew* he'd left the pub. He'd have to say something. 'I was at Eleanor Langton's,' he said, not looking at him.

'Eleanor Langton's,' repeated Lloyd.

George looked up, not sure what reaction to expect. Shock? Disapproval? Or a boys-will-be-boys wink? He got none of those things.

'Times?' Lloyd said.

'I went straight there from the pub,' said George.

'When did you leave?'

'Not until I had to,' he replied bleakly.

'When was that?'

George stared out of the window. 'A little before ten,' he said. 'The snow had drifted off the field, so I went that way. It only took a few minutes to get home.'

Oh, Eleanor, why aren't you on the *phone*? He looked at the ash on the snow. Ashes to ashes, dust to dust. Heaven and hell, life or death. To be or not to be, that was the question.

The inspector was leaving. 'Thank you, Mr Wheeler,' he said, opening the door to find Sergeant Hill waiting in the hall. 'Right, Sergeant,' he said, his voice unnecessarily loud. 'I think we've finished here.' He glanced back in. 'For the moment,' he said, closing the door.

When he heard the front door shut, George went to the window, and watched as they went down the porch steps. As they crossed the driveway, the inspector glanced back, and George automatically stepped back from the window. They got into their car, and drove away.

To Eleanor's, no doubt. George fled upstairs to the bathroom.

Eleanor lay on the sofa, pampering herself with a dry sherry and a box of chocolate mints. Tessa had gone off with her grandmother as arranged, ostensibly to give Eleanor a rest; but Eleanor knew what was really on Penny's mind. If a blood-crazed murderer was going to break in here one dark night, he wasn't going to get Penny's grandchild. Eleanor smiled, as she had at Penny's efforts to get her to go back to Stansfield with them. But it did give her a rest, so she would enjoy it. And of course, there was a knock on the door.

Eleanor's heart sank when she saw the inspector, with the policewoman who had come in during her interview.

'This is Sergeant Hill,' he said. 'May we come in?'

'Yes. Please do.'

They walked ahead of her into the sitting room. Eleanor took a deep breath of cold air before she closed the door.

'I was just having a sherry,' she said, as she joined them. 'Would you like one?'

'No, thank you, Mrs Langton,' Lloyd said.

She smiled. 'I thought we'd agreed on Eleanor.'

She was interested to see the sergeant's immediate and hastily cancelled reaction.

'Mrs Langton,' the inspector said. 'Did you see Mr Wheeler on Christmas Eve at any time?'

Eleanor indicated the armchairs, and sat down on the sofa again. 'Yes,' she said carefully. 'He came here in the morning to ask if I would play the organ that afternoon.'

'Did you see him again?' asked the sergeant.

'At the church,' said Eleanor, noticing that the sergeant wore a wedding ring. Interesting. She wondered about that fleeting look of concern, and thought that she might play up to it. It would be quite fun to land Inspector Lloyd right in it. 'I didn't get the chance to speak to him,' she added.

'And these are the only times you saw him?' asked Lloyd.

'It's up to you what you do about it.' George's words. This was her chance to do something about it. She forgot about making a fool of Lloyd, as she tried to decide what to do.

'Mrs Langton? Could you answer the question?' said the sergeant.

'Yes,' she said firmly. 'I'll answer it. I saw him later. He came here about half an hour after Marian did. I know he's told you he was with his daughter, but if you ask me it's time she was responsible for her own actions.'

166

She didn't even try to gauge what sort of effect her words were having on her audience. She had started now.

'If she finally had the guts to take a poker to her husband, then she should have the guts to admit it,' she said.

'And that's what happened, is it?' asked Lloyd.

'I don't *know* what happened! All I know is what it's doing to George – it's making him ill. It's what he thinks happened – that's why he said he was with her! It's why her mother did what she did. Joanna must be protected at all costs – well, I think it's costing too much. Whatever he's told you, George was here. Until about quarter to ten.'

She looked at them then, for their reaction. They didn't seem very impressed.

'Half an hour after Marian left,' said Lloyd. 'That would be what – half past eight?'

'Something like that,' said Eleanor. 'Maybe a few minutes later. And whatever George has told you, *I'm* telling you the truth.'

'That is what he told us,' the sergeant said. 'Thank you, Mrs Langton.'

They had left before the full impact of what the sergeant had said hit Eleanor.

George. They'd been checking up on *George*.

Chapter Eight

Eleanor took the mini, though the pub was so close, preferring to brave the elements on four wheels. The car park was filling up now that it was lunch time, but she found a space; she hadn't been able to find one on Christmas Eve, or she might never have seen him.

Her foot slipped on the icy ground as she got out, and she walked carefully towards the back entrance. On Christmas Eve, she had had to park in Castle Road; she had used the main entrance. And so had Graham Elstow, coming in as she was going out, the mere sight of him tearing at emotions already exposed by George's visit.

She pushed open the door, and found herself glancing along the corridor to the bar, checking who was there. But Graham Elstow was one person she was never going to bump into again. The phone was being used; Eleanor waited, her face hot with the memory of that day, her heart beating too fast. But the man hung up, and said 'All yours, darling', as though she wasn't in an advanced state of panic. She thanked him, and dialled the number, clutching the coin hard, so that her hand didn't shake too much.

'Byford 2212.'

'Is Mr Wheeler there, please?' Eleanor was surprised at how ordinary her voice sounded.

'I think so,' said the voice. Marian's? Joanna's? Eleanor didn't know Marian well enough to tell, and she didn't know Joanna at all. 'Who's calling, please?'

Oh God, she hadn't thought of that. But come on, Eleanor. Pull yourself together. You've called him before – you have business with him. And what's changed, what's really changed?

'Eleanor Langton.'

There was the tiniest of pauses. 'Just a moment, please.'

She could hear footsteps in the hallway, then muffled voices.

'Hello – Eleanor?' He sounded ordinary too. Not like the tortured man he was.

'George.' She glanced along the corridor. No one around. And the people in the bar too far away to hear. 'I've had the police,' she said.

There was a silence. Then, 'Yes?'

'Yes!' she said impatiently. 'I told them you were with me,' she said.

'Yes,' he said again. 'I thought you probably would.'

He sounded so unconcerned. So matter-of-fact. What if she'd told them that she hadn't seen him? Wasn't that what he'd asked her to do, in his oblique way? Was he relieved or angry that she'd told them?

'But George—' She turned her back on the people in the bar.

'Well,' he said. 'Thanks for ringing.'

Eleanor realised. 'Oh, hell, there's someone with you.'

'That's right.'

'I've got to *talk* to you.'

Another silence. 'Yes – perhaps tomorrow?' The casual tone was beginning to sound a little desperate.

'Tomorrow?' Eleanor echoed. 'Can't you come before that?'

'No,' he said, and she could hear paper rustling. 'No, sorry.'

'All right,' she said weakly.

'Fine. Tomorrow, then. First thing.'

Eleanor hung up, and let out a sigh.

'Stood you up, has he, love?'

She whirled round, her face burning, to see the man who had been using the phone before her.

He looked a little alarmed. 'Nothing personal,' he said. 'Just a joke.' He picked up the receiver. 'At least you got through,' he said. 'That's more than I did.'

Eleanor stared at him. What had he heard? Had she said anything? She'd called him George. Oh, George was a common name – she could have been ringing anyone called George. And why would he care, anyway?

She turned and almost ran from the pub.

'Joanna,' said her father, as he slowly replaced the receiver. 'Did you want something?'

She had stayed in his study after she had told him about the call. If she hadn't, she would have listened in on the hall phone, and conspicuous eavesdropping seemed preferable, morally.

'What did she want?' she asked baldly.

'Just play-group business,' he said.

'Play-group business?' Joanna said angrily. 'Come off it! All that diary consulting – was that for my benefit? You're not *doing* anything just now!'

He slammed his diary shut. 'I will not be cross-examined about my private phone-calls!' he shouted.

That was just the problem, thought Joanna. He probably would be. She sat down. 'That's where you were on Christmas Eve,' she said. 'Isn't it? You were with her. You told me you'd stayed at the pub.'

'Yes.' He sighed. 'It's called bearing false witness, in the trade,' he said.

'And what you were doing with her?' Joanna asked sharply. 'What's that called?'

His eyes widened. 'It's called minding my own business,' he said. 'Just like you were minding yours. You weren't exactly forthcoming about where you'd been.'

But she hadn't lied to him. And she hadn't been . . . She

closed her eyes. 'Is that why Mummy was angry with you?' she asked.

'She wasn't angry with me,' he said, and he sounded almost wistful.

'Was that another lie?'

'No!' He stood up. 'It was a possible explanation for her burning the dress, that's all.'

'Does she know about you and her?'

'Now, look!' He banged his fists down on the desk. 'Whoever this concerns, Joanna, it does not concern you.'

'Doesn't it?' Joanna asked bitterly. 'Then why *did* I find myself lying to the police?'

His body sagged a little, and he sat down heavily. 'I'm sorry about that,' he said.

'Why?' she asked again. 'So that you didn't have to admit that you were with her?'

'I just didn't want Eleanor's name brought into it,' he said, swivelling the chair round, and looking out of the window.

'I'll bet you didn't.'

'Have you told them where you were?' he asked.

'Yes,' she said, but that wasn't entirely true.

'But you still won't tell me? Or your mother?'

'No.' No, no, *no*. She didn't want them to know about the baby. Not now. Not ever, but she had very little option about that. Not until they had to, at any rate.

'Then we'll just have to respect one another's privacy, and hope that the police do the same,' he said.

He was still staring out of the window when Joanna left.

They had spent the afternoon fruitlessly going through the mounds of paperwork that had developed on the Elstow business. Next door, people collated and cross-referenced, and tried to produce some kind of coherent sequence of events from the observations of those not involved, and therefore not likely to be lying. But they were likely to be exaggerating, or imagining things, or simply mistaken.

171

Marian's movements were checkable, and had been checked. She had called on half a dozen people, staying just a couple of minutes at each place, and would have arrived home at about ten, just as they all said she had. Wheeler had been seen walking up Castle Road; Joanna hadn't been seen at all. Someone knew that it was the gypsies. If there had *been* any gypsies, Judy thought, she would have gladly gone and interviewed every one of them. Joanna's information about the overalls had gone down the pipeline, so now people knew that that might be what they were looking for; at least that was something.

Outside, the afternoon had grown dark, and evening had descended. Another day almost over, and they were no further forward.

'The overalls are our best lead so far,' she said, looking up at Lloyd.

'To what?' Lloyd got up and stretched, then sat on her desk. 'To some intruder who went in, saw them, and popped them on just in case he came across someone he wanted very messily to murder?'

Judy shook her head. Lloyd was edgy, ready to dismiss anything she said. He'd been like that since they'd seen Eleanor Langton. 'Are you still convinced it was one of the family?' she asked.

Lloyd looked away in disgust. 'Of course it was,' he said. 'I'm still convinced it was Joanna Elstow, if you want to know.'

'But the doctor confirmed her story,' said Judy.

Joanna had arrived, a little upset, according to Dr Lomax, some time after half past eight. About quarter to nine, she thought. She had stayed for thirty, forty minutes. Something like that.

'The friend of the family,' corrected Lloyd, 'confirmed her story.'

'Oh, Lloyd! Do you think the whole village is party to a conspiracy?'

'I wouldn't be a bit surprised,' he said sourly. 'A domestic.

172

A domestic – you're supposed to get there and find someone in tears saying that she was cutting some bread when the knife slipped. And that's that.'

Judy smiled. 'I don't believe she killed her husband,' she said. 'For one thing, she wasn't there – and for another, I don't believe she wanted to.' She paused. 'I think we should take a closer look at Elstow. He was sober when he arrived at the vicarage in the first place,' she said. 'What made him get drunk?'

Lloyd sighed. 'Becoming involved with that bloody family, that's what,' he said. 'It would drive anyone to the bottle.' He ran a tired hand down his face.

'But he didn't drink,' Judy said. 'Not as a rule. And why would he choose to just then? He was trying to get Joanna back, not put her off.'

'And yet he succeeded, according to her,' said Lloyd, tapping Judy's notebook. 'Does that seem likely to you? He arrives drunk, gets drunker, beats her up, and it all ends happily ever after? Or would have done, if the invisible man hadn't popped in and murdered him?'

Put like that, it seemed highly unlikely, but it had seemed true enough when Joanna had told her about it. If Lloyd had been in a more receptive mood, Judy might have tried to explain that.

'I think our first theory was right,' Lloyd said. 'I think Marian Wheeler was right. Joanna went for him with the poker.'

'But the time of death is wrong,' Judy pointed out reasonably.

'I'm going to get Freddie to have another look at that,' he muttered.

The overalls. White nylon overalls, which George Wheeler had left in the hall, and which had now disappeared. They were important, thought Judy. If they found the overalls, they might get some answers.

Left in the hall. A thought occurred to her. 'Wheeler,' she said. 'He'd know—'

'Wheeler doesn't know if he's coming or going!' snapped

173

Lloyd. 'If you ask me, he doesn't know what day of the week it is, never mind anything else.'

'If your theory's right about Joanna, he'd have to know more than he's telling us,' said Judy, stubbornly.

'Not necessarily. He says he heard the bedroom door close as he went in. That could have been Joanna. Shutting herself in the bedroom with her husband, after she had killed him. Wheeler and his wife go upstairs to change, Joanna creeps down, and into the sitting room, where the original fight took place, and where they found her.'

Judy looked up at him.

'Don't look like that! It fits all the forensic evidence. It explains why she didn't come straight out and tell her parents what had happened. And it means that George Wheeler's telling the truth, and doesn't know what the hell's going on.'

'Except,' said Judy patiently, 'that Freddie says Elstow didn't die until two hours after that, when Joanna was sitting in the pub.'

Lloyd grinned suddenly. 'That's its only drawback,' he said.

'So you're going to ask Freddie if by any chance he's made a two-hour error on the time of death?'

'You never know,' Lloyd said. 'I'm going to ask him to assume that nothing that we have been told is accurate.'

'But we know it's accurate! We know what time they arrived home, we know what time Elstow ate—'

'We only know because people have told us,' said Lloyd.

'The barmaid,' said Judy. 'The people at the afternoon service – why would they lie, Lloyd?'

'People can make mistakes. This is a domestic murder, Judy, whatever way you look at it. The intruder theory is laughable.'

'Maybe,' said Judy. 'But he did meet someone at the pub.'

'According to Joanna,' said Lloyd.

'Isn't there anyone else who might have had it in for him?' she asked hopefully. She had believed Joanna; she wasn't going to admit defeat yet.

'No,' said Lloyd. 'You know there isn't. He didn't gamble, he didn't owe money except in the usual way. We can't find anything on other women – his own wife admits he didn't even drink to excess. The one offensive thing he did was to beat his wife.' He smiled. 'The house *looks* as if a bomb's hit it, but that seems to have been Elstow himself rather than the Battered Wives' Liberation Army.'

'Do you think it's funny?' Judy asked sharply.

Lloyd sighed. 'No,' he said. 'You know I don't. But if you don't laugh at this job . . . ' He shrugged.

You cry, thought Judy.

'Sorry,' he said. 'But what have we got here? We've got a cave-man. Dressed up like an accountant, but a cave-man, all the same. Frustrated and inarticulate – you said that yourself. A man who beats his wife, Judy – you find him with his head bashed in, who do you look for?'

Judy nodded sadly, and Lloyd looked at her, his face serious.

'You've got too involved,' he said. 'You like her. You want to believe her. You don't blame her, do you?'

'No,' Judy admitted. 'Not after what he did to her.'

'See?' said Lloyd. 'What are you defending, Judy? Her innocence? Or her actions?'

She'd walked right into the trap. But there was no triumph in his voice.

'Joanna was home before anyone else,' Lloyd went on. 'Saying she had been locked out.'

'She had been,' Judy said. 'Marian had locked the doors.'

'Why?' asked Lloyd.

'Because she'd found Elstow's body,' said Judy.

'Why lock the doors?' Lloyd repeated.

Judy had just accepted it, until now. Marian had locked up the house in order that no one would find Elstow's body. But why shouldn't it have been found? What difference did it make?

'I don't know,' she said slowly.

'She didn't,' Lloyd said. 'She didn't lock the doors at all. There was no reason to, whether or not there was a body in the bedroom. But there wasn't, because Elstow was in the bedroom, alive. And whoever murdered him locked the doors.' He sat back. 'And then claimed that she had been locked out all along,' he added.

'The time of death is *still* wrong,' said Judy. 'Elstow had been dead half an hour before Joanna got back from Dr Lomax.'

Lloyd made an impatient noise. 'No one was synchronising their watches, Judy! It's all arounds and abouts. Joanna says she got back at around nine-thirty – Freddie says Elstow died at about nine o'clock. Easy enough to lose half an hour that way.'

'*Before* nine o'clock,' Judy reminded him, then realised that she had been steered completely off course. 'And anyway,' she said. 'There's the overalls.'

'What about them?'

'You've seen the house,' she said. 'Whatever else Mrs Wheeler may be, she's a very conscientious housewife.' Lloyd had entertained her to a number of things which, in his opinion, Mrs Wheeler was. 'And it seems that he left these overalls in the hall,' Judy said. 'Mrs W. was doing a washing, wasn't she? I don't think she'd leave a pair of dirty overalls in the hall for long – especially not when it was all decked out for Christmas. I think,' she said simply, 'that she would have washed them.'

Lloyd got off her desk and walked around, which meant that he was actually thinking about what she had said. 'And if she *did* wash them,' he said slowly, 'then the intruder would have had to know that he was going to *need* overalls. And that he could find a nice pair all washed and tumble-dried in the machine.'

Judy nodded. 'And when we took the washing away, Marian Wheeler knew the overalls should have been there,' she said. 'But they weren't.'

Lloyd stared at her. 'Of course,' he said. 'Of course. That's when she bundled Joanna off to bed.' He sat on her desk again. 'Did you notice what she was like when she came back?' he asked.

Judy had. Marian Wheeler had been distracted, unsettled. Her mind seemed to be somewhere else altogether. 'She kept looking at George,' Judy said. 'And he's the one who threatened Elstow in the first place. He's the one who lied about where he was.' At last, Lloyd was really listening. 'Marian Wheeler wasn't protecting Joanna at all,' said Judy. 'She was protecting *George*. Because if Elstow *had* died at five, we would hardly have been asking her where she was two hours later, would we? She knew that. Perhaps it was never Joanna she suspected in the first place.'

Lloyd tore a piece off her blotter, and rolled it into a ball as he thought. 'But when did he do it?' he asked, flicking the pellet at the wastepaper bin, and missing.

'Would Mrs Langton give him an alibi, do you think?' Judy asked.

Another pellet pinged against the metal bin, and landed on the floor. 'She seemed to think she was spoiling one,' said Lloyd.

'Not his,' argued Judy. 'Joanna's. She was very keen to put suspicion on Joanna – and take it right off George.'

Lloyd flicked another pellet, which landed satisfactorily in the bin. 'Arrest the whole lot of them,' he said, getting to his feet. 'That's the answer.'

'Including Eleanor?' Judy asked wickedly. 'You mustn't get too involved, Inspector Lloyd.'

'With her?' said Lloyd, with genuine horror. 'Don't worry.'

They laughed, and the moment could have been seized, but Judy let it go. Two rejections were enough for anyone.

'Elstow met someone at the pub,' mused Lloyd, trying one more attempt at the waste-bin. He missed. 'There are too many little puzzles,' he said, picking the coats off the pegs, and throwing Judy's to her. 'Let's call it a day.'

And they called it a day, going to their separate cars. Judy drove towards home, considering giving her car star markings to indicate its freezing capacity, as her feet and hands began to lose their feeling. Other people looked forward to going home, she thought.

But she was going home to the Hills, and earnest discussions about whether gas or electric central heating was better, about whether their furniture had really been a sensible buy, about how the future really mattered, because it was what you gave your children. 'When they come along,' Mrs Hill had said, with a twinkle, as though she and Michael were newly-weds. And Judy didn't believe that Mrs Hill had missed a word of the Christmas morning discussion between her and Michael.

The Hills might have been sitting with her in the car, pointing out how hard Michael had worked to get their beautiful house, which would be even more beautiful once it had all the necessary things done to it. Pointing out that Judy didn't really *need* to work now, because Michael was doing so well. Pointing out that time was going on – it was hard to believe that it was ten years . . .

She was almost home. Just next left, and then a right, and her twenty-minute journey would be over; she would be safe in the bosom of Michael's family. She pulled the car into the kerb, and sat for some minutes, the engine running. Then she started the car, passed the left turn, stopped, and reversed into it. She stopped again, for a long time, until her breath began to mist the cold windscreen; she wiped it with a tissue, and started the car, indicating right. Back along the road she had just travelled. Twenty minutes later, she passed the police station. Left at the big roundabout at the bottom of the hill. Left, to the old village.

She parked her car beside Lloyd's, remembering the last time. The jolt to her ego of his rejection had been considerable, and she walked almost on tiptoe.

He might have heard the car, and simply not answer the door, she thought, as she pushed open the glass door to the flats.

He might be out. You couldn't tell with the thick curtains and that silly lamp. He'd strain his eyes if he read by it.

178

He would just tell her to go away again, she decided miserably, as she climbed the stair.

When she got to his door, she was out of breath; she had been holding it all the way up. All the way *there*. She gave herself a moment before ringing the bell, then heard the inside door open, saw the light going on. She could see him through the fluted glass. The door opened, and she was inside, in his arms. He was apologising. Why was *he* apologising?

'You're frozen,' he said, letting her go, ushering her into the warmth of the sitting room. He helped her with her coat, and put a finger to her lips as she tried to speak. 'Later,' he said. 'We can discuss things later. Let's get you thawed out first.'

She sat down, while he went to the kitchen, coming back some minutes later with a steaming jug of coffee and the brandy.

'Just coffee,' she said.

'Fine.'

The coffee warmed her, but the silence unnerved her. It must have unnerved Lloyd too, because he began making conversation in the way that he'd told her he did with Barbara. Carefully avoiding any mention of work; even more carefully avoiding any mention of their situation. She took as much of it as she could stand, then waited for a lull.

'I thought you would be—' she began.

'I'm just glad you're here,' he said, interrupting her. He smiled. 'Do you want to eat?'

She shook her head.

'More coffee? Or would you like a brandy now?'

'No,' she said.

He switched off the lamp. 'Kisses by coloured lights?' he said, with a little laugh, and this time he met with success.

They went into the bedroom, arms round one another. The room was chilly; Judy shivered a little as she pulled off her sweater. Lloyd's lips caressed hers as he began to unbutton her blouse.

'It'll be a lot quicker if I do it myself,' she said.

Lloyd smacked her hand away. 'And a lot less fun,' he said. 'You have no soul. *Andante*, Sergeant Hill. *Andante*.'

But Lloyd didn't realise just how many layers of clothes she wore in weather like this. He soon found out, laughing with delight as he discovered what he insisted on calling a vest.

'It is *not* a vest,' said Judy. 'It's a T-shirt.'

'It's a vest. And you thought you could whip it off while I wasn't looking.'

'Shut up,' she said. 'You get yourself undressed.'

'Oh, no,' he said, grabbing her. 'I don't want to miss anything. What have you got on under the trousers?' He took a peek. 'Long johns,' he said.

'They're *tights*,' she squeaked indignantly. 'It's all right for you – your car's got a heater that works. They keep me warm.'

'They don't,' he pointed out.

'Look,' she said. 'They've got feet. They're tights.'

But Lloyd had discovered skin, and was tickling her. They collapsed in a heap on the bed, and the more they laughed, the more *andante* it became, and the more they enjoyed it.

Judy had thought about this moment on the way to the flat. She had thought it would be awkward and intense if it happened at all; at best, she had imagined it would be a kind of self-conscious re-establishment of the status quo. But instead, it was like this, and she lost herself completely in the laughter and the love.

Which was why, when her senses returned, she got up, taking Lloyd's dressing-gown from the door as she went into the sitting room, pulling the belt tight around her. She stood for a moment in the near darkness; she wanted a cigarette, a B-movie cigarette, and she felt in her handbag for the packet, not wanting even Lloyd's seduction lighting. Her hand trembled as she struck the match.

She heard Lloyd arrive in the room; she didn't turn round.

'And I thought it was the faithful come to Bethlehem,' he said, after a moment.

She didn't need him talking in riddles. She inhaled deeply, and expelled the smoke. 'What?' she said, still not looking.

'Joyful and triumphant.'

She smiled, despite herself. 'It was.'

'Then what's wrong?'

The smoke was drawn through the coloured lights, curling round the tree. 'I'm frightened,' she said.

'Of me?'

She didn't dignify that with an answer.

'Of us,' he amended, and this time she didn't have to answer.

He came up to her. 'Because you forgot to keep back a little piece of yourself?' he asked.

She put her cigarette in the ashtray, and turned to look at him. Acting came to Lloyd as naturally as breathing. His voice, his expression, his mood. But he dropped the act with her. He pretended that what was underneath was just another act, but it wasn't; it never had been.

'But it makes you so vulnerable,' she said.

'Yes.'

She hugged him close to her. 'I love you,' she said.

He reached past her, and switched on the lamp, which seemed suddenly brilliant.

'What did you do that for?' she asked.

'Say it again. When I can see your lips move.'

She hadn't meant to say it in the first place. She had spent fifteen years not saying it.

'Where did you get that?' Judy touched the sleeve of the new dressing-gown that Lloyd was wearing.

'Don't change the subject.'

'It's nice,' she said, and glanced down at the one she had wrapped round herself like some sort of fig-leaf; it had afforded her about the same protection.

'The kids gave me it for Christmas.'

'They've got better taste than you,' she said.

'Say it again.'

'They've got better—' She smiled. 'I love you.'

'You've never said that before.'

'I've said it now.' She smiled again. 'Twice. So that should keep you going for another fifteen years.'

'But what does loving me mean?'

'I'm not sure,' she said. 'It means I'm here, when I should be at home with Michael. *And* his parents. God knows what I'll tell them. I'm a rotten liar.'

'So tell them the truth.'

Mrs Hill probably wouldn't believe her if she did, thought Judy.

'Sorry,' he said. 'Forget it. Do you want something to eat?'

'Poor Lloyd,' she said smiling. 'You're hungry.'

'Starving,' he said. 'What would you like?'

'Nothing,' she said quickly. 'I've got to go, Lloyd.'

He let his arms drop away from her, and walked off into the kitchen, slamming the door.

It was bitterly cold, and the wind had come back, moaning through the trees. But George stood in the garden in his shirt sleeves, looking across at the castle, its battlements visible in the clear, starlit night. He was trembling, already. Because it was cold. Too cold to stand out here. The frozen snow glistened as the temperature dipped even further.

The coldest Christmas period since eighteen seventy-something, the radio said. Hypothermia was a killer, they said. Make sure old people wear lots of layers of clothing. Tell them to heat one room only if they're worried about bills. Make sure they have hot meals.

He had ten years to go before he collected his pension, before he was consigned to that section of humanity assumed to be incapable of making sure for itself that it wore warmer clothes in winter – who couldn't even listen to advice on the radio. Ten years to go before other people had to listen to the radio for him, and tell him what it had said. Ten years. He wasn't old. And yet he felt old. Too old to start again.

He could go across the fields, to the castle. To Eleanor. She wanted him there. She needed him. But he wouldn't go. He would stay at home with Marian.

'George?' Marian's voice. 'George, are you all right?'

'Just getting some fresh air,' he said.

He could hear her footsteps crunching on the snow, as she walked over. She came up to him, putting her arm round him. 'A bit too fresh,' she said. 'Come back in. You'll catch cold out here.'

'I always understood that you could only catch colds from other people,' he said.

'And you're testing the theory?' Her arm tightened round him. 'We've just got to carry on,' she said, in a quiet voice.

He looked at her, and smiled. 'You're better at that than I am,' he said.

She kissed him, her face warm against his. 'Don't make yourself ill,' she whispered. 'It's happened. We'll survive it. We've survived other things.'

Lost babies, lost parents, lost dogs. And it was always Marian who kept herself and everyone else together. He kissed her, suddenly and fiercely. But she couldn't help him through this.

'Dinner's ready,' she said.

He gave a short laugh. 'Not much point in my eating it,' he said, patting his stomach.

'Is it just as bad?'

George looked at the castle. 'It won't get any better until this business is over and done with,' he said, and he followed her into the house.

For a few moments, out there in the cold, it had gone. Out in the sharp, breathless cold, there had been no desperation in the pit of his stomach, making him ill.

But now it was back.

Lloyd turned down the gas under his rice, and surveyed the multi-coloured piles of matchstick vegetables, ready for stir-frying. Slicing them up had been good therapy. Removing a table mat and fork from the drawer, he went into the sitting room. She wasn't there.

He picked up the ashtray, in which Judy's cigarette had burned away, leaving ash and melted blobs of nylon ribbon. They were lucky she hadn't set the place on fire. As he put it down, it reminded him of something, and he frowned, looking at it again.

He set his solitary place, and went into the bedroom, where Judy sat, dressed and ready to leave. But she hadn't.

'I thought you were in a hurry,' he said.

She looked up at him. 'I didn't want to leave while you weren't speaking to me,' she said.

Lloyd sat beside her, and took her hand in his. 'I want to explain how I feel,' he said.

She looked away. 'This must be later,' she said.

'Yes.' Her hand still rested in his; his thumb moved back and forth across it as he tried to phrase his statement. 'Judy,' he said at last. 'Going to bed with you is lovely. It's great. Tonight, it was better than ever.' He paused. 'Look at me,' he said.

She turned, her face a little apprehensive.

'But it's not why I want you here,' he said. 'It's not what this is about. And your being here just long enough for us to hop in and out of bed seems . . . sordid, somehow.'

'Sordid!' She turned away again.

'Yes, damn it! Sordid. It's not all I want out of this,' he said. 'But I'm – well, I'm afraid that maybe it is all you want.'

She looked back, her face angry. 'That would be funny,' she said. 'If it wasn't so—' She pressed her lips together, and took a moment before speaking again. 'Listen to me,' she said. 'I've been married to Michael for ten years. Ten *years*, Lloyd.'

Lloyd was listening. But she was saying nothing new. 'So he's got the prior claim, is that it?' he asked.

'No,' she said, her voice exasperated. 'He has, I suppose, but that's not it. Because I don't think it would break his heart.'

Lloyd was lost again.

'Until this year, he spent half his time abroad,' she said. 'He did what he pleased when he was away, and I could have done the same, I suppose. But I didn't.'

'Until I came along?'

'Not even then,' she said. 'Because this *isn't* the same, is it?'

Every time Lloyd thought he'd got hold of something, she seemed to change tack. 'I don't understand,' he said. 'What are you saying? That you were faithful to Michael until I came along and seduced you, or what?'

She closed her eyes. 'No,' she said, opening them again. 'You,' she said. 'If I was faithful to anyone, then it was to you. Because I've never wanted anyone else.' The tears weren't far away when she spoke again. 'So, no – I'm not just after your body,' she said, her voice bitter.

She had been hurt by that; Lloyd put his arms round her.

'I'm sorry,' he said. 'Truly, I am. Take no notice of me.' He held her close. 'But I don't understand why you won't just *leave* him,' he said.

'Because I'm a coward,' she answered, her voice muffled. 'You said I was frightened to leave him, and you're right. I'm scared to change my whole way of life just like that.'

'But you wouldn't be on your own!'

'I know,' she said, standing up. 'And I do have to go,' she said.

'It's this or nothing? Is that what you're saying?'

She nodded. 'Unless it's too sordid for you.'

He looked up at her. 'My tongue gets carried away sometimes,' he said. 'It's Welsh. You have to make allowances.'

She didn't reply. After a moment, he heard the outside door close.

He'd done it again. It was some time before he could make himself move, go into the kitchen, and carry on. And he ate his stir-fry, but his appetite had gone, and he didn't enjoy it. He tried to watch television; some of the proper programmes were back, but they were all, to his jaundiced eye, unwatchable. After the news, which he would have been better advised not

185

to have watched, he went to bed, at an unreasonably early hour for him. He was tired, but he took his book, as he always did.

He opened his eyes when it landed on the floor. Blinking, he picked it up again, and carried on reading, as though to fool it into believing that he'd never been asleep. The words were easy enough, but he didn't know what they meant. Then the print moved and swam before his eyes, and the book slid away again. This time he caught it, admitted defeat, and closed it. But the action involved had made him properly awake, now, and he might as well carry on reading.

He opened the book, almost against his will, at the inscriptions. A hastily written *'Best wishes from'* followed by the indecipherable signature of the author. Underneath, in her neat, clear, writing, *'and from me.'*

But he didn't want to think about Judy, or the arrangement that he no longer wished to live with, or without. He closed the book again, and switched off the light.

He was drifting off to sleep again, when an image came into his mind. George Wheeler. George Wheeler, emptying ash from a dustbin on to the vicarage driveway. Grey ash, black speckled.

Just like the melted nylon ribbon in his ashtray.

Marian Wheeler watched her husband as he got ready for bed. At first, he wasn't aware of it; she watched him become aware, try to ignore it. She watched him become awkward, as if she were a stranger.

He buttoned his pyjama top. 'What?' he said. 'Why are you staring at me?'

Marian took a deep breath. 'What's making you sick, George?' she asked.

'I told you,' he said lightly. 'This business. You know what I'm like – I used to be sick for a week before exams. I was sick in the vestry before I gave my first sermon.'

'Is it because you're being unfaithful to me?' she asked, when he'd finished.

George closed his eyes briefly, and sat on the edge of the bed. 'No,' he said. 'Nothing happened on Christmas Eve, Marian. I went there to get my tie. That was all.' He sighed. 'But I realised that I could stay there or come back here and spend the evening with my son-in-law. So I stayed.'

Marian didn't speak.

'Nothing happened then, and nothing's happened since. I'm not being unfaithful to you.'

'Because you haven't actually slept with her?'

George looked away.

'Why don't you, George?' she said. 'Perhaps it would settle your stomach.'

'Marian—'

'I mean it,' she said. 'If you want to break commandments, go ahead and break them. Don't agonise over it.'

George didn't say anything at all. He turned the bedclothes back slowly, and got into bed.

Marian put out the light, and lay back. She had known about Eleanor Langton's effect on George long before he had noticed it himself; she had prepared herself for the reckoning, unlike him.

Poor George, making a fool of himself over a girl not much older than Joanna; becoming, Marian was sure, the subject of behind-the-hand murmurings amongst the other play-group mothers. Making himself sick with worry and guilt, and for what? A fantasy. Well, Marian would back herself against a fantasy any day.

And yet, she was grateful to Eleanor Langton, in a way; at least she *had* been with George on Christmas Eve, and that proved that he couldn't have killed Graham.

If only she could be that sure of Joanna's whereabouts. But nothing she could say would make Joanna tell her where she'd gone that night. Marian toyed with the idea of a similar assignation to George's; she even considered the possibility of

Joanna's being pregnant by another man. Perhaps that was why she hadn't told them about the baby.

Perhaps it was this man that Graham met in the pub; why he got drunk, why he became violent. It would explain why Joanna had just stayed in the sitting room after she and George had come home, because she wouldn't want to answer questions until she was ready. It would explain why she hadn't taken them into her confidence about where she had been that night. For it would be natural, wouldn't it, to go to him, to tell him what Graham had done.

It explained everything, but Marian knew that it was nonsense. Joanna had been too hung up on her odious husband to have been looking elsewhere.

Chapter Nine

It was nice, not being stared awake by Tessa. Nice, but odd. Eleanor switched on the light, and looked at the clock, to discover that habit and worry had overcome freedom. Six o'clock. That was even earlier than Tessa's start, but she was awake now, and she could never go back to sleep. She lay back, and considered the situation, which didn't seem so bad, after a night's sleep. She felt calmer now that she'd spoken to George, even if it had been an unsatisfactory communication. He couldn't have told the police, or surely the inspector would have asked questions? Or would he? He was fond of drama. The anxiety returned, as she slowly got out of bed.

Not even daylight, she thought, as she ran the bath that at least she could have all by herself, without Tessa's ministrations. She could soak for hours, if she wanted.

The knock on the door made her jump. My God, who came at this time in the morning? Police. It had to be the police. Shouting that she'd just be a moment, she hastily grabbed her clothes, hopping about on one foot as her jeans refused to co-operate. She pulled on a sweater, and opened the door to George. Her mouth opened and closed again.

'When you say first thing, you really mean it,' she said, when she had got her breath back.

'I had a bad night. I could see your light, so I came over.'

He went into the sitting room.

Eleanor followed him in. 'You told them you were here,' she said.

'Yes.' He was by the window, looking out at the courtyard. He didn't look at her.

'So did I,' she said.

'Yes.' He turned from the window. 'Just as well we told them the same thing,' he said. 'Or it might have looked rather odd.'

'It might.' Her eyes searched his, trying to make contact with him through the barrier of his blank, bland stare. 'Why were they checking up on you?' she asked him.

He shrugged. 'They have to suspect someone.'

'I didn't tell them anything else,' she said, bracing herself for his reply.

The smile that had attracted her to him slowly appeared, for the first time in days. 'Neither did I,' he said, and Eleanor felt the anxiety slip away.

His eyes, alive again, took her in from head to toe, and back again. 'Eleanor—' he said, then suddenly, almost audibly, the barrier came back down. 'I have to go,' he said, walking to the door.

Eleanor tried not to think of the man she had met two months ago; the man who had called on Christmas Eve. The man who had fleetingly reappeared with the smile.

'George?' she said. 'When did you start feeling ill?'

He turned, frowning. 'When they arrested Marian,' he said. 'She has to be the mother-hen. Protecting her egg from predators. Offering herself up.'

Eleanor turned away from him. 'Eggs are supposed to hatch out,' she said.

She heard his footsteps coming towards her, felt his tentative hand touch her neck. As she turned, he walked away again, the front door closed, and she was on her own.

Joanna drove out of the vicarage, taking Judy Hill's advice to check the house. There wasn't much conviction about the

190

action, but it was something to do, something that might, just might, make the police start looking elsewhere. There was still an hour till sunrise, so with any luck she should avoid the stares of the neighbours.

Her father's car emerged from Castle Road. She doubted if he'd seen her, other than as another road-user. He had withdrawn into a world where other people didn't exist. Except Eleanor Langton. Joanna had heard him leave even earlier than she had; what was so urgent that he had to visit her practically in the middle of the night? Eleanor Langton was doing her father no good, that much she did know. She had heard him during the night, walking up and down. The last time he'd had as bad an attack as this had been when he brought her home from hospital.

She drove into Stansfield, and took the right turn into the private housing estate where she and Graham had lived, remembering the first time they ever saw it. Before they were married, they had come here, looking for a house. What were now neat if yet to be established gardens had been a sea of mud and builders' rubble, the houses approachable only by planks laid precariously on bricks.

The show house had been one of the expensive ones, beyond their range. So she and Graham had gone to look round one of the others, and she had got whistles from the workmen as she had picked her way up to the front door, still without the steps it needed. Graham had lifted her up, like a child. He had been excited about the house; it was just an ordinary house – one of the bedrooms was barely larger than the larder at the vicarage. *'But it'll be ours,'* he'd said.

They had got into trouble from the site foreman, who had shouted at them about its being private property, and his responsibility if they got hurt. If they wanted somewhere to do their courting, they could find somewhere a lot bloody safer than a building site.

They had bought the house a couple of doors away from that one. Joanna pulled up outside, her heart beating fast. It

191

was almost as though he would be there when she went in, in a mood, as he always was when she'd been home.

Home. That was what had caused one of Graham's rages; when she had called the vicarage home. Was that this time? She couldn't remember clearly. Only the chimes, and Graham's face. What had triggered the violence was lost.

But he wasn't here, not now, not any more. There was no need for apprehension. It was an empty house, that was all.

She walked into the house, through the sitting room to the kitchen, feeling like a visitor, like someone who had come to feed the cat. It was unbelievably untidy, with every surface covered in either dust or whatever Graham happened to have put down and never picked up again. The ironing board was up, with the iron still on it. At least it was unplugged. Graham had been used to having someone who washed dishes and dusted and hoovered carpets for him, especially since the firm she had worked for had done a moonlight, leaving the gates locked and thousands of pounds of bad debts. She hadn't been there long enough to get any recompense, and Graham hadn't wanted her to apply for unemployment benefit. So she'd had no money, and the mortgage meant that there wasn't much left over from Graham's salary. Her mother had given her a fiver now and then, but after the first time, Joanna had made sure that Graham didn't find out.

The kitchen was worse than the sitting room. There were dirty dishes in the sink, and she wished she hadn't come. There were too many memories, too much grease clinging to the cooker, too many coffee mug rings on the formica, too much pain.

Through the archway, over which hung the painting that Graham had bought from a street-artist in Paris on the first day of their honeymoon weekend, to the stairs – and they hadn't seen a brush for weeks. He had been brought up to think that men didn't do that sort of thing, even if they had no alternative. The alternative was to carry on exactly as though

192

someone was going to come along behind and make it all neat and clean again.

The bed was made – even Graham knew how to pull a duvet straight. He had changed the bedding at least once, she thought. It was the blue set, and it had been the pale yellow ones. She remembered everything about their last night in this house, except what had caused it all, just like at the vicarage. It was easier to remember the externals; the chiming clock, the yellow duvet.

She remembered the ambulance men; she remembered Graham saying that she'd fallen downstairs. She had gone along with it, though it was clear that no one at the hospital believed it. Her father thought it was because she was afraid to do anything else, but it wasn't.

She sat on the bed, and looked round the room. Her slippers, which Graham had failed to pack in his remorseful co-operation with her mother, still lay where she had kicked them off that morning.

No, she had gone along with Graham's story for a dozen different reasons. It was easier than admitting to strangers what had really happened. It was unthinkable to go to the police, to go through a court case. And besides, it hadn't all been like that. They'd had *fun*. Often. They'd had fun buying the house, doing it up, furnishing it. The mortgage payments had got difficult once she had lost her job, but they'd managed. The garden had been hard work, because neither of them knew the first thing about it, and she had been wise enough by then not to seek advice from her father. But even it had been fun, and they'd done it in the end. They had a lawn, and flowers. Graham even had vegetables at the back. She stood and looked out of the window, but the snow covered everything.

Beneath the surface, there had been tension. She'd put it down to having to get used to one another. They were from different backgrounds; they had different opinions about how things should be. But everyone had to compromise, she had told herself, when they had had the odd argument, the occasional two-day huff. That had resolved nothing; she could see that now. And so the tension had gone on building, until at last it erupted into violence, and tears, and vows never to do it again. And forgiveness. But he had done it again, and again, until her parents couldn't fail to notice. Their consequent concern had made matters worse; her mother had taken to calling unannounced, and Joanna had started going to see her more and more often to render such spot-checks unnecessary. It was as though everything had been planned, arranged, leading up to that night.

The externals. Like a silent movie. Pulling up outside, like today, after a visit to her mother. Graham, cold-shouldering her when she went in, picking up his evening paper and going upstairs with it. Following him up after a while, to see if she could get him out of his mood. She couldn't remember what she had said, but she remembered that Graham hadn't been listening, and that had upset her.

She frowned. A flash of memory, like a dream. She could see Graham, handing the paper to her, asking if she'd read something.

'Yes,' she had said, annoyed by the interruption. 'I saw the paper at home.'

The little silence. She had dropped the paper on to the bed.

She remembered trying to get to her feet, grabbing at the bed, but all she had got hold of was the yellow duvet, which slid down, taking the paper with it. She could see the paper, as it was kicked under the bed in the struggle. Slow motion action replay.

Then her mind went blank, shutting out the memory, until the moment that she had realised it had stopped, and she could get away from him. She had made it downstairs, then had collapsed at the foot, unwittingly offering Graham his explanation of her injuries. She remembered hearing his voice on the phone. Then the ambulance men, and the hospital. Her mother and father. No Graham. She had asked the doctor to check, just in case. Being told that the baby was all right was the confirmation of what had merely been a possibility, unsought and unmentioned.

The bedroom was covered in Graham's cast-off clothes. The laundry basket was full, as though he'd thought she might come along and do his washing. He'd piled more things on top of it. His wardrobe only had some empty hangers in it; his drawer was stuffed full of unironed shirts. Two dry-cleaning bags lay on the floor, and underneath one she could see the corner of the paper, still under the bed.

She reached down and pulled it out, still open at the page he had wanted her to read. One side was advertisements for used cars, but that wasn't likely, because they had just bought hers when Graham got a backdated increase. News items on the other side. She glanced at them. It was probably just something that had caught his eye. A funny misprint, or a bit of local bureaucracy gone mad.

She read the headings. COUNCIL VETOES SUNDAY OPENING; ASBESTOS SCARE - NO RISK, SAYS FIRM; NEW MOVES IN BUS DISPUTE; PENSIONER ROBBED.

Then, along the bottom, the one that made her eyes grow wide, and her face grow hot. It had to be it. It *had* to be. It couldn't be a coincidence.

Morning. Judy's eyes half-opened, then closed again, despite the angry buzzing by her left ear. After a moment, she sat up, and cancelled the alarm. At first, she wasn't really aware of Michael's non-presence; she had spent half of her married life waking up alone. Then she realised, and remembered. Michael had gone to Edinburgh.

He'd be there by now, she thought sleepily, looking at the clock. And his parents, thank the Lord, would be sleeping soundly in Nottingham.

She had arrived home to find Michael packing; for a moment, she had thought it was instant retribution. And when she had been told that Ian had come down with flu, and that

Michael was going to have to go to Edinburgh in his place, her mistaken impression had struck her as irresistibly funny. She had had to feign a sudden need to race upstairs to the bathroom, where she had pulled the chain and turned on the bath taps, muffling the laughter, nervous, painful laughter, in a bath towel.

Mrs Hill had been discreetly anxious to know if everything was all right; she was doubtless irritated that another month of the limited time at Judy's disposal had apparently slipped away. And she informed Judy that Michael's train stopped at Nottingham, so she and Mr Hill had decided to go up with him, instead of waiting the extra day, since Judy was so busy. He would be glad of the company.

She had driven them all to the station, Michael being unhappy about leaving his car there at this time of the year. They had all remarked on the lack of heat in the car; they hadn't been driving all over Stansfield in it half the night.

Michael had told her that he would be returning on the overnight train arriving in Stansfield at seven thirty-two on Wednesday morning. Judy had said she would meet it, and had queried the wisdom of travelling overnight to a meeting and overnight back again without a break. He had said that nothing would induce him to be in Scotland once Hogmanay had started. Somehow, she thought, that summed up the differences between them.

And the difference between him and Lloyd, she thought, her heart heavy. Once again, what should have been good had turned sour; once again, it had been her fault. She sighed, and was preparing herself to crawl out from under the warm duvet to begin another day, when the phone rang.

Lloyd? She picked it up almost timidly.

'Sergeant Hill?'

Not Lloyd. Constable Sandwell's voice.

'Yes,' she said. 'Good morning, Bob.'

196

'Morning, Sergeant. I'm sorry to ring so early, but I've got Mrs Elstow here, very anxious to see you. I said you weren't due in until nine, but she said she'd wait.'

Judy took that in. 'And you think I should come in now?' she asked.

'Well, it's just that she seems to think that she's found something that will help you with the case, and I thought she might change her mind if she had to wait. You know what they're like.'

'They' covered anyone who wasn't a police officer, in Sandwell's book. He had been seconded to CID, and was proving useful.

'She won't tell me,' he said. 'Or anyone else.'

'Right,' said Judy. 'I'm on my way.'

In under fifteen minutes, surpassing even her Christmas morning sprint, Judy was out in the bitter weather, persuading her car to start. Once it obliged, she got out, and cursed the ice as she scraped it off the windows, realising as she took this exercise that she hadn't eaten since lunch time the previous day, and that she was ravenous.

Back into the ice-box, in which she seemed to be spending her entire life, and off on the twenty-minute journey, which she had made, one way or the other, six times in the last twelve hours.

Something kept teasing her mind; something she couldn't catch hold of. At first, she dismissed it, thinking that it must be a fragment of a dream. But it wasn't. It had something to do with the murder. Something Lloyd had said, but she was certain that she hadn't written it down, which was odd, because she wrote up her notebook every night, and she wrote *everything* down. People laughed at her notes, but Lloyd knew why she took them. She had a dreadful memory. It probably wasn't important. And if it had been something about the murder, she'd have jotted it down somewhere. Maybe just a word, or a question mark against a previous note. She would look through her notes as soon as she got time.

Joanna Elstow jumped up as she walked in, and Judy smiled at her, grateful to her for delaying the moment when she would see Lloyd.

'Good morning, Joanna,' she said, sounding a little like a headmistress greeting a pupil. 'Is there an interview room free?' she asked Sandwell.

'You can take your pick, Sergeant,' he said.

'Good.' She led the way, and went into the first one, closing the door. 'Take a seat,' she said. 'What can I do for you?'

'I've been to the house,' Joanna said.

'Oh?' Judy reached into her bag for her notebook. 'Were there signs of someone else having been there?'

'No,' said Joanna, with a reluctant little smile. 'Or if there was, she must have been as untidy as Graham. And if she was as untidy as Graham, there would have been signs.'

Judy smiled at the logic. 'Well,' she said. 'It was always unlikely.'

Joanna nodded, and pushed a newspaper across the table to her. 'But I found this,' she said. 'Graham asked me to read it.'

Judy frowned. 'When?' she asked, thinking for a moment that Joanna had been communing with the spirit world.

'The day . . . ' Joanna faltered a little. 'The last day I was there,' she said. 'The day I went to hospital.' She leant over. 'Look,' she said, pointing to a news report.

COMA MAN DIES, read the headline, and Judy's eyes widened as she read the report.

'He must have known him,' Joanna said.

Judy agreed that it was unlikely to be a coincidence. 'Though they do happen,' she warned Joanna.

Joanna smiled. 'I know,' she said.

Judy felt foolish then. She always found herself speaking to Joanna as if she were a child instead of a married woman. A widow, she reminded herself. About to become a mother. But a child. A child of the Byford vicarage; a protected, cushioned child who had become the victim of savagery.

Along the corridor, into reception, through the CID room. Keep walking. Don't stop to talk. Get it over with.

'Hello,' said Lloyd.

'I've got Joanna Elstow here,' she said.

Even if they hadn't been at work, with the possibility of someone barging in, there was very little she could say. Perhaps they had said it all last night.

George didn't like guns. He fumbled with the cartridges; it was cold in the study, but he hadn't put on the electric fire.

He thought of Eleanor, and closed his eyes. Standing there in front of him, hands in pockets, barefooted in her jeans and sweater, her hair swept up in a careless knot on top of her head. Young, and beautiful, and free. Free as a bird.

He was awkward with the shotgun; it had been a long time since he'd shot anything. Marian did clay pigeon shooting at the castle, when they held competitions, in the summer. She'd once won a bottle of whisky.

His fingers were stiff; he flexed his hand, and laid the gun down on the desk as he stood up. Marian's prize had reminded him that there was some brandy somewhere. A drink might relax him. Give him Dutch courage, at any rate. He pulled open the cupboard door, and revealed the bottle, with a tot left in it. No glass. He didn't want to go out to the kitchen; he swigged the brandy from the bottle, surprised by the amount, by the suddenness of it on his throat. Pushing the stopper back, he stood for a moment with the empty bottle, remembering its origins.

Joanna and Graham had brought it with them when they'd come over for the silver wedding celebrations. Fourteen months ago. It was just after that evening that Joanna had sported a bruise for the first time, and told them some story to account for it. George threw the bottle into the empty grate behind

199

the electric fire, but it didn't break, didn't even make much of a noise.

'When did you start feeling ill?' Eleanor's question echoed in his mind. When they arrested Marian. Because Marian was offering herself up; guarding, protecting, defending her nest. It couldn't go on. It mustn't go on. He stared at the gun, then hoisted it to his shoulder, as if following a bird in flight.

He pulled stuff out of the cupboard until he could lay the gun down inside, and covered it with the papers and bits and pieces until it couldn't be seen. He closed and locked the door, then went back to his desk, looked at what he had written, and tore it into tiny pieces, letting them fall from his hands into the waste-paper basket.

Eleanor, turning away from him. 'Eggs are supposed to hatch out,' she had said. She must have had to dress quickly, after he had knocked at the door; the sweater label stuck up at the nape of her neck. And he had gone back to her, and tucked the label in.

'Eggs are supposed to hatch out.' Yes. Yes, they were.

If the little bird inside couldn't break the shell, then it died in there.

And here was Eleanor Langton again, Lloyd thought, popping up for the third time in this investigation. He scanned the page. Could Graham Elstow have been going to show his wife something else altogether? It was possible. Anything was possible. But it surely had to be something important, something that over-rode the fact that he wasn't on the best of terms with his wife at that particular moment? Lloyd thought back to the huffy silences which had descended on him and Barbara. You didn't break them for a discussion on the dangers of asbestos, or the desirability of Sunday trading.

He read the Sunday trading piece, in case Wheeler's views had been sought, and Graham had been looking for an argument about Joanna's father. But no, there was nothing there.

Joanna seemed as mystified as they were. The unnamed motor-cyclist on whose bike Langton had been riding pillion was reported as having been 'saddened' by Langton's death. But he wasn't Elstow, because he was also reported as having just returned from working in West Germany for eighteen months.

'We'll check it out,' he said.

Joanna nodded.

They were all in the office now. Joanna sat at Judy's desk, and Lloyd at his own; that way he had the width of the room between them. He could get up, walk round. Affect deep interest in wall charts and floor tiles. It all helped to confuse the enemy.

Judy was talking to Joanna, jotting down the odd thing now and then. She gave him a cool glance as he toured the office with no apparent aim; he wished things could be different, as he had at the pub. But the regret was pushed to one side by the thought that then occurred to him, and he went back to his desk, opening his diary to give himself something to do while he thought it through.

'But you don't recall him ever mentioning Richard Langton?' said Judy.

His ever mentioning, thought Lloyd, automatically.

'No, never.'

Lloyd looked up, and smiled at Joanna. 'Forgive me,' he said, 'but something is bothering me a little, Mrs Elstow.'

She looked across at him, her eyebrows raised in enquiry.

'Sergeant Hill tells me that you and your husband had reached some sort of understanding after . . . ' He finished the sentence with a wave of his hand in the general direction of Joanna's bruises.

'Some sort,' she said dully. 'I think I really only began to understand this morning.'

'Oh?'

'What I was doing to him,' she said. 'What I was letting her do to him.'

'Your mother?' Lloyd stood up, and leant on the edge of the desk.

She nodded again.

'And yet – you didn't make any attempt to communicate with him afterwards,' he said. 'In case it upset your mother.'

Joanna looked at Judy, not at him. 'I didn't want to cause any more trouble,' she said.

'So you left him upstairs,' Lloyd said, his voice slightly raised. 'Not knowing whether he should come down and face the music, or start knotting sheets together.' He shook his head. 'I don't believe that, Mrs Elstow.'

Joanna shot Judy a desperate look, but she was involved with her notebook.

'I – I didn't get the chance,' said Joanna. 'My father took me to the pub.'

'Ah, yes,' said Lloyd. 'The pub.' He pushed himself away from the desk. 'It was your father's idea, wasn't it?'

'No,' she said. 'Not really. It was my mother who suggested it.'

'But it was your father who persuaded you to go?' Lloyd sat down again. 'Yes?' he said.

'Yes.'

'I don't imagine that you wanted to,' he said. 'Not after what had happened. You must have felt a bit rough. And – forgive me again – you must have looked a bit rough.'

'He said it would just look worse later,' said Joanna. 'He was right.'

'So he persuaded you to go with him.'

'Yes.' Joanna sounded wary.

'And having persuaded you, he just got up and left you there, on your own?'

Joanna's mouth opened slightly, but no words came out. Again, she looked at Judy for help.

'Did he, Joanna?' Judy asked.

202

Joanna's shoulders sagged. 'No,' she said.

'No,' said Lloyd. 'Your father left the pub alone, but he left after you, not before you. Right?'

'Yes.'

'When did you leave?'

'About eight,' she said, and there was no expression in her voice. 'I knew my mother was going out, so I gave her time to be well away.' Her hand absently touched the bruise under her eye. 'I wanted to get Graham to come with me to Dr Lomax,' she said. 'But I couldn't get him to open the door. I thought *he'd* locked it,' she said. 'I thought he'd got in a mood again, and—'

Judy looked up from her notes. 'But your mother didn't lock the house up until after nine,' she said.

'My mother didn't lock up the house at all! Don't you see? She thinks *I* killed Graham. She thinks *I* locked the doors. But it wasn't me! Graham let someone in, and they locked the doors so that they wouldn't be *disturbed*. Don't you see?'

'Someone?' said Lloyd.

'Whoever he met at the pub,' said Joanna.

'We can't find any trace of his meeting anyone at the pub,' said Lloyd. 'He came in alone, drank alone, ate alone, and was ejected. Alone.'

'He said he met someone,' Joanna repeated mutinously.

Lloyd stroked his chin. 'Perhaps you'll tell us why you didn't volunteer this information?'

'I couldn't,' she said. 'Not after my father said he'd been with me all evening.'

Lloyd picked up a pen, balancing it on his finger as he spoke. 'And why did he say that, do you suppose?' he asked.

'Because he thinks I did it! They both do!' Her eyes filled with tears. 'So do you,' she said. 'But I didn't. I *didn't*.' She got up, and came over to him, jabbing a finger down on the newspaper. 'What about this?' she said.

Lloyd picked up the paper. 'You think your husband knew Richard Langton,' he said. 'And by extension, Eleanor Langton.'

'Yes, of course I do.'

'Perhaps,' said Lloyd. 'But knowing him hardly constitutes motive for murder.' He looked at Joanna's bruises as he spoke. On the other hand, he thought, perhaps it did. 'And Mrs Langton was at home,' he said. 'All evening. According to both of your parents.'

Joanna stood up, very erect. 'Are you going to check this?' she asked.

'Oh, yes,' Lloyd said. 'We'll check it. Thank you for coming in, Mrs Elstow.'

The door closed behind her, and Lloyd picked up the phone. 'Bob? Come in a moment, please.'

'Let's see what Eleanor Langton has to say,' Judy suggested.

'No,' Lloyd said quickly. 'Not yet.'

'Why not?' asked Judy.

Lloyd was loath to explain why not. Because she made him feel uncomfortable. Because she didn't look at people, she *watched* them. Because if he were to engage in a battle of wits with Eleanor Langton, he wasn't at all sure that he would win.

'Because,' he said, as Sandwell knocked and came in. 'When we go to see Mrs Langton, I don't want to ask her if she knew Elstow, I want to *tell* her she knew him.' He looked up, and handed Sandwell the paper, with the report ringed in red. 'Details,' he said. 'As quickly as that dreadful machine can produce them.'

'There's sometimes a bit of a delay, sir. It depends on whether—'

'No lectures about ROM and RAM and downtime,' groaned Lloyd.

'No, nothing like that, sir.' He opened his mouth, then wilted under Lloyd's stare. 'Sir,' he said, taking the paper and leaving.

Lloyd sat down as Judy began flicking through the pages of her notebook. He smiled as he watched her. No one took notes like Judy did. Perhaps she was going to write a book one day.

'Besides,' he said. 'We've only got Joanna Elstow's word for how she came by it.'

Judy closed the notebook. 'The paper is dated the day she went into hospital,' she said. 'And if we're embarking on a course of taking no one's word for anything, we'll never do anything at all. How can you take Sandwell's word for it that the computer gives him whatever answer it does? Perhaps he'll make it all up.'

'Sandwell has not proved time and time again to be telling lies,' Lloyd pointed out. 'She has. And her parents.'

'You don't like it because it's putting a dent in your domestic theory,' she said.

'No, that's not why,' said Lloyd, thoughtfully and truthfully. 'Why I don't like it is that it's yet another puzzle. We've got more little puzzles than enough.'

Judy opened her notebook again. 'I think I'll write them down,' she said.

Lloyd laughed. 'Writing them down does not solve them,' he said.

'Who says? We think they're connected to the case, don't we? So if they're all written down together, it might . . . ' Her voice tailed off, as a good reason failed to present itself. 'Help,' she finished lamely.

Lloyd was having nothing to do with it. He needed answers to questions, not parlour games.

His shoes had deposited enough of George's ash on the floor of his car to constitute a sample, and it had gone to the lab. At least that was an answer to one question.

He watched as Judy worked her way through her copious notes, in which every little puzzle had of course been entered, and he found himself thinking how soft and shining her hair looked, how pleasing the line of her jaw.

Unprofessional. He had never admired Sandwell's hair, or Jack Woodford's jaw-line, fine specimens though they doubtless were.

She worked carefully, checking every page so as not to miss anything, making a neat list on a sheet of paper. Anything less sordid than Judy was impossible to imagine. And he had probably ruined everything, throwing words about in the way other people might throw crockery. Crockery was less dangerous. Perhaps even someone like Elstow was less dangerous. He had hurt Judy just as surely as if he had punched her.

She sat back and looked at the list, the tip of her tongue brushing her upper lip as she thought hard about something. Unfair, thought Lloyd. She turned to look at him, and neither of them said anything, until they both spoke at once.

'Judy, look, I've—'

'Lloyd – listen to this.'

He held out a hand. 'You first,' he said, because what he had been going to say had had very little to do with the murder of Graham Elstow.

'The things that puzzled us,' she said. 'We know the answers to some of them.'

'Good.'

'We wondered what Mrs Anthony was hinting about George,' she said, and then looked at him enquiringly.

'Presumably she'd noticed that he was taking too healthy an interest in the beautiful Mrs Langton,' said Lloyd.

'Yes. And why Marian Wheeler was still so upset when she was at Mrs Anthony's. She'd just been to see . . . ' She held out a hand, waiting for him to supply the answer.

'Eleanor Langton.'

'And we wondered what Wheeler thought could have made his wife so angry that she would destroy his Christmas present.'

'Eleanor Langton,' said Lloyd, slowly, tipping his chair back as he thought about the little puzzles, and the ubiquitous Mrs Langton at the bottom of every one of them, including today's. Everywhere he looked, there she was, with her long blonde hair and her fine features, and her watchful eyes. Who had provided Marian with her alibi? Who had provided George with his? And who was careful to unprovide Joanna with hers?

'You'll fall one day,' said Judy.

'That's the beauty of it,' said Lloyd, righting the chair, and the allusion was not lost on Judy. 'Any more puzzles?' he asked.

'Who Elstow met at the pub, and why he got drunk,' said Judy.

Eleanor Langton? But they mustn't jump to conclusions. And Sandwell's computer wasn't going to come across for a while yet. Its coaxial cable must have got caught in its zip.

He stood up, and felt a little like an adolescent seeking his first date. 'I . . . er . . . I'd like to go somewhere nice for lunch,' he said. 'And I'd like it much better if you came with me.'

She looked as if she might be going to find some words of her own to throw at him, but then her eyes softened a little. 'Good idea,' she said.

It was a long way to the pub he had in mind, especially when it was necessary to negotiate ungritted country roads and the impacted snow of the by-passed village in which it lived. But it would be worth it for the food, and the atmosphere. They could talk there, perhaps. At least they could relax there.

It had changed hands.

'Not one of my better ideas,' Lloyd said, as they were leaving, encouraged to do so by the simple expedient of the staff suddenly appearing in outdoor clothing, and putting out as many lights as they could.

Judy, who had chosen the less than inspired Chef's Special, laughed, and got into the car, shivering.

It had even been cold. There was a notice apologising, but that hadn't made it any warmer. They had had to stay, since they were miles from anywhere else that sold food at all.

'I'm sorry,' he said.

'You couldn't help it,' she answered.

'That's not what I'm sorry about.'

They were alone in the car park, the staff having beaten them to the exit, and he kissed her, as he'd wanted to do all day. Her response was less than passionate.

'Are you still angry with me?' he asked.

She frowned. 'Angry?'

'About what I said.' He looked down. 'My tongue runs away with me,' he said. 'It always has. You should hear some of the things I say to my sisters – even my mum, once.'

'Your *mother*?'

He smiled at Judy's horrified expression. 'My dad clouted me for that,' he said. 'And he'd have clouted me again if he'd heard what I said last night.' He took her hand. 'He thinks you're the greatest thing since rugby union,' he said, kissing it.

'But you must think it's sordid,' she said. 'Or you wouldn't have said it.'

Lloyd sighed. 'That's the whole point,' he said. 'I don't think. At all. I've never thought anything of the sort.' He let go her hand. 'Am I forgiven?' he asked.

'I suppose so.'

It was as much as he could hope for. He drove back to Stansfield, only to discover that he could no longer delay his visit to the dreaded Mrs Langton. For a visit, if you could believe Sandwell's computer, was undoubtedly called for.

Graham Elstow had been the driver of the car which had hit Eleanor Langton's husband. Elstow had lived with his parents, next door to the Langtons, and had been coming out of the road just as the motorbike had turned in.

'He clipped its rear wheel when he tried to avoid it,' Judy said.

She was reading the print-out while Lloyd drove towards Byford. He was beginning to hate the place, which was a pity.

'The pillion passenger fell off, and went under Elstow's car.' Judy folded the sheets. 'Richard Langton,' she said. 'But the motor-cyclist hadn't passed a test, and shouldn't have had a passenger anyway – and Richard Langton wasn't wearing a helmet, or it might not have been so serious.'

'And the upshot was that Elstow was charged with driving without due care,' Lloyd said thoughtfully.

Judy put the print-out into the glove compartment. 'A bit hard to take,' she said.

'Quite,' said Lloyd. 'She might well be prepared to give Wheeler an alibi, given her relationship with him, *and* this.' He turned almost reluctantly into the castle grounds. 'I rather think that's what Joanna is afraid happened,' he said, slowing to a snail's pace along the narrow road. His car's heater had trumped Judy's car's road-holding qualities.

Eleanor Langton admitted them, a resigned look on her face. 'I'm working,' she said. 'Will it take long?'

'I couldn't honestly say, Mrs Langton,' replied Lloyd.

'Well,' she said, leading the way into the sitting room. 'I don't suppose you'd be here if it wasn't important.'

Other people might have meant that he wouldn't waste valuable time on trifles. But Lloyd was uncomfortably certain that Eleanor Langton knew that she intimidated him.

She stood by the window. 'Please sit down,' she said.

'I'll stand, thank you,' said Lloyd.

Judy sat down, producing the notebook.

'Mrs Langton,' said Lloyd. 'Did you know Graham Elstow?'

'Yes,' she said, without hesitation.

'You didn't tell us.'

'You didn't ask.' She sat down on the low seat by the window. 'Richard and I lived next door to him and his parents,' she said.

'There's a bit more to it than that,' said Lloyd.

Her face hardly registered any emotion. But something changed about it. 'He was responsible for my husband's accident,' she said, her voice clear but quiet.

'And you didn't tell us that because we didn't ask,' said Lloyd.

'No,' she said, looking away from him, out of the window behind her. 'I didn't tell you because I wasn't very proud of what I'd done.'

Lloyd glanced at Judy.

'I met him,' she said. 'That lunch time. At the Duke's Arms.' She turned back. 'I'd gone to phone my mother-in-law,' she said. 'And I met Graham Elstow as I was coming out.' Her fair skin began to grow a painful red. 'I'd had a difficult morning. I'd been talking about Richard, and seeing Graham was the last straw.' She turned her head again. 'I asked him how he'd been for the last three years,' she said. 'I told him how I'd been. Every detail. I told him what it had been like, what Richard had been like. I told him about Tessa, being born to someone who just lay there and did nothing, and said nothing, and never would again.'

Her voice was coming from behind the long blonde hair that covered her face, and Lloyd sat down as she spoke.

'I could see I was upsetting him. Terribly. He'd been a friend of Richard's. I was making him go through it all again. And I couldn't stop. Eventually, he just walked away from me. Into the pub.'

Lloyd sat back.

'And I felt *good*,' she said fiercely, then moved her head to look at him again. 'But it didn't last.'

Lloyd didn't speak.

'It helped, a little,' she said. 'Saying unkind things. I think perhaps you can understand that, Inspector.'

She'd be reading his palm next.

'Then when George came that evening, he told me what his son-in-law had done to Joanna, and eventually he called him by name. And I realised that I was probably responsible for the whole thing. I felt terrible. Then the next thing I knew, Graham Elstow was dead. And I didn't tell you because I

210

hoped I wouldn't have to go through all this.' There were tears in her eyes.

'And that was the only time you saw Elstow that day?'

'Yes, of course.' The answer was ready enough, but her eyes were wary. 'Why do you ask?'

'Someone murdered him.'

Judy had relegated herself to note-taker general, he noticed. Perhaps Eleanor Langton unnerved her too.

'I saw him once,' said Eleanor. 'At lunch time. I had no *idea* he was Joanna's husband! I'd never met her, and I didn't know her surname. People in the village call her Joanna Wheeler. I didn't even know she was married.'

Neither had Constable Parks, thought Lloyd. And the barmaid at the Duke's Arms hadn't recognised her surname. Graham Elstow was a non-person as far as the Wheelers were concerned, so there was no reason to disbelieve her on that score.

'Mrs Langton,' said Judy. 'When Mrs Wheeler left here on Christmas Eve, she was upset. Can you tell us why?'

She nodded, and again a blush suffused her face. 'Something happened,' she said. 'Something very trivial and silly, but . . . yes. She could have been upset by it.'

'Thank you,' said Judy, and she didn't press for details.

'I'm sorry I didn't tell you all this before,' said Eleanor. 'But it really doesn't help you, does it?'

Lloyd stood up. 'Oh, I think it does, Mrs Langton,' he said. 'There were a number of things puzzling us. Small things. But they do have to be investigated.'

She nodded. 'In that case, I do apologise,' she said. 'I didn't realise that I would be hindering your enquiry. But I didn't want to have to discuss my involvement. Especially not with Richard's mother here.'

'You couldn't keep it from her for ever,' said Lloyd.

'No.' She stood up, and went towards the door. 'But she was worried enough without my telling her it was Graham Elstow who'd been murdered.' She opened the door, and Lloyd felt as though he was being dismissed. He *was* being dismissed.

'I upset Graham, and he got drunk and took it out on his wife. So she took a poker to him. And it was all my fault,' she said.

Lloyd looked over at Judy, then back at Eleanor Langton. 'Mrs Langton,' he said. 'That's the second time you've accused Mrs Elstow of killing her husband.'

'Well, didn't she?' said Eleanor bitterly. 'Isn't that what Marian Wheeler's charade was about? And isn't that why George is making himself ill?'

'Mrs Langton,' he said. 'Has anyone indicated to you that that *is* what happened?'

'Of course not,' she said. 'George likes to believe it was this fictitious intruder.'

Lloyd drove back to Stansfield, beginning to feel that he was getting somewhere at last. He wondered what Eleanor Langton had been like before the accident, before she'd had to spend years waiting for someone to die so that she could get on with her life. But, she'd told him what he wanted to know. She was the answer to the remaining two puzzles. And since all the little puzzles could be accounted for by her presence in the Wheelers' midst, it was easy enough to put her to one side, and look at what he had left. A domestic. Wife kills brutal husband.

He said as much on the way back, and Judy didn't argue. But that, he told himself, was possibly because she wasn't speaking at all. So he turned his attention to other matters; he asked her again to talk to Linda, and she agreed, absently. She was preoccupied, barely listening.

'What's wrong?' he asked.

'Nothing,' she said, frowning. 'When I was at school,' she went on, 'I sometimes even forgot my satchel.'

Lloyd laughed.

'It was one of those satchels that you carried on your back,' she said. 'For cycling.'

Lloyd liked the idea of Judy cycling to school.

212

'And I'd eventually be aware that I was too light,' she said. 'That's how I feel now. Too light. Because I'm *missing* something.'

He drove into the police station car park, but Judy didn't get out of the car. 'Why not Wheeler?' she said.

Lloyd sighed. He'd never known her to get this personally involved before. 'Wheeler was with Eleanor,' he said.

'Before we got there, you thought she might have been prepared to give him an alibi,' said Judy hotly. 'What does she do to you, Lloyd? You didn't even *ask* her!'

'She would just have said the same thing,' Lloyd said. 'There was no point in asking her.'

'So you'll take what she says as gospel, but not what Joanna says?'

'You said that if you had pieces over when you'd completed the jigsaw, then they must belong to a different puzzle,' Lloyd reminded her. 'Eleanor Langton belongs to a different puzzle.'

For a moment, Judy subsided, considering her own words. Then she came back into the fray. 'You can't say that,' she said. 'Not when you didn't even ask her about it.'

'Neither did you.'

'I was taking my cue from you.'

'I'd sooner tackle George about it,' said Lloyd. 'Eleanor Langton hasn't got a weak stomach.'

'Huh.'

All right, so the woman had an effect on him. He hadn't asked her, because he knew that she would answer him clearly and concisely, and tell him exactly what she wanted him to know, and no more. He hadn't asked her, because she'd been *expecting* him to ask her, and just for once he wanted to get the better of her.

'She's a witch,' he said. 'I kept expecting to see her familiar curled up on a broomstick.'

Judy laughed.

'It's not funny,' he grumbled. 'Look what she said about saying unkind things.' He looked at her shamefacedly. 'How did she know about that?' he asked, only half in fun.

Judy smiled. 'Because you did much the same to her,' she said.

He got out of the car, feeling slightly better. But there was no doubt that Eleanor Langton made every Welsh superstition in his body rise to the surface and leer at him.

'You fancy her,' Judy said.

Fancy her! Not a chance. Wheeler fancied her, though. No wonder he was a nervous wreck, if he was bedding Mrs Langton. No, Lloyd didn't fancy her. But that just would be Judy's explanation, he thought. She had no soul for Mrs Langton to probe.

'And Wheeler might never have been near the place on Christmas Eve,' she added.

'All right,' he said, as they walked up the steps. 'What's the alternative?' He opened the door. 'That Wheeler went straight home when he left the Duke's Arms, right?'

'Right.'

'So how did he get there? He was on foot, and the main road would have taken him the best part of an hour, remember. And no one, but no one saw him cross the field. They *did* see him walking up Castle Road.' Of course they did. The vicar and Mrs Langton were the object of considerable interest in the village.

They walked through the CID room, and Lloyd stopped to pick up another sheaf of papers. Information gleaned from the full-scale house to house that had now been completed, and none of it, he knew without looking, any damn good. 'Practically the whole village goes to the pub on Christmas Eve,' he said, as they walked into the office. 'It's a tradition. And a lot of them use the shortcut from that side of the village. But no one saw George.'

Judy took off her coat, and sat down.

'Besides which,' he said. 'If your little girl's telling the truth, the house was locked up before George ever left the pub.'

'The barmaid could have mistaken the time,' said Judy.

214

'What? I thought we had to believe what we were *told*.'

'If my little girl's telling the truth,' Judy said, 'she didn't murder her husband.'

Lloyd sat down, his face serious. 'George was in the pub, then went straight to Eleanor Langton's. Eleanor was at home. Marian was out visiting. We've got witnesses to all of that, Judy. And Joanna was at the vicarage, and keeping very quiet about it.'

Judy sighed, at last admitting defeat.

Lloyd nodded. 'If you ask me, Joanna left the pub, and went home. She could and did get in. She put on the overalls, went upstairs and killed her husband. She burned the overalls in the back bedroom, because the fire in her room would practically be out by then. And she knew that she'd be the first person we'd suspect, so she locked up the house, went to Dr Lomax, then came home and waited, saying that she had been locked out. But she wasn't to know that her father had his own reasons for keeping quiet about where he'd been, and before she knew it, he was giving her a different alibi. One that hopefully covered him too, as far as his wife was concerned.'

He tipped his chair back, as the scenario presented itself. 'I don't believe Marian Wheeler did go home to change her dress,' he said suddenly. 'That's why she doesn't know *when* the doors were locked. Why would she go home? She was wearing a coat, and she wasn't going to stay anywhere else long enough to take it off. She finished her rounds of the old folk, and *then* came home. That's when she went up to change her dress – *that's* when she found Elstow.' Oh yes, he thought, it was all coming clear now. 'She thought Joanna had killed him that afternoon. That's when she burned the dress and put her own prints on the poker.'

He let the chair fall forward. 'I think that when we got there, she was as mystified about the doors as anyone. She denied locking them, remember. But then she finds out that Joanna and George weren't at the pub all the time, and she begins to put two and two together. She realises what must have happened, and why the place was locked up. And that's why she was so keen to point out that she *had* locked the doors – check your notebook,' he said, 'if you don't remember. I saw you underline it.'

'I remember,' Judy said dispiritedly. But she still didn't quite give in. 'Why did Joanna tell us about the overalls, in that case?' she asked.

'Someone would, eventually. She thought it might be better if it came from her. So that you would say just what you are saying.'

'Forensic can't tell us very much,' said Judy.

'No,' agreed Lloyd. 'But if we can tell the Wheelers something they don't think we know, that might just do the trick.'

'That they burned the overalls,' said Judy. 'Does that mean you still think the whole family's involved?'

'I think Wheeler's stomach is very involved,' said Lloyd. 'He knew when Joanna left the pub, at least.' He got up. 'Home time,' he said. 'Hours past home time.' He smiled. 'At least you won't get into trouble with your mother-in-law tonight.'

'No, thank God,' said Judy.

'Tell you what. Why don't you come back to the flat for something to eat?' Lloyd asked. 'Make up for lunch time.'

She hesitated, but she accepted. He was winning.

Seven o'clock. Where on earth had Joanna got to? Marian laid the table, still determined that she would go on as normal. At least she could dig George out of the study, to which he had retreated immediately after lunch. He seemed to spend all his time in there. All the time that he wasn't spending in the bathroom, she thought worriedly. It was going on too long. She walked into the study, and stopped dead.

'What are you doing with that?' she asked.

George sighed. 'It was my father's,' he said, a faraway look in his eye. The gun rested on his arm, pointing towards her.

216

'I know that,' said Marian. 'George – please put it down,' she added nervously, as his inexpert finger strayed towards the trigger.

'What?' he said vaguely. 'Oh.' He laid it on the desk. 'It's not loaded,' he said.

'Good,' she said, walking slowly over to the desk. 'Why have you got it?'

'He killed things with it,' George said.

Marian sat down. 'What were you going to do with it?' she asked gently.

George's shoulders hunched a little, like a child's. He reminded Marian of Joanna when she didn't want to go to bed. 'I was just . . . looking at it,' he said.

Marian looked at it. Oh God, what was happening? 'Why, George?' she asked.

He didn't answer; didn't even seem to hear her, or see her. She glanced round the room, and saw the open cupboard, a pile of things on the floor beside it. 'Did you find it in there?' she asked, startled.

He still didn't answer, and she got up to look in the cupboard, as though it could give her some answers. She always kept the gun in the sitting room, locked up. 'George? Where did you get it?'

His eyes seemed to focus slowly as he looked at her. 'The usual place,' he said.

'And you brought it in here?' She looked again at George's cupboard. Normality. Pretend that this is all normal. 'Were you thinking of keeping it in there?' she said, striving to make her voice sound unconcerned. 'Because I don't think it's a very good idea,' she said. 'That lock's very flimsy.'

He'd picked the damn thing up again. Marian carried on gamely. 'After all,' she said, 'if someone broke in, they could get hold of it. We have to keep it secure.'

'It was my father's,' he said.

Was that it? It was his father's, so he wanted it? Anything was worth a try. 'Would you rather I didn't use it?' she asked.

'What?' George looked puzzled. 'Good Lord, no. You use it whenever you like.' He put it down again.

Marian sat opposite him. 'George – don't you think you should see a doctor?' she asked gently.

He looked faintly surprised. 'The stomach?' he said. 'No. It'll pass.'

Marian dragged her eyes away from the gun to look at George himself. 'I think . . . ' she said hesitantly, afraid that the wrong word would spark the quick temper that seemed to have died. Marian wanted to see it back, see George back to his old self. But not while he was like this. 'I think you're a bit run down,' she said. 'Depressed.'

'A nervous breakdown?' he asked. 'Is that what you think it is?'

'It could be,' said Marian carefully.

'*I* think it is,' George said, disconcertingly.

Marian's mouth was dry. This frightened her; George had always just been George. But now, his eyes held an almost accusing look, and she didn't know why. 'What *is* wrong?' she asked.

Suddenly, he came to life. 'You ask me that? Joanna's husband is murdered in this very house, and you ask me what's *wrong*?'

At least bluster was something she understood. 'This started long before Graham Elstow turned up here,' she said. 'You've been . . . ' She plunged in. 'You've been acting very oddly for a long time,' she said. 'Since before that.'

'Before that I had to bring my daughter home from hospital. That's when I was sick before,' he said.

'It's not just being sick,' said Marian. She wouldn't be swayed. 'All that stuff about breaking commandments,' she said. 'What was all that about?'

He didn't answer.

'It started when Eleanor Langton came here, didn't it?' she said.

'Ah.' George sat back. 'My mid-life fantasy,' he said.

218

'Well isn't she?' Marian asked.

'Probably,' said George, his voice tired.

'Don't let her make you ill,' she said. 'Whatever you've done – whatever you do, I'll be here.'

'I know,' said George, and his eyes went to the gun.

Marian stiffened. 'George,' she said, alarmed that she had said the wrong thing. 'Are you in love with her? Or do you just want to kick over the traces?' She paused. 'Break a commandment?'

He gave her a half smile. 'I've broken lots of commandments, Marian,' he said.

Marian stared at him, perplexed. 'Diana Lomax,' she said, bringing common sense to the rescue. 'Go and see her, please, George.'

'She'll cheer me up, will she?'

'She'll recommend someone who can help,' said Marian. 'It *would* help, you know. If you could talk to someone.'

'It does,' said George. 'It helps when I talk to Eleanor.'

'What about?' asked Marian.

'Anything,' George said. 'She's spent a long time just watching people, you know. Listening to them. Not joining in, so she had time to take stock of them, to assess them. She understands people.' He smiled, the strange, faraway smile that he'd had when he was holding the gun. 'A lot of the other play-group mothers don't like her. That's because she understands them, sees through them. It makes them feel uncomfortable.'

'But she helps you?' Marian asked, frowning.

'Yes. She understands.'

'Don't I?'

He shook his head. 'On Christmas Eve,' he said, 'she helped me write my sermon. She suggested it.'

Marian felt a little numb. 'It was her idea, was it?' she asked. 'Shakespeare?'

'Yes. Not the Bible. *To thine own self be true.* I'm not true to myself.'

'Aren't you?'

'No!' he said, with disgust. 'I'm not a vicar, Marian. I'm pretending to be one. I don't believe in any of this. You do,' he said.

'That's why you're breaking commandments?'

He smiled, and Marian didn't recognise this man. 'It's a start,' he said.

Marian shook her head, the sturdy common sense rising again. 'Don't you see?' she said. 'All this is because of how you feel about her. You want to go to bed with her, it's as simple as that. And you think you've got to throw everything up because of it.'

'The Church wouldn't take too kindly to it,' George said.

'The Church wouldn't know,' said Marian. 'Unless she told them. Is that what's worrying you?'

George didn't speak for a long time. Then he sat back, and looked at her. 'I have never heard of any other man sitting down and discussing his potential adultery with his wife,' he said.

'She's making you *ill*, George. And if I thought telling you to forget her would work, that's what I'd be saying.'

'But you think that indulging my fantasy will do the trick?'

'What?' said Marian, guardedly.

'You think if you give me permission, you'll put me off the whole idea,' he said.

Marian didn't answer. Yes, that was the hope at the back of her mind. It had certainly been her hope when she had suggested it before. But now . . . now she didn't care what George did as long as it helped. And there was no way that Eleanor Langton could live up to George's fantasy. He'd find out what a ridiculous waste of energy it had been. She didn't even blame him. Eleanor Langton was blonde, and beautiful, and young. She was lonely and vulnerable, and she had sought reassurance from George. He was flattered, of course he was. But she wasn't worth all this soul-searching, and he'd find that out if he turned his fantasy into reality.

'I just don't want you to feel like this,' Marian said.

George sighed. 'That's not why I'm sick,' he said.

'Of course it is,' said Marian. 'You've been sick ever since you started spending half your time over there. Is that where you were this morning?'

He nodded.

'Why? What do you find to say to her?'

'We've a lot in common,' he replied. 'Graham Elstow, for one thing.'

Marian stared at him, speechless.

'Elstow was responsible for her husband's death.'

She couldn't have heard him. 'What do you mean?'

'He was driving the car that hit her husband,' George said. 'He was in a coma for almost three years.' He shivered. 'Three years,' he repeated.

'Have you told the police?'

'No, of course not.'

'What do you mean, of course not? They should know.' Marian's head was spinning. Eleanor Langton?

'It's up to Eleanor whether she tells them or not,' said George. 'For all you know she has.'

That's what was making him sick. Marian couldn't take it in. George thought that Eleanor Langton had killed Graham Elstow, and he was keeping information from the police. Her mind wouldn't cope with the rest. Faint, vague feelings of betrayal; none that she could put into words. He'd watched her being arrested – practically *forced* them to arrest her . . . She looked at the gun, at George, his face ashen.

'She didn't do it, Marian,' he said. 'She wouldn't. She *wouldn't*.'

'What difference does it make?' asked Marian, her voice weak.

'None.' He clasped his hands, laying his forehead on them, and he looked as if he was praying. Marian hoped that he was.

She stood up slowly. 'Will you let me have the gun back?' she asked.

'Take it,' he said. 'I don't want it. Throw it away.'

Marian took it, and left the study. She was on her way to the sitting room, when she realised that she couldn't keep it in the house. She didn't know this George. She didn't know what he'd do. She walked out to the car, and opened the boot, automatically checking the gun before putting it in.

The cartridges stared back at her, two eyes gleaming in the light from the door.

Chapter Ten

Joanna glanced at her watch as she got out of the car. Almost nine o'clock. She crunched over the ashes to the front door, gloomily aware that her mother wouldn't be pleased. She hadn't even told her where she was. She had been at the house all day; cleaning, dusting, tidying, until it looked like her house again. She felt better, now. But it would be difficult, telling them she was going back there to live. Still, she would do it. Tonight.

The vicarage seemed strange; normally, she could hear her parents talking, or movement, at least. Had the car been there? She opened the door again. No. That was odd; her parents were creatures of habit. Her mother, at any rate. Her father's behaviour over the last few days was far from normal. She went into the kitchen, and stood for a moment at the doorway, a frown forming. This wasn't right. The table was set, but no one had eaten; she could smell the food. She opened the oven door to find a dried up casserole, and she switched it off, beginning to feel panicky. Had there been an accident? She should have rung them, told them where she was. She ran out of the kitchen, and through to her father's study.

He sat at his desk, staring at a lined pad, his pen in his hand. He had written nothing. He didn't look up, or speak.

Joanna swallowed, and went over to him, almost afraid to make a noise.

'Daddy?'

He looked up, his eyes not really taking her in. 'Yes?' he said.

'Where's Mummy?'

'Isn't she here?' he said, but there was no interest in the question. Just an automatic response.

Joanna shivered. 'Did she say she was going out? Did you forget to eat?'

He shook his head.

'What's going on?' Joanna cried. 'What's happened?'

'Nothing,' he said mildly.

'It's freezing in here,' Joanna said. 'Come into the kitchen. I'll make you something to eat.'

He stood up, and followed her.

'She must have told you to get your own dinner,' Joanna said. 'You must have forgotten.'

'No,' he said.

'Where's she *gone*?' Joanna asked again. 'What's wrong? What's the matter with you?'

He looked at her then, for the first time. 'Your mother thinks it's a nervous breakdown,' he said.

Joanna stared at him. 'Has she gone for Diana?' she asked.

Her father smiled. 'They can't listen to your chest for a nervous breakdown,' he said.

'*Are* you ill?' Joanna asked, bewildered, slightly suspicious.

'Your mother thought I wanted to kill myself,' he said, and his voice was calm now. Rational; conversational, almost.

'Why?' demanded Joanna. 'Why did she think that?'

'Because of the gun,' he said.

'Gun?' The word chilled her. 'What gun?'

'My father's shotgun.'

'*Were* you going to kill yourself?' Joanna still wasn't sure that she was dealing with a breakdown.

'I'm not sure,' he said.

'Where *is* she?' Joanna looked round helplessly, as though her mother might materialise.

'She might have gone to Diana's,' he said, as though she had never mentioned it.

'Did she say that was where she was going?'

He frowned slightly. 'Where have you been?' he asked mildly. 'It's late, isn't it?'

Oh, God. He couldn't stay on one subject for two seconds; it was hopeless. 'Have you taken something?' she asked, alarmed by the thought.

'A couple of pills.'

'What pills? How many?'

'The ones you got after you came home from hospital. Just a couple. I thought they might help.'

Joanna ran to the medicine chest, and the bottle was there, still with a good supply of pills. She let out her breath, and took the bottle out, putting it in her pocket.

'Where've you been?' he asked again.

'At home,' she said with a sigh.

'Were you?' He sounded puzzled. 'Were you in your room? I thought you were out.'

Joanna closed the medicine chest, and turned to look at him. '*My* home,' she said.

He stared at her uncertainly, then mumbled something, and fled.

She listened to the now familiar sound of her father's feet pounding upstairs, and sank down at the table. The table set for dinner. The dinner which was dried up and ruined in the oven. Something had happened. Something terrible. Slowly, she rose and went into the hall, but she arrested her hand as it reached for the phone.

She was being silly. Her mother wasn't here, that was all. She had told her father to serve himself, but he had forgotten, mixed up by the pills. It wasn't late, not yet. Not really. She had just heard the clock chime the half hour. Half past nine wasn't late. She mustn't let her father's nervous state get to

225

her. She heard him walking about upstairs; he wasn't well. Her mother had probably gone to get Diana. But she would have *phoned* Diana, said a voice in her head.

She looked at her watch. Quarter to ten. That wasn't late, no matter how you looked at it. So what *was* late? Eleven, she decided. She would give her mother until eleven. Then she would start ringing round. There was no need to panic. She must be somewhere. Joanna glanced anxiously upstairs. She must be *somewhere*, she told herself sternly.

She must be somewhere.

Eleanor Langton got out of the bath, and towelled herself dry, pulling on her bathrobe, and rolling up its sleeves. She had, after a great deal of thought, decided against going to the party. Instead of a quick bath and an evening out, she had had the long luxurious bath she had promised herself, and was washing her hair.

She had been getting ready to go out, having decided that perhaps she could face it, after all; she was coming out of her prison, making a new start, and a New Year party seemed appropriate, even if it was two days shy of the end of the year.

But then she had looked at the ticket. They seemed to think you'd bring a partner, and she had thought that she might feel conspicuous without one. The others had said that lots of people were going alone, what with husbands on shift-work, or husbands who wouldn't go to a disco if you paid them, but they might have just been saying that to make her feel better about not having a partner. Everyone else, she had thought, might turn up complete with a man, and she'd be left alone at the table while they all danced.

Someone might *ask* her to dance. Eleanor had wondered, then, if she could handle that. But what was there to disco-dancing? You hardly knew who you were dancing with. She had never actually danced at a disco, because Richard had run one for years in his spare time and she had helped. She had

226

even played keyboard in a short-lived group that Richard had got together, before they were married.

Another Eleanor, another life. Now she played the organ for the carol service.

She had looked at herself in the mirror, and hadn't been sure about the dress. Perhaps it should be separates; jeans, even. And reflected in the mirror, she had seen the bedroom, so obviously solo. Going to a party might help, she had thought; she might meet someone.

But she *had* met someone; slowly, Eleanor had unzipped the dress, and stepped out of it.

She had just put on the second lot of lather when the knock came to the door. George. She lifted her hair up and looked at her watch on the windowsill. It was after ten. Surely it was George. She squeezed some of the water out of her hair, and opened the bathroom door, dripping shampoo on to the floor. 'I won't be a minute!' she shouted anxiously. 'Don't go away!'

George picked wonderful moments to call, she thought, as she rinsed the shampoo out of her hair. She was pleased that he'd come, that he still needed her. This morning he had been so distant, and odd. And yet, for a moment, she had thought that at last they would make love, and keep the promise that they had been holding in reserve since Christmas Eve. But it had only been for a moment.

'Coming,' she called again, as she wrapped her hair in a towel, and ran along the corridor, throwing open the door.

Again.

'I'm sorry,' said Marian Wheeler. 'I know it's a bit late. But I've got to talk to you.'

Eleanor felt a surge of panic. This wasn't *fair*. 'Yes, of course,' she heard herself saying. 'Come in.'

In the sitting room, she waved a hand vaguely at the chairs, and Marian took off her coat, and sat down.

'I'd better come straight to the point,' she said. 'George isn't at all well, Mrs Langton. But I expect you know that.'

227

Eleanor nodded. 'He told me it was a nervous reaction,' she said. 'That he always got like that if there was an upheaval of some sort.'

'Yes,' Marian said. 'That's true. But I think this time it's worse than that.'

'Do you think he's really ill?' Eleanor asked, alarmed.

'I think he's having some sort of nervous breakdown,' said Marian. 'I'm here because – well, I'm here for several reasons, to be quite honest.' She took a breath. 'Tonight, I found him with his father's shotgun. He said it wasn't loaded, but it was.'

The words hung in the air, while Eleanor stared at Marian, open-mouthed. George? George, who joked about keeping their tentative affair in reserve? George, who winked at her behind Mrs Brewster's back? But no, not that George. George, who could barely think straight any more. George, who had called at six o'clock in the morning, then had hardly even spoken to her. *That* George.

'Why?' she whispered. *'Why?'*

'I've brought the gun with me,' Marian said, hesitantly. 'It's in the car. I wondered if you could possibly put it in the gun room here – I daren't leave it in the house.'

Eleanor agreed, automatically, with a distracted nod of her head. 'Thank God you found him,' she said.

'He may have been waiting for me to find him,' said Marian.

It seemed odd to Eleanor that Marian was here. If George was that bad, shouldn't she be there?

'Shouldn't someone be with him?' she asked.

'Joanna will be back by now,' said Marian. 'I just wanted to get that gun out of the house.'

'Yes, of course,' said Eleanor.

'I think George needs help,' Marian said firmly.

'Yes.' The word came out with a shudder, like a sigh. 'I had no idea he was that bad.' Her mouth felt dry. 'Look – can I get you something? A drink, perhaps?'

'Coffee would be lovely,' said Marian.

· 'Coffee. I'll . . . er . . . ' She pointed vaguely in the direction of the kitchen. 'I shan't be a moment.'

She almost ran along the corridor again, and stood for a moment in the kitchen, taking deep breaths. What was coming next? A third-degree on her and George? Eleanor made coffee, the situation beyond her. And surely not of her making? But that was what Marian thought, or she wouldn't be here.

'Can I help?' Marian appeared in the kitchen.

'You could help yourself to milk and sugar,' Eleanor said.

'Thank you.' Marian took her time, obviously working on her next reason for being there.

'You see,' Marian went on, 'I've spent all evening just sitting in the car, trying to work out what's happened to George.' She looked up, and gave a little shrug. 'You happened to him,' she said.

'We're not lovers,' said Eleanor. 'If that's what you think.'

'Oh, but you are,' said Marian. 'In the old-fashioned sense.' She stirred her coffee. 'It might be better,' she said, 'if it was in the physical sense.' She sat down. 'You see,' she said, 'I think you're the only one who can help him.'

Eleanor's head shook slightly. This wasn't happening. Marian Wheeler wasn't here, practically inviting her to have an affair with George. This wasn't happening.

'Shall we have the coffee in here?' Marian asked, for all the world as though they were swopping recipes.

Eleanor sat down too, still bemused.

'At least get him to see a doctor,' said Marian. 'He will, if you tell him. I know he will.'

George didn't need a doctor. No one thing had happened to George. It was a mixture of *all* the things that were happening to George. Meeting her; his crisis of faith; Joanna, Graham Elstow – Marian's love, smothering him. And was Marian here, now, out of that love? Was she seeking help for George, no matter what she had to do to get it? Protecting him, forgiving him. And not even his attempted romp through the ten commandments could put her off.

229

'He needs your help, Eleanor.'

Eleanor didn't speak. There were things she could say: Mrs Wheeler, my relationship with your husband consists of a few frantic moments in the out-house, and hours of listening to him tell me that you love him, and that he loves you. That doesn't make me responsible for his welfare. That doesn't mean that you can lay the blame for this at my door. She didn't voice her thoughts; what did it matter who or what had driven George to this point?

But it did matter, of course, and as George would doubtless have said, it was up to her what she did about it.

'He seems to value your opinion very highly,' said Marian, and there was no trace of sarcasm.

Eleanor lifted her eyes slowly to Marian's. 'But it isn't my opinion that he should see a doctor,' she said. 'It's yours.'

Marian tutted impatiently. 'He must see a doctor,' she said. 'And he won't listen to me. You're the one who has done this to him, Eleanor. You're the only one he'll listen to.'

'No,' said Eleanor quietly. 'I haven't done this to him. It was already done before I met him. George wants—' She broke off, then decided to go through with it. 'He wants freedom,' she said.

Marian's head went back slightly. 'So that he can do the decent thing by you?' she asked archly. 'Are you holding out for marriage? Is that what it is?'

'No, no, no!' Eleanor shouted. 'Not that sort of freedom,' she said, her voice quieter. She thought for a moment. 'You called us lovers,' she said. 'But we're not, you know. Not in any sense of the word. If George wanted me, he could have me, and he knows that.' She paused. 'But he doesn't,' she said. 'He thinks he does, but he doesn't.'

What *was* she to George, she wondered for the first time. A fellow prisoner? Or just a stick to shake at Marian? The one thing that he hoped would make her angry? And when that didn't work . . . was that what the shotgun was about? Marian had said that perhaps he was waiting for her to find him. Yes, Eleanor could see George doing that, trying to baffle Marian into something other than patient understanding.

Failed again, George, she thought. Failed again.

'I'm just a . . . a sort of focus,' she said.

'A focus?' Marian repeated.

Eleanor couldn't tell Marian what she meant. She and George had both been in prison; but she was on the other side of the bars now, free, while George was still painfully tunnelling out. Hers was the freedom of the newly released long-term prisoner; the world was a frightening, alien place. She and George needed one another, that was all.

'A focus for his dreams?' said Marian.

'If you like,' said Eleanor.

'A damsel in distress, that he had to come and rescue?' asked Marian. 'A sleeping beauty that he had to awaken with a kiss?'

Eleanor felt her face grow hot, and Marian nodded. 'He told me about Graham Elstow,' she said, after a moment. 'About his having caused your husband's accident.' She leant forward. 'He was with you on Christmas Eve,' she said. 'What time did he get here, Mrs Langton?'

Eleanor frowned. 'What?' she said.

'It's a simple question,' said Marian. 'What time did he get here?'

'What are you suggesting?' asked Eleanor, her voice horrified. 'That George killed Graham Elstow? On *my* behalf?' She jumped to her feet. 'Why? Why would you think that? George didn't . . . ? No,' she said. 'He didn't tell you that. Why then? Just because you think he was going to kill himself? Is that why?'

Marian looked up at her. 'I don't think I said anything about George killing *himself*,' she said, barely stressing the final word.

'My God,' said Eleanor. 'If you can't sacrifice yourself for your daughter, you'll sacrifice George. You're trying to blame George.'

'*Blame* him?' Marian repeated, with an uncomprehending movement of her head.

Eleanor sat down again. No. Marian had never blamed George for anything. 'But you can't *really* think it was George,' she said. 'Marian – he was in the pub, and ten minutes later he was with me.'

Marian nodded again. 'And you had thirty minutes,' she said. 'Thirty minutes between my visit and George's arrival.'

Eleanor's eyes widened slightly.

'*That's* what is making George ill, Mrs Langton,' said Marian. 'That thirty minutes.'

George Wheeler splashed water on his face, and looked at himself in the bathroom mirror. If he saw that man walking down the road, he wouldn't recognise him.

Had he been going to kill himself? People asked him questions, all the time. And he didn't have the answers. *To thine own self be true.* Had he been going to kill himself? Marian had gone to the police; she must have done. And wasn't that why he had told her? So that she would protect him from that, too? She would go to the police, not him.

He'd gone to see Eleanor this morning. Why? Because she'd called him yesterday, said she had to see him. He hadn't slept, and then he'd been pacing the floor, deciding to die. Yes, then he *had* been going to kill himself. He'd seen Eleanor's light, and gone to her. Just once, he had thought. He wanted her just once before . . .

Before he killed himself? But his courage had already waned, even then. He couldn't have Eleanor; he couldn't even die.

Had he been going to kill himself?

Eleanor. When had he realised? Not when Marian found Elstow's body, not even when they arrested her. It was later,

232

after that, that it had begun to dawn on him. It was the day after that, in the church, with the sunlight streaming through the stained glass. Eleanor, coming in. Talking quietly. Almost angry when he had told her about Marian; just at that moment he could have sworn that Eleanor had thought *he'd* done it. But then, as she rushed him off to the police station, he had realised. Eleanor had been angry because someone else had been implicated, and she hadn't meant that to happen; she had urged him into the police station, desperate to clear Marian's name.

But she hadn't told them about Elstow's involvement in her husband's accident, and neither had he, even though Marian was under arrest. Marian thought that it was his betrayal of her that was making him ill, and so had he, until now. But it wasn't.

'When did you start to feel ill?' When they arrested Marian, he had said. But it was Marian, of course, who knew when he had really started to feel ill. *'It started when Eleanor Langton came here, didn't it?'*

Had he been going to kill Marian? Marian, who sat there calmly discussing the pros and cons of his adultery, Marian who had confessed to the police because she thought *he'd* done it? Not Joanna, for Marian knew Joanna too well to think that she was capable of it. Joanna had loved Graham Elstow; she had been frightened of him, but she hadn't hated him. No, Marian had been protecting *him*. Her other egg. Or so she believed. But all the time, she had been protecting an intruder, defending a cuckoo's egg.

'Eggs are supposed to hatch out.' Eleanor understood. He was trying at last to break out of the shell, and that was what was making him ill. Yes, he had wanted to blast his way out with his father's shotgun, and he could never be sure which way he would have pointed it, if he'd had the nerve to pull the trigger.

Lloyd carried the empty plates into the kitchen.

'It was lovely,' Judy called through. 'Well worth the wait.'

'Good things take a little time,' Lloyd called back, smiling. 'I've told you before. *Andante*.' He piled the plates in the sink, and took mugs out of the cupboard.

'I could have made something in ten minutes,' she said.

'I'm sure you could, but I wanted one decent meal today,' he said, hunching up his shoulders as he waited for her reaction.

She arrived in the kitchen. 'I can show you a school report,' she said. 'It says, "Judith shows an interest in and aptitude for domestic science." So there.'

'What happened?' Lloyd put the sugar bowl on a tray with the mugs. 'Black or white?' he asked.

'White.'

'Take that through, will you?' he said, indicating the coffee jug.

'Do you trust me to?' She took it.

He poured milk into a cream jug, then remembered that he had cream. 'Cream or milk?' he called.

'Milk.'

He shrugged. No soul. It was good to see her back to her old self again, but it did make him feel more than ever like a bottle of aspirin. He carried the tray through, to find Judy looking at his Christmas cards. 'You won't find it there,' he said. 'If anyone had the nerve to put it on a card, it would go in the bin.'

She turned, smiling. 'I don't have to,' she said.

'You're bluffing.'

'Am I? All right,' she said, sitting on the sofa. 'Call my bluff.'

'How?' He picked up as many things as he could carry from the table, and went through to the kitchen. Judy was under strict orders to do nothing. This was an occasion. He came back through. 'How can I call your bluff?' he asked.

'If I'm bluffing, give me permission to tell Jack Woodford,' she said.

Her eyes glowed with mischief. But she *was* a rotten liar, as she had pointed out last night, and she didn't look as though she was bluffing. She must be, though. How could she have found out?

'Well?' she said. 'Can I tell him?'

'No.' He picked up the salt and pepper and table mats, and turned to see her grinning at him. 'If you know,' he said, 'you must have gone to Somerset House.'

She shook her head. 'It isn't Somerset House any more,' she said. 'And that would have been cheating.'

'Certainly would.'

Back in the kitchen, he illogically put away the table mats and the salt and pepper, and left, closing the door on the piles of dishes. 'So you are bluffing,' he said, as he came back in. 'I'm not calling it,' he added quickly.

'Am I allowed to pour the coffee?'

'No! You're to be waited on hand and foot.'

'So how come I had to carry the coffee in?'

'It's good luck,' he said solemnly, pouring the coffee. His first name had haunted him all his life. She didn't know it. 'How could you have found out?' he asked.

'You took me to visit your father before he went back to Wales,' she said.

Lloyd joined her on the sofa, relaxed, now. 'Then you're definitely bluffing,' he said, drinking some coffee just to see Judy wince. He liked it when it almost burned his mouth. 'If it's possible,' he said, 'my father is more ashamed of it than I am.' Even his father just called him Lloyd. And his mother had settled for a shortened version, which could have been the diminutive of something less awful.

'What did he call you when you were a baby?' she asked. 'He didn't call you Lloyd then, surely?'

'I don't know,' Lloyd said. 'The baby, I suppose. That was his problem.'

Judy's dark eyes regarded him as she gently blew at the steam from her coffee. 'No,' she said. 'He didn't tell me.'

Lloyd laughed. 'You gave in too soon,' he said.

'I've not given in.'

He frowned. 'What's my father got to do with it, then?' he asked.

'You and your father went off to look at some furniture,' she said. 'To see if you wanted an old dresser, or something.'

An old dresser or something. A genuine . . . He began to feel uncomfortable again. Because that bit was true. 'So?'

'So I was left alone,' she said. She left a pause. 'With the family Bible.'

The family *Bible*? They didn't have one. Did they? Oh, God, yes. He could remember it. A huge black one that he'd grown up with and seen every day, and to which he had never paid the least attention. But even so, they didn't write *names* in it.

Judy sipped her coffee.

'I'd know,' he said. 'If they'd written babies' names in it.'

'How? Your sisters are older than you. There weren't any babies after you.'

Lloyd finished his coffee, and his mug still steamed. 'What are *their* names?' he demanded.

'Megan and Amelia.'

He poured himself more coffee. 'I've told you that,' he said. 'I must have.' Megan and Melly. That's what he called them. He never thought of Melly as Amelia. But then his father sometimes called her Amelia. That's where she got that from. But he couldn't be sure.

'All right,' he said. 'If you know, tell me.'

She looked horrified. 'You said you'd flatten me if I ever used it,' she protested.

'You *are* bluffing.' He pointed at her. 'But just in case you're not,' he said. 'Don't you ever utter it. Ever. Not even when you're *alone*. Or I'll—'

'Flatten me,' she said.

'Worse. I'll put a notice up in the CID room that you wear a vest. That'll put a dent in your image, Sergeant

Hill.' He smiled. 'I'm very glad you're here,' he said, giving her a squeeze.

'I'm glad I'm here.' She lay back, her head on his shoulder. 'Talk to me,' she said.

'What about?'

'Anything. It doesn't matter. I don't listen anyway.' She closed her eyes. 'Anything except double-glazing and cavity wall insulation,' she said.

Lloyd smiled. 'Well, that leaves the field fairly open,' he said. 'What would you like? The influence of Roman culture on ancient Britons?' He kissed her, and her response was rather more to his liking than it had been in the car park of that dismal pub. 'An analysis and comparison of the French and Russian revolutions,' he said, as she began to loosen his tie. 'Flora and fauna of the Florida everglades . . . ' Her mouth touched his as he spoke. 'The pre-Raphaelite Brotherhood,' he said.

'Eleanor Langton,' she said.

'The habitat of the natterjack toad,' he carried on, and kissed her as she laughed.

'You said she was in all evening,' said Judy.

'The decline of Twelfth Night as a popular festival.' She wasn't wearing a vest tonight. 'The effect of television on the British film industry,' he murmured in her ear, as he undid her bra.

'But she might not have been.'

'Can't you think of anything else? Pick a subject.'

She smiled. 'The pre-Raphaelite Brotherhood,' she said. 'Marian saw her at five past eight, for about five . . . '

Lloyd drew her into a long kiss, but it had to end.

' . . . minutes, and George got there at about twenty to nine.'

'In the middle of the last century,' Lloyd began, his lips on her shoulder, 'three artists – Rossetti, Holman—'

'And it only takes a few minutes across the fields,' she said.

'Holman Hunt, and Millais,' he went on, his lips travelling with the words, 'decided that they didn't think much . . . she'd

237

get there at twenty past,' he said, tackling her zip. 'At the earliest.' Or long johns. She'd catch her death.

'Plenty of time to do it,' said Judy.

'I know,' said Lloyd. 'But I'm in the mood *now*.'

'Eleanor had plenty of time to kill Elstow.'

Lloyd sat back. 'Except that if your little girl's telling the truth, then she would have been there by the time Eleanor Langton arrived,' he said.

'Joanna could have been and gone by twenty past.'

'In which case, she wouldn't have found the door locked, would she?'

'Are you saying that Joanna *is* telling the truth?'

'No,' he said, with great patience. 'I'm saying that if it was Eleanor, then there's no reason to disbelieve Joanna. And if there's no reason to disbelieve Joanna, then it wasn't Eleanor. You like logic problems – sort that one out.'

Judy took his hands. 'Sorry,' she said.

'I'll forgive you,' he said. 'But only because I'm damned if that family's going to spoil this evening.'

Judy smiled, and lay back, taking him with her. 'What family?' she said.

'Will you stay the night?' he asked.

'Oh, Lloyd, I can't,' she said.

'You've never spent the night with me.'

'I *can't*,' she said. 'Please, Lloyd, I don't want another row.'

'Why can't you?' he asked. He didn't want another row. He wanted her to stay.

'I have to meet Michael's train at half past seven in the morning,' she said.

'There is a half past seven in the morning here,' Lloyd said.

She kissed him. 'I'm sorry,' she said. 'It would be too obvious that I hadn't been home. There would be too many questions.'

Don't go on at her, he told himself. Don't spoil it again. He smiled. 'And you can't tell lies,' he said.

She shook her head.

'What you need,' he said seriously, putting his hands on her shoulders, 'is a piece of magic chalk.'

'All right,' she said. 'I'll buy it. What's magic chalk?'

'Well,' he said. 'Dai's going home from work, and calls in for a quick drink. And there at the bar is the most beautiful blonde he's ever seen. He can't believe his luck when she buys him a drink. So he sits down, and chats her up a bit, and then she says would he like to come home with her and make love to her.'

Judy smiled.

'Would he not?' Lloyd went on. 'So Dai throws caution to the wind, goes home with her, and makes love to her for hours. But all good things must come to an end, and Dai's getting dressed to go home when he sees the time. "My God," he says. "Look at the time. What am I going to tell the wife?" '

'Are you making this up as you go along?'

Lloyd grinned. '"Don't worry, Dai," she says. "I've got some magic chalk here, see?" And she gives him a piece of chalk. Well, it just looks like ordinary chalk to Dai, but she swears it's magic. "Just put it behind your ear," she says, "and tell your wife the truth." '

Judy moved closer to him as he spoke. 'You *are* making it up,' she said.

'Dai doesn't fancy that at all,' said Lloyd. 'But the blonde just smiles again. "Trust me," she says. "It's magic." So Dai goes home, taking the chalk with him.'

'Does this go on all night?' Judy asked. 'So I'll have to stay – like Whatshername telling stories?'

'Scheherazade,' said Lloyd. 'Now, he doesn't have much faith in this chalk, but he's got no chance otherwise. When he gets home, he puts it behind his ear, and goes in. "Where have you been, then?" says his wife. And Dai takes a deep breath. "I've been making love to a beautiful blonde all night," he says. "Don't give me that, Dai Griffith," says his wife. "You've

239

been down the Legion playing darts – you've still got the chalk behind your ear!'"

Judy laughed, but then her eyes widened, and the smile faded. She twisted away from him, reaching for her handbag.

'Leave it!' he ordered. 'Don't dare bring out that notebook!' Gun-dogs were supposed to *obey*.

She leafed through the pages, and looked up. 'It's all here, Lloyd,' she said. 'We had all the pieces. You were asking the right questions, all along.'

Lloyd looked over her shoulder at her notes, but he couldn't decipher the mixture of Judy's own form of speedwriting, the odd clear word and dozens of question-marks and asterisks. 'I hope your official notebook doesn't look like that,' he said.

'Why did Marian Wheeler go all the way to Eleanor Langton's, and then all the way back to Mrs Anthony's?' Judy said, her eyes bright with triumph. 'Why go to Eleanor Langton's at all?'

He had indeed asked those questions. It seemed to him that they had been answered, but obviously not.

'Why did Marian Wheeler deny locking the doors, and then insist that she had? Why lock them in the first place?'

He thought that they had established that Marian Wheeler *hadn't* locked the doors, whether or not Judy's little girl was telling the truth. Which, judging from Judy's almost indecent excitement, she was.

'Why bother going home to change her dress?' asked Judy.

'You wrote that *down*?'

'Yes,' she said, surprised. 'What I *didn't* write down was when you told me just to tell the Hills the truth.'

Lloyd was relieved to hear it.

'And I thought how they wouldn't believe me if I did,' said Judy.

Lloyd sat back, and looked at her. Feed in a few wild scenarios, and Judy would sift through them, rejecting everything but the facts, because she had no imagination to get in the way of the truth. She gathered facts. Some were tiny and vital; some were pages long, and useless. But they were all in there, like that dreadful computer of Sandwell's. Much more fun, though. It wouldn't be sitting there, beaming from ear to ear.

'Go on,' he said.

'Marian was alone in the house with him,' Judy said. 'So she had to have an alibi.'

He nodded slowly.

'And that's why she went to see Eleanor Langton. It *was* a trumped-up excuse. It had to be Eleanor, because she had no obvious friendship with Marian – in fact, gossip would say just the opposite. But Eleanor would be certain to know all the details – know that the time of Marian's visit *mattered*. George would tell her everything, and Marian Wheeler knew that.'

Lloyd sighed. 'And then Mrs Anthony,' he said, feeling weary. 'Whom Marian has known from childhood. She *knows* the old lady's as sharp as a tack. If anyone was going to notice her new dress, it would be Mrs Anthony.'

'That's why she stayed there long enough to take off her coat,' said Judy. 'Unlike anywhere else. Then she spilt some coffee, to give herself an excuse to go home.'

'Where she burned the dress,' said Lloyd. 'For us to find, along with all the other evidence.' Of course, of course. If she had simply denied murdering the man, the chances were that they would find some evidence anyway. So she just gave them a bit more. 'And she did her trick with the poker,' he said. 'To make it look like faked evidence.'

'And if she had trotted out her alibi,' Judy said, picking up her notebook, 'we would have been a lot less inclined to believe it. But as it was,' she said, 'she let us discover her alibi for her. And congratulate ourselves on how clever we'd been. *Don't give us that, Mrs Wheeler*,' she said, in a very fair imitation of Mrs Dai Griffith's accent. '*You've been down the Legion, playing darts.*'

Lloyd stood up, and began to pace round the little room. 'She had to lock up the house,' he said. 'She couldn't risk

241

Elstow being found before she'd finished leaving evidence for us.'

'And she had to keep it locked,' said Judy. 'Because she still didn't want him found too early. Or we might have got too accurate a time of death.'

Lloyd nodded. The trouble with alibis was that you couldn't really be in two places at once.

'She had to lose half an hour,' said Judy.

He nodded, his back to her. Easy enough to lose half an hour, he'd said. And when she confessed to killing Elstow, she simply made it half an hour later than it actually was. Half an hour which she had spent beetling back and forth across the village.

He ran a hand over his face, and stood staring at the Christmas tree. 'And she burned the overalls in the back bedroom,' he said, turning to face Judy. 'Knowing that when we found burnt clothing upstairs, we wouldn't *look* for any other fires.'

'I wonder how she felt when she saw George spreading them all over the driveway,' said Judy.

Lloyd shook his head.

She closed the notebook, looking sad, and still a little confused. 'She must have known we would suspect Joanna,' she said. 'She even told us she thought Joanna had killed him. How could she *do* that to her, Lloyd?'

'She didn't.' Lloyd sat down heavily. 'The locked doors,' he said. 'The Mystery of the Locked Bloody Doors. That was the one piece of evidence that we *weren't* supposed to know about.'

Judy frowned.

'Marian and George always went to the pub on Christmas Eve,' Lloyd said. 'Every year. And every year, they stayed until ten-thirty, singing carols. So she packed George and Joanna off in the belief that they'd do the same, and would therefore have cast-iron alibis. She would be home first, and no one would ever know the house had been locked up at all.'

242

'But they didn't stay,' said Judy.

'No. They didn't. And Joanna arrives home at ten past eight to find herself inexplicably locked out.' He looked across at Judy. 'She thinks it's her husband being bloody-minded, and goes off to see the doctor. She doesn't tell her parents that, because she doesn't want them to know about the baby. When she gets home again, she waits for them to come home. They get in, and now *she's* the one who feels bloody-minded. So she does what her mother asks, and doesn't go up to see her husband. Off they all go out again, and when they come back and find Elstow . . . ' He bowed his apologies to Judy. 'In all innocence, she tells us that they were locked out. Which puts Marian in a fix, because she didn't want us to know.'

'And then, she realises that they *weren't* together all evening,' said Judy. 'You said that too.'

'So she has to tell us that she *did* lock the doors. To prove that it couldn't have been Joanna, because she couldn't have got in. Only she didn't know about Joanna's earlier trip home, did she? She thought she had covered her when she said she'd locked the doors at nine. Those doors,' he said. 'They were bothering me all along.'

The phone rang, and there was a moment before Lloyd snapped back, and picked it up. 'Lloyd,' he said.

'Sorry to bother you so late, sir, but I thought I'd better ring you. We've had Mrs Elstow on the phone, saying that her mother's gone missing.'

'Missing?' said Lloyd. 'Has she now?'

'Young lady sounded pretty desperate,' he said. 'I've sent WPC Alexander – didn't think I should send Parks. Not on his own, anyway.'

'Right,' said Lloyd. 'Thank you. Let Parks get his beauty sleep. I'm on my way.' He almost hung up, then put the receiver back to his ear. 'I'll pick up Sergeant Hill on the way,' he said, with a wink in her direction.

'But I think,' he said to her as he replaced the receiver, 'that you should probably do up at least some of your clothes.'

She had been gloriously unaware of her *déshabillée* through-out both his bringing it about, and her triumphant unearthing of the truth. Lloyd straightened his tie, and grinned.

'Ready?' he said.

Marian had wanted to kill Graham Elstow when she had stood by Joanna's hospital bed. She had wanted to, but the thought of actually doing it hadn't occurred to her. Not then. And she had wanted to kill him when she had gone to the house for Joanna's clothes, with him in attendance, mumbling apologies at her as she packed. But she hadn't thought of actually doing it, because Joanna wasn't going back. So he didn't matter any more, and Graham Elstow hadn't so much as entered Marian's mind from the moment she had left that house with Joanna's suitcase, until Christmas Eve, when he turned up at the vicarage.

And she hadn't thought about killing Eleanor Langton at all, until now.

She had come looking for help, that was all. George needed help. He was ill because he was so convinced of Eleanor's guilt that he was displaying the symptoms; Marian had enjoyed the effect that her words had had on Eleanor, who sat at the kitchen table, her head on her hand, her coffee cold beside her.

Marian had thought that George's infatuation with her was a passing phase, something that at worst a few illicit afternoons would have cured. The towel round Eleanor's head accentu-ated the fine bone structure, the youthful, unlined face. She wouldn't have blamed George if he had given in to a physical attraction.

Eleanor slowly unwound the towel, and her hair fell down in damp golden strands. The movement caused the bathrobe to fall open slightly, revealing long, shapely legs. Marian compared herself with the girl who sat opposite. Twenty-six, seven? Slim. Elegant. Wearing only a bathrobe, and she had thought that it was George at the door, just like last time.

244

And yes, Marian would back herself against a fantasy any day. But Eleanor Langton was no fantasy. Whatever George wanted, one thing was clear. One thing was certain. And it was more potent than all of Eleanor's physical attraction. Eleanor Langton wanted George.

Eleanor absently rubbed her hair with the towel as she looked at Marian. 'You're wrong,' she said.

'Wrong?'

'Perhaps George does think I killed Graham Elstow,' she said. 'But that isn't what's making him ill.' She sat forward slightly. 'He needs the freedom to be himself, Marian,' she said.

'Freedom,' repeated Marian thoughtfully. 'Yes, perhaps you're right.'

And she thought again of those cartridges, in the gun that George had pointed at her. She stood up.

'Perhaps you're right,' she said again. 'But at least we can make sure that he doesn't get it at the point of a gun. I'll go and get it.' She turned on her way to the door. 'If that's still all right with you,' she said.

'Of course,' Eleanor said tiredly. 'It should be out of harm's way, whatever he was going to do with it.'

'Quite,' said Marian.

She walked along the corridor to the front door, leaving it open as she stepped out into the icy night. There was a thick layer of frost on the car already, and for a moment, she thought that the boot lock had frozen. But it gave at last, and she took out the gun, leaving the boot open. Slipping her hand into the pocket of her jacket, she felt for the cartridges. Light streamed across the courtyard from the open door, and eventually Eleanor would come out, to see what was wrong. And she would come up to the car. Closer. Closer.

It was a dreadful accident. Dreadful. I couldn't leave the gun in the house, not with George behaving like he was. So I thought the best place would be the gun room at the castle. I only ever use it there anyway, and the castle could always use

245

an extra gun. I was so stupid, not checking it. But George
had thought it wasn't loaded – that's what you told me, wasn't
it, George? It was dreadful. Eleanor came with me to get it; I
took it out of the boot, and it just . . .

Marian would never forgive herself for not checking the gun.
But she would forgive George his lie. She would be patient,
and sympathetic, and understanding.

And he would come back to her, just like Joanna.

They left George and Joanna with WPC Alexander. They
didn't know where Marian was, they said; they had rung
everyone they could think of. And Judy had seen Joanna's
face when Lloyd had said that there were some more questions
he wanted to put to her mother, if she contacted her or her
father. Joanna had not been surprised.

They were on their way to the castle, for inscrutable reasons
of Lloyd's. 'What if she's in bed?' Judy asked, as Lloyd carefully drove at five miles an hour through the castle grounds.

'Then we'll go away again,' he said. 'But you heard George
– he thought that Eleanor had killed Graham Elstow, and
Marian knows it.' He glanced at her. 'And I think Marian
would be very keen to drop that snippet of information into
Eleanor's lap,' he said.

'But do you think she's still here?' asked Judy. 'It's late,'
she pointed out. 'By most people's standards.'

'No,' said Lloyd. 'But Mrs Langton just might know where
she's gone. Or make a good guess,' he added, with a laugh.
His tiredness was evident in the Welshness of his accent,
usually carefully controlled and measured. 'Besides,' he said.
'Eleanor Langton's been the answer to all the other puzzles,
hasn't she? Let's see what she can do with this one.'

The castle appeared on their left, huge and black. 'I don't
think you should drive right in,' said Judy. 'It really is very
late, Lloyd. We might frighten her.'

Lloyd pulled up at the gatehouse, and they walked over the
frozen, snow-covered gravel, through the massive entrance,

into the castle proper, their footsteps deadened by the snow and the fourteen feet thickness of the walls.

They heard Eleanor Langton's voice softly calling Marian's name.

Marian Wheeler said something that they couldn't catch, as she and Lloyd arrived at the turn into the courtyard. Lloyd, a yard or so to her right, couldn't see what Judy could see.

It happened so quickly; it happened so slowly. She had seen it in films, when they slowed the action down. She had thought it was just for effect, but that was how it was.

Eleanor Langton, walking towards the Wheelers' car. Marian Wheeler, hidden by the open boot, gun raised, pointed at Eleanor, her finger on the trigger.

'Mrs Langton!' Judy's own voice, echoing round the ancient buildings. 'Stay where you are!'

Marian Wheeler turning. Turning instantly, turning in slow motion. Turning, her finger pulling the trigger.

Seeing the ground rushing towards her, as the shot shattered the still night. Hearing glass break, feeling pain tearing at her leg. Running feet; Lloyd calling out. Hands touching her. 'Get inside!' Lloyd's voice. Lloyd's hands. Blackness.

Opening her eyes. Lloyd was kneeling beside her. 'I'm all right,' she said. 'I'm all right.'

'Thank God.' He pressed his forehead to hers.

She tried to get up, but she felt dizzy, and leant back against the wall.

'Wait,' said Lloyd. 'Take it easy. You were out for a couple of minutes.'

'Was I?' She frowned. 'My leg,' she said. 'It hurts.'

Lloyd looked down. 'It's cut,' he said. 'Quite badly. You must have caught it on one of those spikes when you went down.'

Judy looked at the wrought iron, foot-high spikes which carried an ornamental chain round a flower bed.

'Is she all right?' Marian Wheeler's voice, afraid; it came out of the darkness. She was close, but Judy couldn't see her.

247

'I'm all right, Mrs Wheeler,' she said, grunting with the effort of getting to her feet. She leant on Lloyd. 'I think you got one of the castle windows,' she said, trying to sound positively jolly.

'I didn't mean to shoot at you,' said Mrs Wheeler. 'It was *her*. It was *her*.'

Lloyd put his arm round Judy's waist. 'Come on,' he said. 'Sit down in the car.' He led her to the Wheelers' car, and opened the door for her. From there, Judy could see Eleanor, inside the house, framed in the light from the doorway.

'She was going to take George away from me,' Marian said. 'I couldn't let her do that. I let Graham Elstow take Joanna, and look what happened.'

Judy looked at Lloyd, who shrugged. 'Let her go on talking, I suppose,' he said quietly, in answer to her unvoiced question. 'Can you see her?'

Judy peered into the deep shadow of the castle, and shook her head.

'It should be all right as long as Eleanor stays in the house,' Lloyd said, crouching down. He gently lifted the torn cloth away from Judy's leg. 'I think I should rip it some more,' he said. 'Keep it away from the wound.'

Judy nodded, and closed her eyes while he dealt with it.

'Are you OK?' he asked doubtfully.

'Yes.' She glanced down unwillingly, and looked away again. 'I don't think it's as bad as it looks,' she said. 'It hurts like hell – isn't that a good sign?'

He smiled, and stood up. 'Mrs Wheeler?' he said. 'The sergeant's hurt. I think she should go to hospital.'

'Then take her. I didn't mean to hurt her.'

Lloyd sighed quietly. 'I know that,' he said. 'But I don't think we can leave without you.'

There was silence.

'We know what happened, Mrs Wheeler,' he said.

248

'But I had to kill him,' she said. 'We'd never have got rid of him. I had to. I had two hours to work out what to do. It was quite clever, don't you think?'

Judy shivered.

'Yes,' said Lloyd. 'It was quite clever.'

'Joanna's having Graham Elstow's baby,' Marian said. 'She thinks I don't know. But I was washing her poor face, and I heard her. I heard her. *Let the baby be all right.* I *heard* her. A baby. A baby! He'd have rights. Even if she left him, he'd have rights. Over *my* grandchild. We'd never have got rid of him. I had to kill him.'

Judy closed her eyes, as the pain throbbed through her leg.

'Mrs Wheeler,' Lloyd said, his voice soothing. 'Why don't you come out where I can see you? And you don't need the gun, do you?'

'Oh, yes,' she said, sounding surprised. 'It's all over. Don't you see? It's over. I just wanted to explain.'

The throbbing increased with Judy's heartbeat, as she looked at Lloyd. She put her hand on his, where it rested on the car door.

'No, Mrs Wheeler,' he said. 'It's not all over. People will listen. They'll help you.'

'They'll send me to prison.'

Practical, sensible, thought Judy. But then Marian Wheeler was a realist.

'Yes,' said Lloyd. 'They might. But even if they do, they'll still help. You know that.' He paused. 'You've helped people, Mrs Wheeler. So now they'll help you.'

She moved then, and they could just see her shape standing out from the shadow of the castle walls. Judy patted Lloyd's hand.

'Mrs Wheeler,' he said. 'I really think that Sergeant Hill should go to hospital. Will you come with us?'

The sirens were faint at first; they grew louder, until the sound filled the air, punctuated by a shotgun blast.

Post-Mortem

Exhaust fumes hung in the cold, still air; sirens whined down as the cars' engines were switched off. Lights flashed, and the winking colour on the pale, ancient stone seemed almost festive. Judy stood watching, supported by the car door, unable to help.

Lloyd, grim-faced, walked through the chaos towards her, shaking his head.

'All right, what's going on here?' A torch played on their faces. 'Inspector Lloyd?' said the voice, disbelievingly.

'A woman's just shot herself here,' Lloyd said angrily. 'She's dead, I'm sure, but I want the doctor here. Now.'

The sergeant ran back to his car, and reached in for his radio. After a few minutes, he came back, still looking confused. 'I've to tell you that Freddie's at the station, and he's on his way,' he said.

'Good,' barked Lloyd. 'Now you can tell me what this circus is *doing* here!'

The sergeant looked offended. 'The burglar alarm went off in the station,' he said. 'We were using it as an exercise.'

'The *burglar* alarm?' Lloyd repeated, then sighed. 'The window,' he said to Judy. 'She broke a window.' He took a short, calming breath, and explained in more detail to the bemused sergeant.

He turned back to Judy. 'Do you think you can walk to the house?' he asked.

'I'm sure I can.' She limped to the doorway, her arm round Lloyd. Eleanor Langton stood just inside, shivering.

'Do you mind if we . . . ?' Lloyd began.

'Of course not,' she said.

'Mrs Langton,' he said gently. 'You'll get pneumonia if you don't get dressed.'

She looked down at herself almost in surprise. 'Yes,' she said. 'Yes, I will. Then I'll make you a hot drink, Sergeant Hill. I don't think you should have anything stronger – they say it isn't . . . ' She foundered. 'There's a first aid kit in the kitchen,' she said. 'I'll bring it.'

Judy smiled. 'Don't bother,' she said. 'You get dressed.'

Lloyd helped her to the sofa. 'I think your leg should be up,' he said, easing off her shoe, and pulling the coffee table towards her.

'I'm not dripping blood all over the carpet, am I?' she asked. She wouldn't look.

He smiled, shaking his head, then sat down beside her. 'Some coward you turned out to be,' he said.

'She was going to *shoot* her, Lloyd!' Judy said, springing to her own defence.

'And you thought it would be a much better idea if she shot you,' said Lloyd.

'I didn't think anything! I just warned her.'

'I don't understand,' Lloyd said. 'You're frightened to change the way you live, but you're quite happy to get in the way of a deranged woman with a double-barrelled shotgun.' He stood up. 'I have to get over to the vicarage,' he said, with a sigh. 'Break the news.'

Judy nodded. Poor George, she thought. Poor Joanna. 'Lloyd? Tell Joanna I'm sorry I couldn't come myself.'

'Sure.' He looked at her for a moment. 'I thought you were dead,' he said.

She caught his hand, and squeezed it. 'So did I,' she replied.

*   *   *

Joanna gave her father a little encouraging smile as he went off with the inspector. She had wanted to say she was sorry, but she couldn't, because her father must never know the terrible thing she had thought, when she had finally rung the police.

Her poor, gentle father.

The inescapable truth, which should have been shattering, had come almost as a relief. Almost as though she had known all along. Perhaps she had. And perhaps so had her father, who may have convinced himself that Eleanor Langton had killed Graham, but had failed to convince his stomach. And now, her mother was dead. But she couldn't take that in. Not yet.

She waited until the sound of the police car's powerful engine had dwindled to nothing before she closed the door.

'I've made a big pot of tea,' said the policewoman. 'You come and have a cup of tea with me, love.'

Joanna allowed herself to be steered into the kitchen, where the fire burned brightly and WPC Alexander bustled plumply round her. She had offered to go with her father to the castle, but he had said she should stay. Two hours ago, he couldn't have summoned up the will to make such a decision, but he could now.

Because with the inspector's terrible news had come a reawakening of her father's spirit.

At least she hadn't lost him.

Eleanor found as many containers as she could for coffee, which she was providing on a conveyor-belt system for the people who were working out in the bitter cold. It seemed ridiculous that just across the courtyard there were dozens of cups and saucers in the café, and she couldn't get into it. She found herself thinking that she would have to speak to her employers about that, as though this happened every week; she almost made herself laugh.

Thank God Tessa wasn't here, though in truth, the events of the night had barely affected Eleanor herself. A shout, a shot. Another shot.

Now that they had told her what had happened, she knew how close she had come. But at the time, it had just been a confused sequence of sights and sounds, like a scene from a badly directed play.

She handed the tray to a grateful policeman, and picked up the first aid kit. Sergeant Hill had refused several offers of medical assistance, but Eleanor thought she really ought to do something.

'Ah, just the job!' A tall, thin man with an unexpected smile appeared in her kitchen and took the box from her. 'Doctor,' he explained.

'Oh, good,' she said. 'I'm sure I wouldn't be very good at it.'

'Neither will I,' he said. 'But you have to give the public what they want.'

George had nodded his confirmation that it was Marian, then had walked away, feeling detached from it all. Perhaps it was the pills. For a long time, he stood unnoticed in the shadow, watching as the numbers dwindled, and only Chief Inspector Lloyd and the officer who had driven him remained. When the ambulance came, bumping over the frozen ground to Marian, he slipped into the courtyard.

The door was open; he walked in, and could see Eleanor at the end of the corridor, sitting in the dining room. She stood up as he went in, her face pale.

'The police are waiting for me,' he said. 'I just wanted to be sure you were all right.'

She nodded, but her eyes were worried. 'George?' she said. 'Did I cause all this?'

'You?' He took her hand. 'Oh, Eleanor. No.' He shook his head. 'No.' he said again.

They were putting Marian in the ambulance; they asked if he wanted to wait until it left, but he shook his head. It was odd, he thought, as he was driven back home. Now that everyone else was feeling sick, he didn't.

Not any more.

*　　　*　　　*

253

Lloyd watched as the ambulance drove away with Marian Wheeler's body, and rubbed his eyes. Would she have come with them if the damn squad cars hadn't arrived? He passed the shattered window that had brought them, and shrugged. He'd never know now. All he knew was that his immediate future would be filled with enquiries and questions and statements, and the depressing likelihood that the file would quietly be closed on Graham Elstow's murder.

He shivered, and arrived at the cottage as Freddie was leaving.

'Bloody cold out here,' said Freddie, his breath streaming out as he spoke. He smiled. 'I never thought I'd get that close to Sergeant Hill's legs,' he said.

Lloyd rubbed cold hands together. 'Isn't there something about medical ethics?' he said.

'I have to take my pleasures where I find them,' said Freddie. 'Most of my patients are past their best.' He opened the car door and threw in his bag. 'Like Mrs Wheeler,' he said.

'Must you be so cheerful?' Lloyd said. 'The woman has just blown her brains out.'

Freddie grinned. 'I'd sooner look at Mrs Wheeler's brains and Judy Hill's legs than the other way round,' he said.

Lloyd smiled reluctantly.

'The leg's not bad,' said Freddie. 'The wound, I mean. I've bandaged it up – but she should get an anti-tetanus injection.'

'Now?' asked Lloyd.

'Now would be best.' He got into the car. 'And she should take it easy for a few days,' he added. 'But they'll tell her all that at the hospital.'

Lloyd lifted a tired hand as Freddie reversed out of the courtyard, and roared off into the night. He knocked quietly at the door.

Eleanor Langton gave him a little smile as she opened it. A real smile. 'Come in,' she said. 'I'll make you a cup of coffee – you look frozen.'

'Great,' said Lloyd. 'Thank you. Are you all right?'

'Yes,' she said. 'I didn't really know what was happening until it was all over.' She walked down the corridor a little way, then turned back. 'Your sergeant saved my life,' she said.

Lloyd nodded briefly, and walked into the sitting room, where Judy sat, her now bandaged leg still resting on the coffee table. 'Right,' he said. 'A quick cup of coffee and then we have to get you to hospital.'

'Hospital?' she said.

'Freddie's orders. Besides, I want a real doctor to look at it.'

She laughed. 'Freddie is a real doctor,' she said.

Lloyd raised his eyebrows. 'Laugh-a-minute Freddie?' he said.

'That's just how he copes,' said Judy. She patted the sofa. 'Come here,' she said.

Lloyd sat beside her on the sofa, as she gingerly removed her foot from the coffee table, and moved closer to him.

'We have to sort ourselves out,' she said.

'Yes,' Lloyd agreed. 'But I don't really think this is the ideal place,' he added, with an uncomfortable glance at the door. 'She'll be back any minute.'

'Oh, but it is the ideal place,' said Judy. She looked down for a moment, then her head came up resolutely. 'I'm not very proud of what I've been doing,' she said. 'To you or Michael.'

Lloyd took her hand.

'I should have left him when it started,' she went on, then shook her head. 'I should never have married him in the first place.' She looked away again. 'For a moment tonight,' she said, 'I honestly thought I was dead. And I've wasted too much of everyone's time. Michael deserves more than this, and so do you.' She smiled sadly. 'So I'm leaving him,' she said.

'Are you sure?' Lloyd gently touched her bandaged leg. 'You'll never have a better piece of magic chalk.'

'I'm sure.'

Her lips touched his, gently at first, then with an urgency that took him by surprise. They broke away as the normally

255

silent Eleanor positively banged her way down the corridor, rattling cups.

Lloyd frowned. 'You set this *up*,' he said, incredulously.

Judy grinned. 'They don't call you a detective for nothing,' she said.

'You *told* her? About us?'

'She told me,' said Judy.

'I told you she was a witch,' said Lloyd, as Eleanor just happened inadvertently to bump into the door with her noisy cargo.

'Sorry I was so long,' she said. 'I made a couple of sandwiches.'

A sandwich and a cup of coffee later, Lloyd went to bring his car round from the gatehouse. He stood for a moment looking down at the moonlit village. It was exactly like the Christmas card he'd got from the Woodfords.

And this place had made him shiver, he thought, touching the rough surface of the wall. Perhaps his Welsh superstition had been right.

Mrs Anthony could have told them. She hadn't been hinting about George at all. She had been telling them, in words of one syllable, about Marian. And hadn't he said that they would find an old lady who would solve it all for them? Pity they hadn't been listening.

Murder at the Vicarage, he thought, as he got into the car. He must read it again some time.